PRAISE FOR MARTIN SHANNON

…a breath of fresh air in the urban fantasy genre.

— EDISON T. CRUX - AUTHOR OF THE ENOC
TALES

Martin hits the weirdness that is Florida right on the nose. The magick is clever, the laughs are big, and these people are my neighbors.

— G. MICHAEL REYNOLDS

You will love every crazy minute.

— KA MILTIMORE - AMAZON BEST SELLING
AUTHOR OF BURNED TO A CRISP

FREE STORIES

Don't miss all the excitement that happens between each volume in the Tales of Weird Florida series. Sign up at www. martin-shannon.com to stay up to date with Gene and the gang as they navigate the dark and treacherous backwaters of Weird Florida with each new short story.

BLOODY DEED

MARTIN SHANNON

PART I
BIRDS OF A FEATHER

1

DOWN AND OUT

*B*ike tires churned with each pump of my legs, but try as I might, I couldn't outrun the fading day. The last rays of a setting sun sliced through the scrub pines and found their way into my eyes, forcing me to look away lest I add blindness to my current list of problems.

I was late.

Clank! Clank!

An expensive lawn mower bounced along the dirt road behind me, the remaining tools of lawn care trade strapped to it with a complex weaving of frayed bungee cords.

You grow it, he mows it. My wife is such a comedian.

I pulled up the edge of my shirt and wiped the road grit from my face. Porter and I hadn't been married a year, yet it still felt strange to call her 'my wife.'

Right, like fiancé was less awkward?

I was lost in thought comparing the merits of both equally life-changing terms when a passing truck roared down the dirt road kicking up enough sand and wind to push me into a narrow mud-lined culvert.

What's the hurry?

The behemoth's taillights faded into the dusky haze. A bent Dade County license plate dangled from its rear end and glinted in the light.

Miami... figures.

I shook my head and dug in, pumping my legs and dragging the lawn tools back onto the dusty road.

This is life now.

To say things hadn't worked out exactly liked I'd planned after graduation was a gross understatement. First, the high points. Porter had said 'yes' and we'd been married a few months now. In a twist of remarkable luck, we'd even reached the point where her brothers had begun to tolerate me at family gatherings.

That was the extent of the awesome in my life.

Now, the low points.

We were poor.

We weren't standing in the bread lines or rubbing sticks together for warmth poor, but we certainly didn't have much of what the songs says it took to get along.

I swerved to avoid trash on the roadside and quickly turned around to make sure I hadn't lost any of the yard tools.

Nope, still there—damn.

Right out of college my wife had been able to get work rather quickly—she had friends and wasn't afraid to call them.

Unlike me.

It should have been more difficult for a journalism major to find something these days, but not my wife. Porter'd picked up the phone and in an hour had an interview. That interview had lead to an offer, and that offer had netted her a job. In less than seven days, my wife had gone from college graduate to leasing agent at a beautiful apartment complex just outside of Tampa. It was good to be back in the home town, even if we were on the furthest possible edge of it.

I pedaled faster to avoid sinking in the soft sand, still dragging the mower behind me.

Ah, the mower.

At present that expensive hunk of steel and plastic was basically the pinnacle of my post-graduate achievements. Just like my wife, I too had sent in all manner of applications, resumes, you name it, but not a one of them went anywhere—I even got turned down trying to sell plasma.

They didn't even want my blood.

After being kicked to the curb for what the woman at the counter described as 'abnormal plasma' with a self-righteous scrunch of her nose, the yard business had been basically the only thing left. Still, Porter believed in me, so much so she'd been willing to do the unthinkable—take out another loan.

"It's a lease, Gene," she'd said the day we picked up the yard slicing terror behind me. "So don't break it."

And so far I hadn't, but that was purely by chance, as it certainly appeared that mower wanted us both dead.

It seemed like every job I did had some issue: hidden rocks in the tall grass that got caught on the blade and launched into the homeowner's car, walking face first into a hornet's nest resulting in three anti-histamine shots in my abnormal-plasma-filled butt, and even now, the job that was supposed to put us in the black was practically out past Riverview and damn near likely to get me run over.

I glanced back at the mower again before ducking a low hanging pine branch.

Still in one piece...

Another moving truck roared past and I turned my head to avoid the sand blasting that would follow.

Dade County again? Somebody's heading south in a hurry.

The dirt road jogged to the left, and I pedaled harder to keep my bike from spinning out in the loose sand.

Cutting grass hadn't been a bad idea, as ideas went, and so

far the yard business had paid a few bills, but we were also paying the lease for the equipment, as well as a myriad of other things I hadn't expected when we got out of school.

Like debt, lots of debt.

But this was the big client; do a good job here and we'd be set and maybe be able to pay down some of those loans. This whale came courtesy of one of my wife's contacts. She'd gotten word that one of the local yard outfits had closed up shop and this client had come available.

"It's a big job, Gene. Think of the money," Porter had said, handing me the address.

A quick check of the map confirmed our suspicion—it was a big job, a really big job. The owner had a piece of land not far from an old derelict poultry farm out past US Highway 301. This had put me on the road to what Porter's family referred to as 'God's Country' and doing my damndest to not get run down in the process.

Still, thanks to my wife, I was staring down the barrel at over an acre of the green stuff.

Did it have to be this far away?

I pumped the pedals and kept an eye out for the turn, hoping I didn't get pushed off the road by yet another high-speed hauler.

This was *not* how I expected life after college to be.

I turned around to check the weed whacker; my bungee cords were still holding, and that meant the other gas-powered rental was still attached to the lawnmower's dirt smeared top.

The blower was another matter entirely.

It clung for dear life between the mower's push bar and the bag, bouncing precariously out of its frayed strap and ready to topple into the street at any minute. Now, any sane and normal person would have stopped their bike and made an adjustment —I was neither.

My name is Eugene Law, and I'm a Magician. I don't do card

tricks and I'm not much for bending spoons. I deal in the cosmic powers of the universe, or at least I used to. Lately, I'd been trying my best to avoid Magick all together, lest it blow up in my face yet again.

Over the last few months Magick had become a sore subject in the Law household, and seeing as my wife was about as Magickal as drywall, that meant I was the source of those problems. I couldn't put my finger on when, but somewhere along the way the cosmic power in my body had gone haywire. It was certainly still there, still swirling around in that nebulous place it preferred to dwell, but like a bad renter, it wasn't willing to lift a finger to help me out.

I'd tried everything: new sigils, complex Latin, the actual reading of Magickal texts—the ones I was still willing to open— but nothing helped. It was as if my Magick had a mind of its own and was more than happy to do what it wanted, and if that happened to coincide with my requests that was fine, otherwise I was screwed.

I glanced at my watch.

Speaking of screwed... You're going to be late. Can't cut grass in the dark. A little Magick should be fine, just don't over do it.

It was a bad decision, but I didn't have time to stop and re-attach everything. It was Magick or run out of daylight.

I reached out with my power, drawing up those cosmic energies from the wellspring of my chest and sending them out into the world. "Et ligabis..."

The Latin was simple, as was the effect. It should have helped those bungie cords catch the blower and keep it from ending up on the street. At least that was how I envisioned it working.

So much for envisioning.

The blower kicked on and sent a whirling cloud of sand and dust into the air that made it next to impossible to see. Sadly, it didn't actually fall off the back of the mower, as that would have been helpful. Instead it caught between the straps and sand blasted me right off the road.

I hit the culvert and lost control of the bike. The handlebars turned sideways and jabbed me in the gut while at the same moment my front wheel caught on a stray root. The entire acrobatic sideshow brought the lawn care caravan to a sudden stop, launching me into a marvelous face-first meeting with a roadside pine.

2

BLACKOUT

*S*and.

Death tastes like sand.

I'm not dead.

That proclamation from my addled brain did little to assure me of my status as one of the living, so I tried what any normal not-dead person would try—I opened my eyes.

No difference.

It was just as black with my eyes open as it was with them closed.

Okay, so I might be dead.

Not one to accept death quickly, I tried different positions of open and closed eyes until the first inklings of a wide and stubby palm frond began to take shape.

Are there palm fronds in Hell?

It didn't feel like Hell.

And you have a lot of experience with this, do you?

I didn't, but for some reason I always assumed Hell would have a lake of fire. Nearest I could tell there was no lake of fire, but to confirm that suspicion I would have to move my head.

Ouch! Ouch! Ouch!

Every muscle in my neck screamed out in pain at that modest attempt at movement. I fought through the worst of it, and twisted until I found what looked like the light at the end of the tunnel.

Don't go into the light, Gene!

The rational side of my brain was more than happy to continue providing solid recommendations as to what that light was, but it was drowned out by the more creative and rapidly panicking side.

Aliens!

The single beam split and became two bright bulbs of eye-blinding fury. I was forced to shut my own lids lest I lose what little adjustment to the dark I'd accumulated. The low rumble of a car engine, along with the snapping of dry branches caught under tires confirmed my suspicions.

It's not aliens, unless they drive cars now.

The headlights slipped past me as the car rolled to a stop along the narrow culvert. With the offending beacons gone I felt confident I could look again, but what greeted me in the soft red glow of the Cadillac's tail lights did little to make me feel better.

The mower!

Aliens would have been better, much better, than the busted-up husk of my rental mower dripping oil like spinal fluid on the muddy ground.

Porter's going to kill me.

I tried to move my arms, but found them pinned at odd angles under my sore and mostly non-functional body.

Slam.

The black Cadillac's driver door must have opened while my brain had been too busy processing the broken shell that had been the mower. I thought about saying something, but found my lips weren't moving exactly right, a byproduct of being pressed into the sand I imagined.

Crunch. Crunch.

That wasn't the hard pounding sound of boots on the gravel and soft sand, that was something different, something decidedly more luxurious.

I tried to crane my neck to get a better look at the newcomer in the warm glow of the taillights but the simple act of twisting those poor ligaments further sent a new wave of pain through my body.

"Look at you."

I didn't recognize the voice, but then again it wasn't like I would, Tampa was a city of a few hundred thousand, and I didn't know all of them.

But maybe Porter does...

I tried to respond, again forgetting my lips had swelled to roughly twice their normal size. "Hulp."

Black slacks and a pair of fancy shoes filled my vision, this wasn't the uniform of a trucker taking a shortcut through rural west Florida, this attire said money.

"Wrong place, wrong time. Eh?"

You could say that again.

My impromptu visitor crouched down in front of me, his polished shoes sinking gently in the soft sand. Those jet black slacks traced their way up to an equally black jacket, and underneath that a black button-down shirt.

This guy takes monochromatic to a whole new level.

I'd seen a few rich people in my day, so I didn't dwell too long on his attire. It was his face that trapped the air in my lungs. Clean-shaven and practically hairless, he smiled in the red light, but it wasn't a friendly smile, it was more like the smile a badger might use right before it ate your eyeballs.

"Uh..."

He held up a perfectly manicured hand to his lips. "Shh... Let's see what we have here."

This guy clearly didn't appear interested in extending a

hand, and in fact, having him this close sent a fresh dump of adrenaline into my already shaky body. I tried to untwist my arms, but they weren't responding exactly as they should have been—in other words, they didn't move.

Mr. Monochrome didn't appear to be intimidated by my impotent attempts at flopping about and instead ran a long narrow finger across my cheek.

Boom.

The effect was immediate.

Some Magicians were great at hiding it, others weren't, but when it came to direct skin on skin contact, it was damn tough to keep a fellow Magick user from knowing you carried around an unhealthy helping of cosmic power in your chest.

What the hell?

The last Magician I'd run across was Morgan Crowley, and I wasn't ashamed to say that experience had soured me more than a little on the idea of palling around with other Magickal people, places, or things. In fact, that was part of the reason my old roommate and I had lost touch. When I left him, Ed Lovely was still neck-deep in trying to save the world from the forces of darkness, while I was more interested in passing finance and keeping Porter happy, and not expressly in that order.

Judging by the highly suspect gentleman standing over me I really should have put more time into the 'fighting forces of darkness' opportunities being around Ed had afforded me.

All of this would have been enough to send my already pounding heart to max, but that wasn't even the half of it. Mr. Midnight held something up on his finger. Sure, the light was dim, but I didn't need a blinding headlamp to tell that was blood on his finger, my blood to be precise.

Hey, I need that!

What he did next sent a shock through my already confused system.

He licked his finger.

That fashion-conscious Magician licked my sandy blood off his finger like he was tasting a nice brisket, and judging by the look on his face he appeared to like it.

"Magick blood, delectable, but there's something else, I can't put my finger on it."

You just put your finger on it, and you're not doing that again.

I didn't care if my powers weren't working quite right, but I sure as hell wasn't going to lay there while that one-color freak job figured out how many licks it took to get to the center of this Tootsie-Pop.

I reached into my chest, digging deep for the cosmic power I knew would be swirling down there, hungry to be unleashed and not really caring much about the target.

"No, not tonight." The practically hairless man shook his head gently as if he were talking to a child.

Now he'd done it—I was pissed, really pissed.

Being licked like a chew toy while laying basically upside down in a culvert somewhere in Riverview can do that to a guy. This had not been my day, not by a long shot. There was a spectacular chance I'd lost anything that resembled my security deposit on the mower, and now this guy was going to tell me what I could and couldn't do, all while tasting me like an undercooked steak.

Oh, hell no.

The Magick roared to life in my chest. It expanded like a kid's party balloon and twisted into shapes that would make a clown blush. It was hungry and wanted out in the worst of ways. All I needed to do was supply it with the words and a destination.

The words? Damn it.

My swollen lips were having a tough time with English, there was no way they'd get Latin any better—I wanted to knock this guy into next Tuesday, but my mouth wasn't up for anything remotely that complicated, and as it turned out, neither was he.

Click!

My Magick hadn't counted on the subtle and mundane click of a telescoping metal rod. It all happened really fast, but somehow I went from a swirling cauldron of cosmic power, to a twenty-something on the receiving end of a metal baton upside the head.

The last thing I remembered clearly was remarking at how the baton was black too.

This guy was nothing if not consistent.

3

FOWL PLAY

That's it, I've got to be dead now.
   I tried to move but my wrists were caught up in what felt like chains.

There has to be chains in Hell.

I pulled on my arms but found them stuck in a semi-permanent position above my head.

Yep. Feeling very Hell-like now.

I figured it was time to open my eyes, but they didn't agree and tried to close again every chance they got. Before it had just been my lips that were swollen, now the rest of my face had joined in on the fun. Thick and puffy, my cheeks were making it next to impossible to get much beyond a blurry and narrow view of wherever I was.

Once again no lake of fire.

Sadly, it might have been better for me had I actually seen a lake of fire, because my current location left far too much to the scary part of the imagination.

My original guess was right—I was bound by what looked like heavy chains that kept me attached to a concrete wall. Mine weren't the only set of chains in the room, there had to be at least a dozen or more hanging from the distant walls, but none of them held any prisoners.

Lucky me.

Somewhere deep in my head panic was rising like a cresting wave, but I still didn't have enough rational thought in my twice-struck brain to pay much attention to it.

My animal brain had a different plan.

The adrenaline dump came hard and fast, flooding my muscles with an erratic life-affirming juice and urging me to yank on the chains like a crazy man. This made zero impact on the hardened steel, but had the secondary effect of tearing at the skin around my wrists like sandpaper. My heart rate skyrocketed, and I sucked down air in mad gulps. I tried kicking my feet, but they were too bruised to do much more than flop around like yesterday's catch.

This insanity continued for a few seconds before the last of the life-preserving adrenaline died down, and with it the strength to fight back. My arms dangled from the chains like spent noodles, while a single line of bright red blood slipped down my dirty wrist.

Blood.

Visions of Mr. Monochrome flashed in my mind, his finger covered with my blood and a feral smile on his hairless face.

Click. Click.

I shook away the nightmare and tried to find the source of that clicking sound.

"Is someone here?"

My voice carried in the large and cavernous room. It bounced off the walls and echoed back at me twisted and scared.

Click. Click. Click.

It was almost like scurrying, but with a decidedly metallic bent. I squinted in the dim light, not quite able to make out the furthest edges of the concrete prison. My eyes weren't in the best of shape—a black metal rod to the head will do that to a guy.

"If you can hear me, I'm trapped too."

The human eye is primed to detect movement, even the tiniest amount is enough to get our primordial brain stem hot and set it tracking, and that's exactly what I got. A flash of pink shot down the far wall. Too far away for me to make sense of, but also too small to be a person. The quickly vanishing thing couldn't have been more than a foot or two tall.

"Hey!" I said, pulling on the chains and sending a fresh trickle of blood down my arm. "I'm over here. Help me!"

Click! Click!

There was the sound again, but this time closer—too close to be honest.

"Hey!"

More movement in the shadows drew my attention.

What the hell are—flamingos?

Plastic yard birds, the kind you'd find in the front lawns of old time retirees or laying in stacks in the souvenir stores that lined the beach appeared just beyond the edge of my blurred vision.

"Uh…"

What I'd thought had been just a few, turned out to be a good bit more. A plastic flock of at least two dozen clicked their way into the halo of light surrounding me. They walked on long metal rods, no different than what you'd find on real, honest to goodness yard art. It gave them an awkward, and somewhat humorous bobbing gait.

"Um. Hi, guys, or would it be gals?"

Long necks rose and fell in time with their comical steps, but something didn't feel right, and with each step closer their black and pupil-less eyes shortened my breath.

"Okay, that's close enough. Unless you've got a plan for unhooking my wrists."

The flock gathered just beyond my legs and milled about as if waiting for something.

"Wrists, guys," I said, holding up my chains. "Any of you got a plan for my wrists? Maybe you could lend me a leg and we'll try to pick our way out of this?"

Their tiny bird heads tracked my raised arm, then my wrist, and when the first drop of my blood hit the dirty floor, they pounced.

You haven't lived until you've been rushed by a flock of soulless plastic yard birds.

"Holy shit!"

The birds rolled across my body like a wave, the sharp ends of their metal rod legs stinging my tired knees as they tore into the blood on concrete.

"Whoa! Let's not get any ideas, guys."

Too late.

The crowd cleared just long enough for what had to be the largest of the yard ornaments to approach. A long and elegant neck extended up to sniff the air, while its black and beady eyes zeroed in on the blood on my wrist.

"No, trust me, I've got abnormal plasma. You don't want it—bad stuff—it'll give you indigestion. You ever read about those birds that eat rice and explode? This is totally exploding blood. Yep, last set of plastic flamingos that snacked on my body juice —boom." I tried to pantomime an explosion with my bound wrists. "Tough way to go out if you ask me. Nothing but shards of plastic and bent metal. Didn't even have enough to do a proper identification for next of kin. It was a dustpan burial. No mourners..."

The lead bird's metal rod legs clicked on the hard concrete, stepping gently around my knees and past my thighs. I yanked my wrist back, but that only made the blood trickle more.

"Okay, okay. So maybe I lied..."

That long and elegant neck extended, its beak reaching to my bloodied arm.

"But, I'm sure it still tastes terrible. I mean, I eat like crap. You know what they say, 'garbage in, garbage out.' You don't want to eat garbage right?"

It would appear the yard bird did, his beak was now only inches from my exposed wrist.

Magick, Gene!

So far the cosmic power trapped inside me had only succeeded in making things worse, not better, but there was something about being hopelessly cornered by blood-drinking yard art that made me think it might be a good idea to try again.

The bright yellow plastic beak sniffed at my arm and I swore its coal-black eyes lit up with delight.

Oh, hell no.

I reached for my Magick, pushing past the tired muscles and dull headache, and digging for the power I knew was anxiously waiting for an opportunity to escape. It was there, but something wasn't right. The Magick that I'd expected to be full and ready to rock, instead, limped like a whipped dog.

How bad did I get hit in the head?

I didn't have time to contemplate just how close I'd come to a concussion, because my least favorite plastic yard animal was now just millimeters from my bloodied wrist. It reared back its head like a snake and zeroed in my trickling lifeblood.

"If you could just leave me a little to go on that would—"

I didn't get to finish my request before a second bird launched itself out of the flock. The creature's tiny plastic body slammed into the much larger alpha and knocked it to the ground.

What came next could only be described as a 'bird fight.' Plastic necks slapped against each other, while sharp metal rods clinked like swords.

The smaller bird was a fighter, and even though it might just be trying to win a bigger slice of the bloody Magician pie, I pulled for it just the same. The ferocity of that little mauler couldn't be denied and after a few rounds it looked to have gotten the advantage—or so I thought—but in an instant the scuffle turned and my savior found itself pinned by the metal legs of the much larger bird. It twisted in a silent squeal and scraped against the rough ground unable to fight back.

Come on, little guy. Get up!

The larger flamingo reared its neck for what I assumed would be the killing blow, when something inside me snapped. Magick that had been flopping around in my chest shot out in a completely unexpected burst and smashed into the larger bird. The alpha toppled off its perch, giving the smaller flamingo a fighting chance.

Well, that was unexpected.

4

WILLIAM TELLS

*T*he yard art battle raged across the dirty concrete. Metal clanged and plastic popped as both birds fought for dominance. The rest of the flock gathered around the melee, content to leave me alone while what I assumed would be a new alpha was selected, that is, all but one.

This little bird didn't follow the flock. It approached cautiously, those spindly metal rods clicking against the hard ground.

"Shoo!" I tried to brush it away with a foot, but it hopped my leg and continued its advance.

"Hey, get! I'm not dinner. You hear me?"

The plastic fowl pivoted past my knee on thin metal legs, its beady black eyes locked in on mine and unwavering. All around us the other birds shifted this way and that, following the tumultuous battle raging on the concrete, but not this one. None of that appeared to faze this bird, it had eyes for one thing—me.

"Go!"

The flamingo ignored me and crept closer, its head bobbing gently in the dim light.

Son of a bitch!

Black eyes stared up at me from their perch on my thigh.

"Do your worst you stupid lawn ornament. I can take it. You ever had a staring contest with a Yaga Doll?"

The flamingo's neck swung gently from side to side like the twisting dance of a cobra, its coal-black pupils never breaking contact with mine.

"I am Eugene Law, maybe you've heard of me. I've walked the Gloom and lived. I'm not afraid of—"

The bird raised a metal leg, then stabbed into my thigh, the sharp metal gliding between the soft tissue and muscle.

"Argh!"

The bird's eyes refused to break off their stare, and its head continued to sway in a mesmerizing fashion. My own heart pounded in my chest and tears formed on my cheeks, but I didn't look away. If this bird wanted to figure out who was boss, then he'd find he picked the wrong Magician to screw with.

I reached for my Magick, but before I could manage more than a trickle of cosmic power, the yard art removed its metal rod from my leg.

Dark red blood welled up on my jeans from this latest hole in my beaten body.

"Damn it, you stupid bird. I swear I'll—"

The poorly formed insult faded on my lips as the small creature bent down and let its beak drift gently across the wound. My blood tinted the creature's orange plastic beak a dark red.

"What the hell?"

I'd felt Magick before, Morgan Crowley's clockwork precision, or the wild surge of Shorty's fiery green eyes, but neither of those prepared me for this bird.

A passionate and animalistic energy raced up my leg and across my chest like a wild fire. The cosmic power lit up my brain like the Fourth of July, sending once groggy neurons firing on all cylinders.

We were communicating.

It wasn't so much thoughts as it was feelings or emotions. In that moment, the tiny plastic flamingo shared brief flashes of imagery, disjoint at first, but rapidly taking shape with the help of my hyperactive brain cells. Plastic flamingos, too many to count, drifted past in my head, their beaks chattering and squawking.

The flock...

As quickly as the image appeared it vanished, leaving me cold and alone in a terrible darkness.

Alone...

That image faded as well, and I found the little plastic bird had nestled against my chest, its beak gently pressed against my chin.

We are flock.

"Uh, listen, I don't know about that. I'm married and I'm not sure she'll be cool with a... whatever you are."

Clank!

A distant dead bolt dropped into its lock and in an instant the pitched battle for yard ornament superiority vanished. One moment the bright pink birds had been skittering across the floor, and in the next they disappeared completely.

"How'd they do that?" I asked my little companion, but she was gone too.

What the hell?

The distant door swung open slowly, its heavy wood dragging on the dusty concrete and filling the empty room with a grating scrape like fingers on an impossibly large chalk board.

I closed my eyes and hoped I might have a chance to catch Mr. Monochromatic off guard.

The sound of sniffing, like a hunting dog tasting the air, greeted me from the other side of the room. I held my breath.

Is that a dog?

"His heart is loud. William still hears good," a voice said, raspy and distorted. "His breath is warm and full of life. And he's William's, all for William."

My eyes snapped open, and I immediately wished I'd kept them closed.

The man was gaunt—impossibly so—his skin stretched tight over bones that looked oversized in the dim light. Long claw-like fingers with broken nails scraped at the air, while obscenely oversized jaws stretched out like pulled taffy, dangling gently in the hazy dark.

He took a deep breath through a nose that appeared to be no more than a hole in his face.

"It's been so long since they let William have the good blood," he said, his wide jaws waggling with each word. "But William has been a good one. He hasn't had so much as a lick of even a single tasty morsel. He has left them all for Deacon. Not a single one. Not one, not one!"

The gibbering man clapped his long and claw-like fingers together in a broken melody. "He puts them on the truck, bound and gagged, and stuffed with rags. He sends them far from home."

The man clicked his heels with each macabre stanza. "He ties them tight and makes it right. He sends them far from home."

I scrambled against the chains, but the murderous man only sang all the louder, his voice rattling against the empty walls.

"He feeds them right and holds them tight, but never takes a bite. He sends them far from home."

Magick, Gene!

I tried to push past the terror and reach for my Magick, but it was elusive and hard to hold on to. My heart was moving too fast, and I couldn't slow down my harried breathing.

"He does all these things because he must, but the Deacon sees it cause he's just. His reward is great, a feast on the plate."

The twisted man's song must have been approaching its end,

as his little jig took him to my feet. "Shall William start with the toes? The nice and crunchy toes?"

The man's face split open from beneath his nose like the fleshy wings of a large bird. Buried inside those jowls his jaw expanded to reveal a short and crooked stinger. The fleshy and serrated probe slipped from his flapping jaws. Pointed and glistening in the dim light, it danced across the insole of my dusty shoes, dipping between the laces and caressing my sock covered skin. "It smells of grass and sand, but its blood it will be grand!"

I pulled my legs up. "Holy shit!"

Bile rolled around in my gut and I thought for sure I was going to lose whatever was left in my stomach. I fought against the waves of nausea, but they kept coming, each one stronger than the last.

William took a deep breath through his whistling nose hole and ran a clawed hand along my leg. "Dark meat for dark hearts? We could grind it up and make tarts?"

The ghastly Doctor Seuss's fingers probed my bruised body like he were sizing up a piece of meat. I tried to reach for my Magick again, but my nervous system was on overdrive. My hands shook and my heart beat like a kick drum. I couldn't focus on anything beyond the long fingers and hungry jaws of that twisted and gangly thing.

"What is this?" he said, pausing to inspect the puncture wound in my thigh.

Do it, Gene!

I grasped at my Magick, and willed everything I could into a frantic scramble for power, but the cosmic forces in my chest were on tilt as much as I was, and they slipped out of my mental fingers just as fast as I could reach for them. It was like trying to catch the wind or carry the sea. My Magick was a rabbit and we had a fox at the door.

"It has spoken to the birds? Impossible, there are no birds in here. William keeps the birds out. Deacon says to keep the birds out, and William always does what Deacon says. William must be good. Deacon gives him the good blood, the tasty blood. No birds here. Sangre Reina says no birds with the tasty ones."

William's clawed hand clamped down on my leg, his sharp nails digging into my flesh, while his loose shirt fell open to reveal a sick and twisted sigil melted into the skin. Jagged lines like the beating of a broken EKG machine criss-crossed his sternum. Fleshy arms, like the legs of an insect, unfolded from the narrow valleys between his ribs. They poked at my wound and the dark blood pooling around it, their tiny hairs prickling at my skin.

"It was a bird! No one must know. William is good or Deacon would not have given him a tasty one. He will eat the tasty one and then all will be forgiven."

The gangly man's flapping jaws unfolded wider, the serrated and fleshy stinger glistening in the dim light. "For best taste, start with the face."

Oh, hell no!

5

WE ARE FLOCK

*W*illiam's dirty nails reached for my face and I lost it. A Gene-sized batch of pent up panic launched a sneaker solidly at that gangly thing's saggy mid-section. The impact was soft, like kicking a hotel pillow, but still had enough force to push that rhyming monster out of face-eating range for the moment.

"It's feisty. William likes them wiggling," the beast said, trying to right itself.

I dug deep for my Magick, and clawed for anything that might heed my call.

Please!

The cosmic energy trapped in my chest fluttered and drifted frustratingly in and out like a plastic bag in the breeze. There was no Magick for me in that moment, but something else came to answer my call.

We are Flock.

The bird!

The flamingo appeared out of nowhere, its plastic beak rubbing against the palm of my hand.

Huh?

The images came fast, almost too fast, but I got the general gist of what it wanted. I twisted my arms to expose the manacle's lock. Narrow, rod-like legs slipped into those key holes and released the chains that bound my wrists.

More images flooded my mind. This time though they came too many and too fast. I couldn't keep up with the bird.

Slow down!

But the little plastic animal didn't slow down. She was trying to tell me something but I couldn't catch up with the complexity of her message.

William got to his knees just in time to see the flittering flamingo.

"Shoo. No bird! This isn't your dinner, this is William's tasty treat."

The bright pink flamingo jumped into my lap and pressed itself against my chest, while its neck nuzzled my chin. The next image was easy to understand—it was me, holding it like you'd cradle a football.

You want me to carry you?

The bird's black eyes stared at mine, and its little head tilted gently to one side.

William's chest feelers reached for me, while saliva dripped from his unfolded face.

I didn't have a choice. My Magick wasn't answering the call, and this little bird appeared to have a plan. I just hoped that plan wasn't sitting in my lap while William ate my intestines like rope-sausage.

Here goes nothing.

I scooped the tiny bird up and held her to my chest.

Move!

The flamingo didn't have to tell me twice—that image was clear enough exactly as it was.

I scrambled out of the path of William's insect-like claws.

The gangly thing froze mid-strike, his red-rimmed eyes

searching the wall I'd been sitting against only moments before. "Impossible! Impossible! Deacon says no one joins the birds. No one!" William's claws raked at the wall in frustration.

Why hadn't he followed me? I wasn't more than a few feet from him, but my cannibalistic jailer only continued to search the wall. Why hadn't he turned to face me?

We are Flock.

The tiny bird nestled her neck against my chest and I took a few gentle steps backward. William sniffed the air like a rabid dog.

"It must be here. The tasty treat couldn't have gone far. Deacon will be angry," the twisted man muttered, running his long claws along the wall. "Deacon will not know. No one will know. William will find the tasty morsel and gobble him up. Then no one will know. William is good."

I took another gentle step backward and kept a close eye on his wildly searching arms.

More images flashed in my head.

Outside. Away.

I hugged the bird against my chest.

I can't agree more little buddy, but he'll see us.

The flamingo twisted its neck just enough to look me straight in the eye, and even though those shiny black plastic coals couldn't move, I'd swear they rolled at me.

What?

If plastic birds could sigh, my new friend did exactly that.

We are Flock.

William spun around, and his searchlight eyes taking in the wide room. "It escaped the locks. The tasty morsel escaped the locks. It must have a key. It must have sneaked a key from Deacon. Lousy Deacon, promises William a tasty treat then sneaks the treat a key. Deacon wants William to be in trouble. Deacon wants the Sangre Reina mad at William."

How the hell is he not—I am invisible.

It was the only logical conclusion.

The little plastic bird bobbed its head with considerable frustration on her almost expressionless face.

William sniffed the air, taking in great puffs through his whistling nose hole. "Too many morsels have been here. William can smell them all. Soft hair and pretty skin. Always pretty skin. It must have gone out through the door. William will find it, and then William will eat it."

The gangly thing charged and if it wasn't for a decent bit of quick footwork, I'd have taken William full on in the chest. If I had, that would have been the end of our little trick—even invisibility has its limits.

William tore past me, his face resealing while the chest feelers collapsed back beneath his shirt. He grabbed the door's handle and flung it open with enough force for it to leave a dent in the concrete wall.

"William is coming, tasty treat! He will find you and he will eat you!"

The wiry man raced into a darkened hallway, leaving me and my new friend alone in the empty prison.

I don't think so.

The tiny bird bobbed its head in assent then pressed it against my chest.

We are Flock.

I pat the flamingo's head and whispered. "We sure are little buddy. What do you say we get the hell out of here?"

I CLUTCHED the yard art to my chest like a drowning man. I wasn't about to let go of my only way out of this maze and the plastic bird didn't seem to mind. She appeared to know the complex layout of this place pretty well and occasionally used her head to direct me down one hallway or another. We heard William's voice in the distance more than once, but my plastic companion always pointed out an alternate route and kept us one step ahead of that monstrous thing.

It wasn't long before we pushed through the last door and stumbled into the humid evening air. A large moving truck sat parked just beyond the building, its engine idling in the cricket-laden dark.

"This is the last of them, right?" a voice said, coming around the edge of the truck.

Instinctively, I ducked behind a large trash can. The tiny bird sighed.

We are Flock.

I shook my head.

We are invisible, you're right. I forgot.

I stepped around the trash can to get a better look at the truck, and what appeared to be the driveway back to the road. In doing so, my elbow caught the edge of the can, and knocked its lid off and onto jagged pavement.

Clang!

"That you, Willie?"

I froze and the little bird froze with me. A large man poked his head out from the far side of the wide moving truck. "Willie?"

He stared right at me, but whatever Magick that little flamingo possessed worked, because the wide-bodied trucker didn't move.

"That thing gives me the willies," a voice from the truck's cab called out.

"You ever think that's why they named him that?"

The truck driver adjusted his hat. "Ha! That's a good one. We got to get on the road"—he looked at his watch—"cargo needs to get down south before we're late. That bitch'll be hell on us if we're late."

"Watch it. She's got eyes and ears everywhere. This shit beats running drugs, and the pay is way better, so don't fuck it up."

"Right, right." The large man checked the lock. "You have any idea what they do with them?"

"Do I look like I care?"

Somewhere deep in the building William's voice cried out again.

"Come on," the driver said, banging the side of the cab with his hand. "Let's get the hell out of here before that thing comes out."

"You got it."

The second man climbed aboard and the truck slowly pulled away from the loading area.

Now!

I tucked the bird under my arm and made a mad dash for the bumper. Like the high school jock I never was, I landed awkwardly on the rough steel ledge, and clutched at a dangling strap lest I end up back on the pavement the hard way. We hadn't made it far from the squat building before its doors burst open and a clearly angry William shouted something in the night air.

His words were lost in the rumble of the engine.

I held onto the flamingo and the strap as we bounced through the dense pine trees. We reached the dirt road and hadn't quite gotten up to speed when something shined in the faint moon light from a nearby culvert.

My bike.

"Come on, girl. Let's go home."

PART II
FLOCKED OFF

6

TAR AND FEATHERED

"*G*ene?"

William's long fingers reached for me, his jaws quivering in a soundless scream.

"Gene."

A serrated tongue snaked along my leg, lapping at the blood that was everywhere at once.

"Wake up, Gene!"

"What!" I shouted, my eyes popping open and taking the morning sun in a blinding flash.

"You were having a bad dream." Porter stood at the end of the bed attaching her earrings. As usual, my wife was up and ready with the dawn. She had a full day in the leasing office ahead of her and she liked to be the first one there.

"Low person on the ladder has to climb twice as hard," she'd said back when I asked why she was in there before the rest of the team. "I get the coffee going and prep the lobby. It's the little things, Gene. It's always the little things."

I fell back into the bed and pulled the fancy blanket over my head. "Ten more minutes."

Porter continued to move around the room like a precision

buzz saw. "You've got more jobs today. I've left your list on the counter. Try to remember to eat something before you go."

"Ugh." I rolled over and pressed the still partially swollen side of my face against the pillow.

Was it real? Did all of that happen?

I coaxed my tired brain into rewind and walking me through the events of the prior night. I remembered the ride out to Riverview, dragging the mower, and losing control. I had flashes of waking up in the dark and then the Monochromatic man.

My heart beat a little faster at the thought of his feral smile.

"I'm getting a waffle. You want one?" my wife called from the kitchen.

My stomach rumbled.

"Yeah." I kicked off the blanket only to find a narrow puncture wound on my leg, nicely healing, but an instant reminder of the events of last night.

We are Flock—the bird!

I'd put the bird in our utility closet, along with the battered mower.

The mower!

Porter opened the freezer and I could hear her tearing at a package of frozen waffles. We rarely had time to cook, and since this was the display unit we really couldn't afford to keep it in anything other than pristine condition. All that had been part of the deal. Our apartment was used to entice new renters, which meant no cooking, no mess, and very little in the way of living.

Clunk.

Porter loaded the toaster.

I swung my feet off the bed and checked myself in the standing mirror the interior designer had been nice enough to install. The bruises were there, but already fading fast. My Magick may not be working right, but at least it remembered how to stitch me up.

You can't tell her.

I fished a clean shirt out of the dresser and pulled it over my head, checking again to make sure none of the more impressive welts were showing before finding a pair of shorts.

Satisfied the puncture hole was hidden, I pulled the blanket back up to make the bed. We'd have people walking through our model apartment by mid-morning and it had to look perfect.

I hadn't gotten past fluffing the pillows when Porter's scream sent me flying over the bed.

"Gene!"

William's salivating jaws appeared in my mind.

He followed you home! He's coming for your wife!

I reached for my Magick and burst out the bedroom door in full attack mode.

"Is that oil?!"

Porter stood in the tiny kitchenette. With her arms folded, she stared daggers into a glistening trail of black that ran through the apartment like a rope of melted licorice. It snaked across the formerly spotless rug, around an off-white couch I was not allowed to sit on, and pooled nicely in front of the sliding glass door that led to our patio.

"Uh..."

The trail of toxic black continued onto the patio, cutting a perfectly staining line across the porous concrete before vanishing under the utility closet door.

"Gene! You got oil all over the apartment!" Porter ripped her waffle and mine out of the toaster and slammed them down on a waiting plate.

"I... Okay, we can fix this..."

Like hell you can.

My wife crossed our tiny living room like a hurricane, yanking open the sliding glass door and stepping around the pooling oil on her warpath toward the utility closet.

The bird.

Porter grabbed the knob, but it refused to turn. "Unlock this door!"

Shit, I locked the door.

The events of last night continued to come back to me. Together with the flamingo, I'd dragged the mower back, but in my delirious state, I'd brought it through the apartment. I remembered placing the tired bird in a small duffel bag that had been wadded up in the corner of the closet. It didn't seem to mind, and I hadn't been able to think of a better place at the time.

"Gene, there's more oil coming out! Get the keys."

I shook my head. Porter was right, inky blackness seeped out of the door seam with each pull on the knob.

Shit!

I found the keys on the counter and made my way to the patio next to her, doing my best to avoid the already spilt mess in the process.

Just open the door. Don't worry about the bird. You left her in the duffle, remember?

I put the key in the lock and took a deep breath, then opened the heavy door.

"Why is the closet full of stupid plastic flamingos?"

What?!

My wife was right, there had to been a dozen bright pink and plastic birds stacked like firewood in the narrow closet.

"I… I got them from a client," I lied, not exactly sure how to explain the pink medley to my wife.

Porter pulled them off one at a time and tossed them aside. I cringed, expecting them to go on the offensive, but nothing happened. In fact, they didn't appear to be any more than cheap plastic yard art.

I don't get it.

"Oh my God!" Porter unburied the mower and took in the full extent of the damage for the first time.

I wanted to tell her it looked worse than it was, but truth be told, it was pretty damn bad. The front edge was partially crumpled in, and the blade had bent upward, catching the engine mount and expertly puncturing a hole in the oil pan.

"What did you do?" my wife demanded, her face quickly turning red in the rising morning sun.

"I…"

How much do I tell her? Do I tell her I crashed on the way to Riverview? If you do that, she's going to wonder why you didn't get back until late. Do I tell her about William? The Flock? No. You've got a good life here and the less Magick crap that interferes with that the better off you are. It's over. You got away and there's no way they find you here. She's starring at you, you better figure something out, and fast.

"Oh, Gene," Porter said, a tear shining in her eye. "We work so hard. Do you know what this is going to cost us? I'm doing everything I can—everything, and this… I just can't process this right now."

I couldn't find the words before my wife walked past me and out the apartment door. Her heels echoed on the distant hallway, each pounding strike a hammer blow to my chest.

"Squawk?"

The dingy duffle bag jiggled, sliding off what remained of the plastic birds before landing with a thump next to my feet.

I unzipped the bag and found the plastic bird's black eyes starring up at me. The urge to pick her up was strong. All I had to do was scoop her up in my arms and vanish. I could go anywhere, disappear, drop out of life.

We are Flock.

I shook my head. What was I thinking? I had a life here, and even though I'd clearly screwed that up massively this morning, it certainly wasn't worth running away.

"Not today, little buddy," I said, gently pushing the bird back into the duffle and zipping it closed. I wasn't certain, but I could have sworn the tiny bird sighed.

Think, Gene.

The oil was a mess, but the mower was worse. I considered my Magick but dismissed that thought as quickly as it came. That was a recipe for making a big problem a thousand-fold worse.

You need help.

I went back in the apartment and slid the dirty bird bag under our bed, petting the tiny creature softly for good measure. "I'll be back."

It didn't take long to find the phone number I was looking for in one of the drawers of our kitchenette's tiny desk. I punched up the digits and held my breath.

"Hola," came a voice on the other end of the line.

"Alonzo?"

"Eugenio? What's up, buddy?"

"I've got a problem."

"Again?"

"Yeah."

"How bad?"

I placed the phone against my chest and surveyed the damage. "Do you know how to get oil out of carpet?"

"I'm on my way."

I thanked him at least a dozen times then put the phone down and glanced at the clock. I had an hour before the first potential residents could be walking through our decidedly un-showable showroom model.

Rapido, my friend. Rapido!

7

MR. FIXIT

Bang! Bang!
   I sprung to my feet and flung the door open. Alonzo stood on my welcome mat, a bevy of cleaning supplies in one hand, and in the other, three plastic pink flamingos.

"You redecorating, Eugenio?" he said, shoving the plastic birds in my hand.

"Uh, yeah. Porter's mom gave them to us." I accepted the yard art and set them on the counter. I didn't have time to make sense of that now.

"No yard decorations on the grounds."

"Right." I nodded, guiding the older man into the apartment.

Alonzo always reminded me of my days spent watching Saturday morning cartoons as a kid. If there were ever a man that was the Spanish template for Fred Flintstone it was Alonzo. A barrel-chested, brick-layer of a man, with callused hands and leathery brown, sun-scorched skin.

He rubbed at his mustache and starred at the glistening oil. "Why did you bring the mower through the apartment?"

Why did I?

Truth be told, I couldn't remember. Much of last night was a blur and for some reason I must have thought it made good sense to roll the oil leaking mower through the apartment.

"I was—"

"Drunk?" the maintenance man asked, completing my sentence for me and providing an excellent alibi.

"Yeah."

"Eugenio, you've got to cut back. How many times is this?"

"Uh…"

Alonzo set his bucket down and bent his knees to get a better look at the oil stain. "I'll help you count. First, you clogged the disposal with potato skins."

"I was trying to make a Shepherd's pie for Porter."

Alonzo put his head at eye level with the oil. "Uh, huh. You also found a way to overload the thermostat and left scorch marks on the wall."

"Yeah, but that was during a heat wave and I…" I said, letting my voice trail off. I'd been trying to use my Magick to chill the apartment faster. That was back before I really noticed how uncontrollable it had become.

"And each time have I told Porter?"

"No."

"Eugenio, this is bad," he said, handing me a bag of cat litter.

"What's this for?"

"Soak up the oil and save some in case Porter decides to kick you out and just get a cat. It might be easier for everyone."

Very funny.

The next thirty minutes was spent working through the oil in as orderly a fashion as we could muster. Alonzo did most of the directing, while I worked up one hell of a sweat following his instructions. Eventually we got around to the patio, the utility closet, and the lawn mower.

"Eugenio! What did you do?"

Alonzo may have worked for the complex, but he and I were

tight, and as such I felt reasonably comfortable laying out some of what happened to him. "I crashed."

"Into what? A commuter plane? Did you finish by hitting it with a sledgehammer?"

"Very funny." I helped the older maintenance man remove the mower from the utility closet. "It's not that bad."

"It isn't?" He tilted the body of the behemoth up to check the undercarriage. "Hmm..."

"See," I pointed to the bent blade, "just need to get that blade fixed... right?"

Alonzo wiped off the oil and pointed to the punctured pan. "And replace the oil pan, and it looks like the blade shroud is bent. This is a rental, isn't it?"

"Yeah."

"Ouch."

I sighed and leaned against the sliding glass door, letting the cool glass soften the coming financial blow.

"How much do you think it'll cost to fix?"

"Two hundred, at least."

My stomach dropped out from under me and I was suddenly quite happy I'd chosen to lean against something. "No... Really?"

The maintenance man nodded, popping the throttle in and out. "Might have to check the cables too. How fast were you going?"

"Not that fast!"

Alonzo shook his head and let out a low whistle. "If you say so."

"Shit," I said, banging my hand against the door. "Porter's gonna kill me."

"Yep."

"You aren't helping."

The older maintenance man smiled and finished cleaning

the last of the oil off our patio. "Well, I might have an idea, but you aren't going to like it."

"What? What's your idea?"

"Sweep that up," Alonzo said, pointing me to a pile of unused litter.

I grabbed the push broom and went to work on the offending gravel. "Well?"

"I'm thinking. Here," he pointed to the monster mower, "hold the pull-bar while I tighten this cable."

I set the broom aside and grabbed the pull-bar, doing everything I could to keep my hands rigid and steady.

"Yeah, that'll work," the older man said, a furtive smile on his face.

"What?"

Alonzo wiped the sweat from his chin with his shirt. "Help me get this cleaned up and we'll see if we have a spare uniform that fits you."

"Uniform?"

My plans to recuperate and figure out what the hell to do about the multiplying yard ornaments vanished in the twinkle of Alonzo's walnut eyes.

"Yup, I think I've got an old one you can use."

"Great…"

"Afterwards you and I can run that monster over to my brother's place in Ybor. He fixes all manner of motors and he might be able to help you out."

"I don't have any—"

"Money?" the older maintenance man said, checking the throttle cable.

"Yeah."

Alonzo stepped back and landed a strong hand on my sweaty back. "You work like this the rest of today and you won't have to worry about it."

"Seriously?"

The older maintenance man laughed. "Yeah. I can't have Porter murdering you. If she got arrested, we'd lose the most beautiful girl in the office."

"I don't know whether to take that as a compliment, or to—"

Alonzo cut me off and pointed toward the inside door. "She's coming."

He was right. The telltale pop of my wife's heels on the hard concrete echoed in the narrow hallway.

"How'd she know it would be... She called you didn't she?"

The maintenance man nodded. "A few minutes after you did."

"So you knew all along?"

Alonzo smiled and motioned for me to scoop up what remained of the cleaning supplies. "Uh huh, but it was your idea to get the mower fixed."

"Right, the mower. What do we do?"

Alonzo pointed to the wide green space beyond the patio. "We let your wife show the unit and we push that monster out front through the grass.

Much smarter.

Porter's voice echoed in the hallway. "So this is our one-bedroom unit. It has a cute kitchen and..."

"Come on, Eugenio!"

I hesitated. Something in my head held me back.

The birds!

There were more of them now. If that were even possible.

"What are you doing?" the maintenance man asked, but I was already inside and it was too late to answer.

I scooped up the suddenly multiplied plastic birds and searched frantically for a place to put them. I settled on shoving them in our tiny pantry. The hard pink bodies barely fit wedged between the cereal boxes and ramen noodles.

Squawk?

"The bird!"

Porter's key hit the lock at roughly the same time I reached the bedroom. The duffle wasn't under the bed anymore, it now lay on the floor, half-unzipped with the bright pink head of my new friend sticking out of it.

Clunk!

"So where did you say you two were from again?" my wife asked in that pristine and cheerful voice she reserved for special occasions or client showings.

"Oh, Maddie's from Alachua. That's just outside of Gainesville, are you familiar with that area?"

"Very," Porter said, a hint of annoyance in her voice. "As you can see the living room is cozy with a great sliding glass door to take you out to a private patio."

Squawk?

"Shh." I clamped a hand on the tiny bird's beak. "We've got to go."

Images flashed in my head, all I had to do was pick up the bird and walk right out, and she would do the rest. I unzipped the bag and cradled the tiny plastic fowl.

More images followed—freedom, power, destiny. The tiny bird flooded my mind with thousands of options in the blink of an eye.

We are Flock!

Nowhere was off limits and nothing was beyond our grasp. Together with this little bird, I could be unstoppable.

"So, this is the bedroom." My wife pushed open the door and kicked the empty duffle under the bed in a single fluid motion. "You'll see its got a large window as well, and a door directly to the bathroom."

I didn't hang around for the rest of the tour, instead the tiny bird and I slipped out through that adjoining bathroom and into the living room.

Crack!

I stopped to find a pink plastic flamingo broken under my shoe.

Where are these things coming from?

I scooped the broken pieces up and tossed them in the trash before slipping out the door unseen.

We were Flock, and we had things to do.

8

BURNED EGGS

A warm breeze funneled through the narrow hallway between the first floor apartments. The little plastic bird pressed its neck against mine and together we walked softly between the units.

Hungry.

The tiny pink bird filled my mind with a flash of images—someone was having breakfast and it smelled pretty good to us.

Like she was guiding a plow horse, the flamingo jabbed me with her beak and directed me toward our neighbor's unit—Mark and Alyssa.

Mark made his money working for his father-in-law's firm. He was a pretty successful young attorney, or so he said. Our neighbor was keen on making sure everyone knew just how good he was doing. I placed an invisible hand on their door and leaned in to listen at the cool steel.

"I'm going to be late!" Mark said, even muffled by the door, his voice was easy to pick out, it smacked of authority with more than a hint of entitlement.

"Fine, just get out of here then. I don't care."

That was Alyssa. I had no idea what she did other than

lounge around the apartment during the day blaring soap operas at max volume. I knew this because lately I'd been spending my day lounging around our apartment. It was hard to be angry with someone for doing the same thing you were doing, but I had the moxie to pull it off.

Hungry...

The little bird was right—I was hungry. Someone on the other side of that door had made eggs.

"Eggs?" I whispered to the tiny bird.

It shrugged its shoulders.

I guess even birds like eggs.

Movement inside the apartment caused me to spring back, and not a moment too soon. The door swung open, and a perturbed Mark burst out. His leather briefcase swung fast and I had to jump back a second time to avoid taking it full on in the man-parts.

"Can you at least try to do something today?" The young attorney flipped his head to the side in that annoying hair flicking motion both Porter and I hated oh so much.

"Whatever. How about you focus on not disappointing my dad?" Alyssa said, she hadn't gotten dressed yet, then again I wasn't sure we'd ever seen her outside of her two potential states. Alyssa was either in pajamas or dressed to the nines in a form-fitting number with five-inch heels. There was no in between with that one, and since it was before ten pm it was clearly pajama time.

Mark appeared to have a few choice responses prepared but Alyssa's stern eye kept his mouth shut. He adjusted his tie and stomped off toward the parking lot.

Now!

The little bird didn't know much about verbal communication, but it knew timing. I slipped in through the open door before Alyssa could slam it shut. Neither Porter nor I had ever been in Mark and Alyssa's place, and at this point I'd been rather disappointed by that fact. I'd always assumed lawyer money would outfit one hell of an apartment and I was keen to see it.

I was wrong.

Alyssa pushed her thick, long hair behind her ears and flopped down on a clothes-covered couch. She fumbled for the TV remote as I took in the rest of the two bedroom unit. Newspapers and glossy magazines lay in collapsing stacks throughout the kitchenette. Porter and I didn't have much in the way of countertop space, but we were wealthy landowners compared to Alyssa and Mark.

Sizzle. Pop!

"Fuck!" Alyssa shouted, pulling herself out of the couch and away from the weather segment to check on the eggs. "Shit, shit, shit."

They weren't quite burnt, but they weren't quite as good smelling as they'd been a few moments ago.

The tiny bird perked its head up and sniffed at the air. I could sense the concern in its plastic body like I felt the pressure drop before a storm.

What is it?

The bird didn't answer. She provided no images beyond a general sense of unease.

Alyssa tossed the skillet into the sink and turned on the water, filling the small apartment with a cloud of hissing steam. The young woman slammed her hand on the counter. "Stupid, stupid!"

My flamingo choose that moment to pull hard for the door. "What is it?" I whispered, hoping my voice was covered by the pounding faucet.

"Your bird doesn't like me, Gene."

I froze, my hands struggling to hold on to a no longer placid plastic animal. I knew that voice, even if I hadn't heard it in years. The sound of that melodious tone took me back to a singular moment all those years ago. In an instant, I was standing on the Floor of Unresolved Fears all over again, the street preacher's hands crushing Samantha's withered skull.

I backpedaled fast, clearing the tiny kitchen and beating a path to the door. A path now blocked by a suddenly very well-dressed Alyssa. Gone were the pajamas, and in their place was a form-fitting dress, that left very little, if anything, to the imagination. "Is this better, Gene?"

The tiny bird scrambled to be free of my hands. It sent a barrage of images into my mind, too many to count.

Let go!

"Oh, does your little devil bird want to go? You joined a Flock, eh? See, I knew you had a dark streak in there. I didn't expect it to be quite so perverted, but hey, we work with what we've got." Alyssa took a step toward me and let her fingers trace the line of her low-cut collar.

The images became a blur. It was too much. I was flooded with a shuddering wave of pure emotion.

Fear!

The little flamingo's beak swung around and snapped at my face.

"Argh!" I shouted, dropping the plastic bird the moment she bit into my cheek. "What the hell?"

The creature hit the ground and vanished, its clicking metal feet quickly fading on the hard tile.

"What can I say?" The Alyssa-looking thing shrugged its perfect shoulders. "I have that effect on people."

"What are you?"

Our neighbor smiled and shook her thick mane. "You're asking the wrong question, Gene. You keep asking the wrong question. You should be asking, 'Who am I?' Or more importantly, 'Who do I want to be?' "

"I remember you from—"

"The Gloom?" Alyssa said, taking another seductive step

toward me. "Such a boring place. I'm glad you didn't decide to stay there too long. You're needed out here. Out in the real world with me."

"Who are you?"

Alyssa only smiled and spun around to show off the unzipped back of her sultry dress. "Zip me up?"

"I…"

The beautiful woman shook her head and giggled. "Fine, this is just too much for you, I get that. Should we go back to something more comfortable?"

My heart was pounding too hard to respond.

"I'll take that as a yes." Alyssa turned around and became the spitting image of Morgan Crowley.

That pounding heart lodged solidly in my throat.

"Is this better?" my former girlfriend said, her hair a brilliant green and her bright eyes digging into my brain like an ice pick.

"Morgan!"

"No, silly. I'm no more Morgan than I was your ample-chested neighbor, although I am learning you really do have a 'type,' don't you?" The Morgan-looking thing squeezed her breasts in an almost perfunctory manner. "I can't say I understand it, but that's always been the fun of human beings. You are such complex little creatures. Long on emotions, and short of intelligence, but that's not why I like you, Eugene Law."

I glanced at the door, but Morgan had me blocked.

The patio!

"You've got that special something. It's subtle." My ex-girlfriend took a deep breath as if she were enjoying a nice bouquet. "Just the right mixture of pain, loss, and moral ambiguity. I think you'll succeed where all the others failed. I've got high hopes for you, Eugene Law."

I backed toward the patio door, all the while trying to keep the woman who shouldn't be standing there distracted. "If it's Magick you're after, I'm afraid you're shit out of luck. My powers are all over the map, in fact I'm convinced they hate me more and more with each day."

Morgan followed me around the couch, her bright green hair catching the light of the morning sun. "Oh, sweetheart, that's nothing. You're still learning the ins and outs. You just need a good teacher. I'd be happy to take over that role."

I checked the sliding glass door; it was unlocked. "I think I can manage."

"No, you really can't," my old roommate said, Ed Lovely taking the place that had been occupied by Morgan only seconds ago. "You were smart enough to avoid this idiot and his failure of a life, but I'm starting to get the feeling you aren't going to get where I need you to be. You're too busy letting the Magick run you. That's not how this works."

I reached behind me and let my fingers catch on the sliding door's handle. "Stay away from me!" I shouted, pulling the door open and letting the humid air rush into the cool apartment.

"I'll see you again soon, sweetheart," Alyssa said, her chest practically falling out of her dress.

I ran across the short-cropped grass and past the well-manicured bushes, hitting the blacktop and practically running into Alonzo and my mower.

"Eugenio, you ready?"

Yes!

Anything was better than another one-on-one session with whatever that thing was.

Anything.

9
ROBED IN

"*G*eronimo!" Alonzo called down before dropping another large palm branch on my head. It was the fourth one this morning and arguably the nastiest one yet.

"Got it." I stepped aside just enough to get whipped across the shoulders by the offending branch.

"Drag 'em around front," the older man called down his perch on the ladder.

I know.

I grabbed the ends of the spindly fronds and hauled them into the parking lot. The palms scraped across the blacktop behind me, leaving a trail of stripped blades and dirt. I stopped about halfway across the asphalt desert and wiped my face with the bottom of Alonzo's old work shirt. It had to be over ninety degrees by now, and it wasn't much past eleven.

Just keep going...

I took a deep breath and resumed my drag toward the dumpster, stealing glances at the apartments around me and wishing I was inside one of them right now instead of frying myself slowly on the unforgiving blacktop. There wasn't much to see. Most of the young and hip tenants, like Mike and Alyssa, had long since left for high paying office jobs.

You don't know what those are, Gene.

The complex wasn't all mega-money hipsters though, it did house a few retirees, and I wasn't far from the building they tended to lease out of. Unit 'C' was nearest to the dumpster and a tiny grassy area that served as a dog-curbing mine field for the community's elder residents.

Three floors up I caught the flapping of fabric in the breeze, a breeze that had not made it down to ground level.

Mr. Jenkins stood on his balcony, newspaper expertly rolled under his arm, while his opposite hand cradled a cup of coffee. He stared off into the distance behind a pair of tinted glasses. The old man's spotted head held only a few remaining hairs, all of which danced in time with the whispering wind. According to Porter, Mr. Jenkins was the complex's longest tenured resident; rumor was he'd lived here in a small house before the apartments had been built, and part of his buy-out had been a rent-free unit for life.

The original developers and their lawyers must have been pretty smug about the whole thing, but I imagined they hadn't expected the old man to live as long as he had.

The breeze kicked up enough for me to feel it, and in turn it caught the seam of Mr. Jenkins' robe, throwing the sides wide open and providing me with the answer to an unpleasant bit of trivia I hoped I was never asked about.

Mr. Jenkins is not a fan of underpants.

I turned my attention from the impromptu flashing and focused on getting this next bundle of queen palm fronds to the dumpster.

"Hey, kid!"

He's not talking to you.

"I'm talking to you," an ornery Mr. Jenkins called down again. "Where's Alonzo?"

"Uh, he's around the other building," I said, wrangling the unruly palm bundle.

"Do you know when he's coming back?"

What do I look like? His secretary?

The palm bundle shifted in my fingers, slipping down far enough that I had to use a knee to hoist it back up. "No, sir. I'm sorry."

Even from three floors up I could hear Mr. Jenkins sigh. "Well, damn it. How much do you know about fixing toilets?"

I hopped forward on one foot, precariously balancing the heavy palms while trying not to end up in the heap with them. "Uh... that depends."

Mr. Jenkins smacked his newspaper against his leg. "Excellent, finish up that nonsense and come on up right away. I'm in unit three-oh-three. Be sure to wipe your feet."

The palm branches crashed perfectly into my already built up pile, this time only taking a small bit of skin off my already sore hands.

"Uh, sir. I..."

The balcony was empty, Mr. Jenkins and his largely useless robe were long gone.

Shit.

"Go see what his problem is, Eugenio," Alonzo said, clearing the corner with a bucket of hot tar. "Once you're done, we have a roof to patch."

For what had to have been the first time in my life, the thought of fixing a broken toilet really sounded excellent.

"Got it."

I TRUDGED up the steps to the third floor dragging Alonzo's bucket of plumbing supplies with me. The man had everything in that plastic bin: spare pipes, drain snakes, epoxy, even a smattering of fixtures in various states of usable. The five-gallon bucket clunked against my leg, and was sure to be leaving a painful mark I'd get to enjoy at the end of the day.

I paused at the breezeway between the units to look down on the complex. The leasing office golf cart shot past, and I could have sworn I caught the edge of Porter's hair snapping in the wind.

Okay, so maybe I was a little envious, but could you blame me? We'd both graduated from the University of Florida. We both had degrees, and we both were capable and well-adjusted adults.

Mostly.

But she was the one that got the job. She was the one that got every job. If she so much as sniffed at an opportunity it damn near jumped in her lap and kissed her. Me, on the other hand, if I even looked at a potential job opening I'd receive a pre-emptive call telling me not to apply.

I set the heavy bucket down and let the cool breeze wash over me as the tiny golf cart zipped around the corner and out of sight.

It hadn't started out like this. Neither of us had been what you'd have called 'well off' when we'd graduated, but we hadn't been scraping together nickels for warmth either. Still, all of that ended when Porter's Dad went into the hospital. Her mom needed all the help she could get, and even with Porter's brothers still in Missouri and doing what they could, my wife felt it was important to send money to help cover the mounting bills.

Neither of us could have known at the time just how hard it would be for me to find employment, or just how many random things would go so wrong in the process. To make matters worse, Porter's Dad wasn't getting any better, and soon we might have to find a way to scrape together enough cash to get her up there one last time.

I sighed and shook my head, then picked up the bucket and started searching for Mr. Jenkins' unit.

Three-o-one, three-o-two... Ah ha. There you are, three-o-three.

I should have guessed it as much when I noticed the welcome mat sitting in front of the door was roughly as unwelcoming as Mr. Jenkins himself.

Solicitors will be eaten.

I set the bucket down and knocked gently on the hollow metal door. "Mr. Jenkins, it's me, Eugeni—Gene."

"Who?" a gruff voice said from the other side of the door. "We don't want any."

Somewhere inside a dog barked.

"I'm from maintenance." I rattled the bucket of plumbing tools against my leg.

"Huh? Go away or I'm calling the cops."

"I'm here to fix the toilet."

The dog barked a few more times before I heard the telltale crinkling of a plastic bag. "Here, take this and pipe down—I got a Magician to come and fix the toilet."

Bark!

"I know, right? What are the chances?"

10

PLUMBING THE DEPTHS

I froze, mouth agape, and hand still in that half-knocking position laying against the painted metal when the door swung in and the negative pressure practically pulled me into the apartment.

"Don't just stand there. You'll let all the mosquitoes in," the elderly man said, his pale fingers yanking me by the arm into the dimly lit room.

I felt the crackle of Magick the instant his fingers touched me.

Magician.

My brain was still processing Mr. Jenkins last words to his dog, which made it very difficult to take in the confining nature of the tiny apartment.

Dog.

Mr. Jenkins' pony-sized pet padded up to me. He was easily over a hundred pounds, and very little of that appeared to be muscle. His long black and brown fur did little to hide the dog's robust appearance.

"What do you think, Marco? Is he a decent test?"

The large dog pressed its nose against my hip and breathed deeply, then proceeded to sneeze a few times.

Bark!

"Yeah, I think so, plus he says he can fix the toilet."

The mountain dog wagged his tail and whacked it against the counter.

Thump. Thump. Thump.

Mr. Jenkins nodded his head, sending his wispy hairs dancing in concert with the rest of his frail body. "Yes, yes. The lovely ladies on the second floor are getting tired of letting me use their commode."

Marco shoved his nose against the pocket of the old man's robe. Mr. Jenkins dug in and produced a dusty treat. "Last one, now, I've got work to do. Don't pester me."

The dog growled and pawed at the dirty tile in the tiny entrance way—a spot that barely held the three of us and Alonzo's bucket.

"He'll be fine. I know what I'm doing."

Bark!

"That was *one* time, and frankly it wasn't my fault."

Snort!

"Fine, I'll ask him," Mr. Jenkins said, throwing his hands in the air and giving an inadvertent view of his opening robe.

Underpants. Thank God.

"Kid, are you pregnant?"

"What?! No."

"See," Mr. Jenkins said, motioning to the dog. "And I bet he's not lactating either, right?"

"No. I'm… what does any of this have to do with fixing your toilet?"

"Nothing." The old man pointed me toward the bathroom. "The dog's just a mother hen. See, he's not pregnant, nor lactating. Are you happy now?"

Hrmph!

The mountain dog padded away and laid down on the patio, then promptly rolled over and turned his butt to face the old man.

"That's more like it," Mr. Jenkins said, moving me to a position just outside the bathroom door. "Now if you'll just stand here for a second, we can run the test."

"Don't you have a toilet that needs to be fixed?"

Mr. Jenkins paused and placed a hand to his face. "You're right. I think we ought to get that toilet fixed first. Just in case."

"Just in case of what?"

The old guy didn't answer, instead he opened the door and pushed me into the dingy bathroom.

Mr. Jenkins was clearly not a fan of cleaning products, his sink had enough rings to make Saturn blush, and the toilet appeared to have decided it would rather clog itself in protest then spend another day in these conditions.

"All right, so there's the problem." He leaned over to point at the offending bowl.

"It's clogged?"

"In so many words, yes."

"Have you tried—"

Mr. Jenkins threw his hands in the air. "I've tried the Hercomer Healing, the Nine Ninnies of Nelvim, Elvick's Eviction, plus at least five different rituals, and I even bought some of this stuff." The old man grabbed a box of something designed to fix a septic tank. "It says right here it's got active enzymes. Do you know what they do?"

"No."

"Nothing."

I set down the plastic bucket and peered into the abyss. "Have you tried a plunger?"

"What's that you say?"

I fished Alonzo's wooden-handled clog remover out of the bucket and held it up. "This, have you tried one of these?"

"Yes, of course. Do I look like a fool?"

Somewhere from the patio a dog barked.

"He didn't ask you!" Mr. Jenkins shouted.

"Well, if you've already plunged it I don't know what else I can do," I said, moving the plunger back to the bucket.

"No, stop, maybe it just needs another good whack. I mean, maybe I loosened it. Go ahead, give it a go."

Mr. Jenkins' toilet needed more than one good whack. After twenty plunges I stopped counting, but that didn't stop the old man from urging me on. "Come on, kid. You can do it! Put your back into it. Are you gonna let this modern marvel beat you? No sir, you show that commode who wears the pants!"

"I'm wearing shorts," I said, wiping the sweat from my face.

"Oh, well, you really ought to think about wearing pants."

"Why's that?"

Mr. Jenkins pointed at my legs. "Those aren't much to write home about."

Sigh.

The old man took a seat against the sink and grabbed the top page off the stack of newspapers laying next to the toilet. "Don't want to get any water on these…"

"Uh huh," I said, pausing to catch my breath.

"What do you think of this place?" He pointed at a thumb-nail-sized and grainy picture of a small white house.

"Looks fine."

"No it doesn't. It looks like hell."

Water splashed on the floor. "Okay."

Mr. Jenkins scooted his slippered feet out of the way of the vile liquid and folded the paper over to put the picture front and center. "Yeah, Mallory Lane. 69 Mallory Lane… sounds perfectly terrible, doesn't it?"

"Sure."

A half-dozen more poundings and finally the porcelain

throne relented. A couple of burps of stomach churning gas and water, and the bowl drained beautifully.

"You did it! Nice work, kid."

"Thanks." I rinsed the rubber end of the plunger off in the old man's tub. "Well, I've got to run."

Don't remember... Don't remember...

"Oh, wait, I almost forgot. I need you to help me with a test."

Damn.

"Listen, Mr. Jenkins. I'm touched you think I could help you," I said, going for maximum buttering. "But I'm not sure there's anything—"

"Nonsense, kid. You're a Magician, right?"

"I... Yeah, but—"

"Excellent! Come on, I'll show you."

I placed the plunger in the bucket and followed the old man back into his living room. Marco the dog had taken up residence on a fur-covered couch and barely opened an eye at my arrival.

"Okay, if you'll just take a seat here," Mr. Jenkins pointed to a recliner that sat opposite the chair, "then we can get started."

I set the bucket down and hesitated. "I don't know..."

Visions of terrible Magick rolled through my head like a bad horror movie. In one scene, I was consumed by the chair, and in another I was torn limb from limb by the cheap furniture's thick arms. Most of the visions involved terrible pain of one kind or another.

Too many late night movies...

"Bah." The old Magician pushed me back into the recliner with a surprising amount of strength for his wiry frame. "You're a Magician. You'll be fine. Now, here's what I need you to do." Mr. Jenkins proceeded to explain a massively complex set of sigils and Magickal machinations. Even in my heyday with Morgan, I would have been hard pressed to follow his unconventional train of thought.

"So, you got it?" he asked, leaning in to give me an excellent view of his uneven facial hair.

"Uh."

The old man threw his hands in the air. "Damn it! Listen, just hit me."

"Excuse me."

Mr. Jenkins cinched up his robe, sealing off the view of his tighty whiteys and improving my morning immeasurably in the process. "Hit me."

"You want me to punch you?"

"No, you ninny. I want you to hit me with the best Magick you've got."

"What?" I said, pulling myself out of the recliner only to be pushed back into it.

"No, you've got to stay seated."

"Huh?"

Marco barked from the couch.

"Yes, I know it's limited in its present state, but this is just a test, we'll scale up as needed."

"Listen, I'm not sure I can—"

The old Magician cut me off and slapped me clean across the face. "Can you now?"

Hell yeah I can.

I reached for my Magick, digging into that reservoir of cosmic power just itching to be set free to wreak havoc in the real world.

"Well? Come on, kid. I don't have all day."

The Magick swirled in my chest and I drew it out like a crashing wave. "Ledo!" I cried, sending the energy into a fist and headed right at that smug old man's face. In my mind, I saw him fall over and clutch at a broken nose, but that wasn't what happened, instead of a knockout punch between the eyes, my Magick settled on a petite showering of flower petals.

"Huh, I did say hit me, right?"

What the hell?

I reached down again, but this time the Magick evaded my grasp, just like it had with William breathing down my neck. Back then I thought it was the stress of being near eaten alive, now I wasn't quite so sure.

"I…"

The old man tilted his head to one side and pursed his lips. "Performance issues?"

"No. Just give me a second and I'll do it."

Mr. Jenkins nodded and leaned in for the punch. "Sure, sure. Sometimes you gotta get warmed up. Put it right here," he said, pointing at the grey stubble of his chin. "Don't worry about hurting me. It's a new design I'm working on, 'Jenkins' Jelly.' "

I took a deep breath and focused, pulling everything I could out of the reservoir of power that welled up inside me. I sent all of that power directly at the old man. Back in Gainesville, Morgan had said I hit like a dump truck, and I was ready to show that old Magician just how much horsepower I kept under the hood.

Thump!

I opened my eyes to find myself staring at a modest-sized sack of uncooked oats sitting in Mr. Jenkins' lap.

"Uh… Listen, never mind. We can do it another time. It's no problem. This sort of thing happens to everyone at some point."

"Has it happened to you before?"

Mr. Jenkins whipped his head back like I'd offered him a pit viper sandwich. "No, of course not, but don't sweat it, kid. I'm sure it's a one-time thing."

"Actually, it's been happening to me a lot lately."

Mr. Jenkins stood and helped me out of the chair. "Oh, that's a problem then. I'd worry about that."

"What?!"

Marco rolled over and barked at the door.

"Gene, meet me on the roof when you're done," Alonzo called from outside.

"Well, thanks for fixing the commode, Gene. Sorry about all the Magick stuff. I'm sure you'll figure it out."

Bark!

"Oh no, Marco." Mr. Jenkins grabbed my bucket and handed it to me. "I'm most certainly not in the business of addressing performance anxiety issues."

Bark! Bark!

"I don't care how much he reminds you of a younger version of me."

Growl.

"Right, a younger and better-looking version of me, just don't forget who gets you the 'Mar-vee-poo' peanut butter treats."

The mountain dog sighed and rolled over on the couch.

"That's what I thought." The old Magician guided me to the door of his oddly shaped apartment.

"Wait, do you know why—"

"No idea, kid. Things like that just happen. I tell you what though, I'll keep the oats—never can be too regular—and if you find yourself in a Magick pickle, you come see me and I'll lend you a hand."

Mr. Jenkins had the door open before I could formulate a response. "But... I..."

"Roof access is at the end of the hall to the right. Good luck!"

Wham!

The door to unit three oh three slammed shut, leaving me in a narrow breezeway with a bucket of plumbing parts and more questions than answers.

11

CALIENTE

*A*lonzo handed me a lukewarm bottle of water. "You've done good, Eugenio."

We leaned against the cool body of his truck as it lay under the shade of a great oak tree near the back of the property.

"Thanks," I mumbled between long gulps from the bottle. My lips felt like they were sloughing off in chunks, but surprisingly I found them still attached when I wiped a hand across my face.

Go figure.

The older maintenance man caught me pressing the half empty bottle against my cheek and chuckled. "You got some sun today."

Ya think? Porter's gonna kill me.

I stretched my legs out in the cool grass. "Yeah, a little."

The day hadn't ended after patching the roof, not by a long shot. Alonzo's 'to-do list' had been stuff of legend—hercules would have thrown in the towel had he been handed that monster.

Together with the litany of impossible tasks, we'd raced up and down the property all morning. Somewhere around lunch time he'd pulled a microwave out of the back of his trailer like a stage magician and nuked us a couple of burritos. I hadn't complained, those piping hot rolls of beans and rice hit the spot in a way I'd found hard to imagine before today.

The rest of the afternoon had been spent repairing a hole in the fence where it appeared kids were sneaking in and out at night. It wasn't long after attaching the final few feet of rolled metal chain that we decided to call it a day and that was how we ended up here, in the shade of the oak, and enjoying the final light of the setting sun.

I tilted the bottle and drained the remaining water in one swallow.

Alonzo stood and rubbed his back, taking my empty bottle and his, and throwing them in the nearby dumpster. "Ready to go?"

"Go?" I asked, my voice breaking like a pre-pubescent teen.

"Yeah. Let's get your mower to Miguel."

I raised a hand to block the last rays of a setting sun. "Now?"

Alonzo nodded and pulled open the truck's passenger door. "Well, only if you want a free dinner in Ybor."

"You had me at free," I said, dragging my beaten body off the ground and depositing it on the hot vinyl passenger seat.

"I thought so." The truck's engine rumbled to life and two dim headlights popped on to illuminate the darkening pavement.

I leaned against the door and let my eyes drift in and out, but it wasn't long before a quick smack on the leg from Alonzo ejected me from my haze.

"Porter..."

He was right. My wife had just finished locking up the leasing office and was on her way down the sidewalk toward our unit. She carried her heels in her hands like she always did after a hard day on her feet.

"You want me to stop?" the older maintenance man asked, slowing the truck.

"Yeah. Give me a second, okay?"

"Sure."

Alonzo slowed the truck to a standstill, and I climbed out the passenger side. Porter held up a hand to block the sunlight cutting across the horizon. "Gene?"

"Yeah."

"What are you doing?"

I pointed to the mower laying like a murder victim in the bed of Alonzo's trailer. "I'm making it right."

"What do you mean?"

"I spent the day working for Alonzo. In return he said his brother would fix the mower and we'll be good as new."

It was hard to tell, but I thought I saw a tear in my wife's eyes, but it could just as easily have been the sun. "Really?"

"Really."

"Gene, that's great!"

My wife leapt off the curb and threw her arms around me. This was a much more emotional response than I expected, but hey, I wasn't going to turn down a hug from Porter—not now, and not ever.

It was with my wife in my arms that I noticed something along the edge of the perfectly manicured bushes that lined the front office.

A pink plastic flamingo, or more truthfully, three of them.

The Flock is growing.

I didn't have much time to contemplate this concerning turn of events before Alonzo rolled down his window and hollered to Porter and I.

"You got a good one, señorita."

My wife let go and wiped her eyes. "I know. He can be a pain from time to time, but—"

"But he knows to call Alonzo when he gets in over his head," I said, finishing Porter's sentence.

"Exactly." She slapped me on the butt before turning her attention to the maintenance man. "You taking him out for beers?"

"Better. Dinner in Ybor. You want to come?"

My wife politely shook her head. "No, I'm up to my armpits in paperwork. Thank you for keeping us from losing the security deposit on the model unit."

"No problem." Alonzo smiled.

Porter gave us one last wave goodbye and started back toward the apartment, but hadn't gone a few feet before she stopped. "Oh, Gene, if you can believe it, Alyssa stopped by the leasing office today. You know, our neighbor, the one we never see?"

My heart dropped into my toes and I'd swear half the color drained from my sun-burned face. "Yeah?"

"Yeah. She wants to get drinks with me tonight. A little girls night. Isn't that awesome? I haven't been out with a girlfriend since God knows when."

"Uh, sounds great. Be safe, okay?"

"I'll be fine. You're the one going to Ybor. Alonzo, keep an eye on him, okay?"

"You got it. Come on, Eugenio."

Porter waved and blew me a kiss, something she hadn't done in years. "Don't wait up for me!"

I climbed into Alonzo's truck, but my heart was suddenly not in it. I couldn't tear my eyes off the side-view mirror and the slowly disappearing Porter.

Please be safe.

IT DIDN'T TAKE us long to reach Ybor City, or at least it didn't feel like it, as I'd spent the entire drive worrying about Porter and whatever it was posing as our next-door neighbor. My mind was stuck on an endless loop, vaulting back and forth between abject worry and improperly placed exuberance.

She'll be fine. But, what if that thing... She'll be fine.

"Gene? You falling asleep on me?" Alonzo asked.

I opened my eyes to find us stopped at a light off Seventh Ave waiting for a dozen chickens to cross the street.

"Why did the chickens cross the road?" the off-duty maintenance man asked, turning down the radio.

"To get to the other side?"

Alonzo shook his head. "To get cervesas!"

He let out a deep belly laugh at his silly joke as the last of the feral birds hopped up onto the curb and sure enough appeared to saunter right into the nearest watering hole.

"That's Ybor." Alonzo patted my shoulder before gunning the engine and roaring through the light.

Ybor City was a unique part of old Tampa, one I honestly didn't spend much time in. In the early nineteen hundreds it was quite a happening place to be, with cigar factories and a booming population of Spanish and Cuban immigrants. Sadly, that hadn't lasted—the Great Depression saw to the end of prosperous Ybor City. The quaint town with its narrow brick streets and vibrant culture collapsed in the face of economic ruin and never really recovered. Today it was a dangerous part of the city, one you didn't go in after dark unless you had friends there, knew exactly where you were going, or both.

Alonzo pulled off Seventh Ave, leaving behind the most iconic part of Old Ybor City, with its hanging lights and odd mixture of bars, dance clubs, and scantily clad women, and drove us into the industrial underbelly of the old town. The compact man guided his truck down a couple of side streets, then onto a narrow dirt driveway, before we passed under a large banner proudly proclaiming "Miguel's Small Engine Repair" in both English and what I assumed was Spanish.

Alonzo navigated the packed dirt lot with skill born of experience. He swerved to avoid potholes and soft spots, then pulled the truck and trailer into an open spot not far from the large garage.

"Okay. Now, before we go in, there are some things you need to know about Miguel. He's got a daughter, Sofia. She's a sweetheart. A little weird, but most kids her age are." Alonzo sighed and looked out the window almost wistfully. "Oh, to be eighteen again, am I right?" The barrel-chested man didn't give me a chance to respond. "Anyway, he got in some trouble a few years ago. He's not a bad guy, but he got caught up with a rough element and had to keep food on the table and a roof over his daughter's head. He's got a solid mistrust of just about everybody, but you should be okay if you stick with me."

"Uh, okay," I said, catching the faint sounds of an argument coming from somewhere nearby. "You hear that?"

"Yeah..." Alonzo dropped the truck into park and opened the driver's door.

I followed the maintenance man's lead and climbed out of the cab on tired legs. Together we walked across the hard sand toward the garage. I hadn't noticed it before, but not far from that large steel building was a small house, not much bigger than my apartment.

The narrow house leaned ever so slightly to one side, its corrugated steel walls struggling to keep the ramshackle roof from falling in. A small set of wooden steps lead up to a screen door, out of which bright light poured onto the tall grass, along with the sounds of a scuffle.

"Get your hands off of me!"

"Sofia!" Alonzo shouted, running past the garage and heading straight into the tiny home.

Crash!

A side window shattered, and through the broken glass the screams of a young woman's voice reached my ears.

I dug for my Magick, then hesitated.

What if I make it worse?

"Get off—" Alonzo's voice was cut off by an inhuman growl.

Could I actually make it worse?

I wasn't ready to test that theory quite yet, and instead did something far more questionable—I raced in after him.

12

FANGS AND FLAMES

"Alonzo," I cried, stumbling right into the middle of a living room stand-off. It was like a scene of out some old spaghetti western done up in cheap furniture and paneled walls. In the center of the room, positioned somewhat oddly on an otherwise empty coffee table, lay a shiny metal toaster. Beyond the toaster, and next to an overturned recliner was my boss, his neck cradled menacingly in the arms of a man I didn't expect to see again in my life.

The man-in-black.

Directly next to me, with her back to the door must have been the young woman I'd heard screaming only moments before. Her tight leathers, nose ring, and skull-cap hair said street tough, but it was the steely look in her eye that worried me. "Who the hell are you?"

"I work for Alonzo." I pointed at my borrowed work shirt. "See, maintenance, says so right here. How about you two let my boss go so I can get paid?"

"Eugenio, get out of here, and take Sofia with you," Alonzo cried, clawing at the iron grip of that pale white hand.

The man-in-black tilted his head slightly, as if trying to process my appearance. "You."

"Me."

"But William—"

"Creepy cookie-monster? I gave him the slip."

"A problem I will remedy." The monochrome man dug a finger into Alonzo's neck. "Give me the Duplickity, Sofia, or your uncle dies."

"I told you, I don't have it."

"Don't lie to me, Leech. I can see the bird's kiss on your leg."

Bird's kiss?

Sofia's hand drifted down to cover an angry red scab on her milky white legs.

The bird...

"They wouldn't have me."

The man-in-black pressed his finger tighter against Alonzo's neck, soliciting a thin line of blood. "I don't believe you."

"Do you think I'd be standing here if I had, Deacon?"

So that's Deacon.

"You're lying. The bird is missing, and I know you took her." The man-in-black ripped his hand across Alonzo's neck, sending my boss falling to the ground and struggling in vain to keep the blood in his body. "You have a choice. Give it to me and I will let you take your uncle to the hospital using a Slip."

"Alonzo," Sofia gasped, her hands shaking. "And if I don't..."

"Oh, I won't let him die," Deacon dipped his finger into the rapidly pooling blood. "The Swarm could always use another feeder."

Sofia's voice wavered. "You wouldn't!"

Deacon gently traced a hand across the dying man's chest and sent the first feelers of a twisted and exotic Magick into the dusky air. "I would, and so much more. Give me the Duplickity and your uncle may yet have a normal life."

"I told you I don't have it."

I'd felt the twisted edges of that Magick before, while pinned beneath William's jabbering body, and I felt it again now, moments before the girl let out a primal, and practically feral yell, then launched her tiny body at Mr. Monochrome.

She hit him hard, her jaws unfolding like complex origami.

What the hell?

Mr. Monochrome didn't appear fazed. A quick twist of his hips and he had the young girl careening into a paneled wall behind him, her claws leaving deep gouges in the cheap wood.

Claws!

My brain was struggling to process all the data points streaming in, but it knew none of them mattered if I let Alonzo bleed out. I raced across the narrow room, bounding over a coffee table and knocking the odd looking toaster sitting on it to the ground before getting a hand on Alonzo's neck. The fresh blood sent a wave of nausea through my body. He was still breathing, but barely. "Get up! Come on, we've got to get out of here."

"You aren't going anywhere." Deacon pulled me off my fallen boss and tossed me across the cheap carpet like a rag doll. "I should have done this when I had the chance."

The man's pale-white face and ashen lips split open along an invisible seam below his nose, swelling like a sail and revealing a wide and hissing stinger.

Oh, hell no.

I reached for my Magick, unlocking the internal controls that kept it in check and giving that power a direct path into the real world. "Ledo," I shouted directing that force at Deacon's oversized-jaws. My Magick erupted in an explosion of power, but instead of hitting him in the face with an invisible fist of righteous fury, the man-in-black ended up with a soggy waffle right between the eyes.

"Argh!"

It may not have been what I wanted, but it bought me

enough time to get back to the twitching maintenance man. Sofia took this opportunity to clamp herself on the monochrome man's back before he could dislodge the waffle completely. She'd shrugged off her jacket and let the open sides of her tank top fly free in the air. Six long and fleshy appendages unfolded from the sides of her body and latched on to Deacon.

We gotta go.

I scooped an arm under Alonzo and dragged him toward the door. Blood dripped from his neck like cheap wine. "Come on."

The man-in-black swung wildly, but Sofia remained hooked to him like a spider monkey. The sides of Deacon's jacket flared out to reveal a much larger and more pronounced set of insect arms, each with a sharp claw at the end. Undeterred, the young woman's wide jaws reached for his neck, but they were no match for his arms. With a grunt, those new appendages peeled Sofia off like a clinging tick.

"Don't let him reach the toaster," Sofia cried before slamming her back against the dirty panels.

The toaster?

Too late.

Deacon's hands slammed down on the handles and sent a shock wave of Deep Magick across the room. Heat poured out of the shiny metal box, and flames sprung up around it like weeds, melting the carpet and sending twisting eddies of acrid smoke into the air. It was a Magick-pouring fire machine and neither Alonzo nor I were going to survive much longer if we didn't figure a way out of this tiny-house torture chamber.

I stumbled toward the fading maintenance man and pulled him up. Together we hadn't made it more than a few feet before a fresh wave of Magick crested behind me. The monochrome man's power was cold and precise. It snapped like a whip and caught a recovering Sofia off guard. "Flagellum!"

A score of brilliant black tentacles erupted from one side of his insect arms like inky black constrictors. They snaked around the teenager's neck and hands, hoisting her up into the smoky air.

"Give me the bird."

Sofia snarled and fought against the unholy restraints, then turned to face me. "Get him out of here!"

That's your cue, Gene! Time to go.

The fire reached the ceiling and sent the first pieces of scorched drywall crashing down around us. I shielded by eyes, but the man-in-black didn't have the same compunctions and directed his other hand at me.

Shit!

A fresh set of black tentacles shot out from the other half of his spidery arms. They snaked through the air and zeroed in on my neck. I lost my grip on Alonzo and fought at the tightening noose.

"You want your Duplickity, Deacon?" Sofia's voice strained against the growing flames. "There it is." She pointed to a single pink flamingo nestled against the side of the overturned couch. "And there." Sofia kicked her feet toward another plastic bird against the window sill.

Deacon dropped me and turned his black threads toward the rapidly appearing pink birds.

Just then something hit my chest, a little plastic something I wasn't quite sure I'd ever see again.

We are Flock.

"Hell yeah we are little buddy," I said, clutching the tiny bird to my chest.

The man-in-black's tentacles scooped up plastic birds by the armful. "One of these has to be it." Deacon kicked the toaster upright and popped the handle up, turning off the heat like he'd switched off the gas.

"Run, Alonzo!" Sofia shouted.

"I don't think so." Deacon pulled the young woman close and

let his wide jaws wrap around hers. Like mating puffer fish, his fleshy folds crushed hers and left the maintenance man's niece fighting for breath. Her eyes rolled back in her head and those spidery appendages disappeared along her ribs. Armed with the toaster, and hands full of plastic birds he sent a fresh set of black tentacles ripping across the across the burning walls. Supports cracked and panels buckled.

While the fire had been more than happy to do the bulk of the work, the man-in-black was willing to finish the job and bring the rest of the place crashing down around my ears before vanishing in a burst of smoke and fire.

Crap!

The little bird filled my mind with images of a burning Gene clutching a lump of melted plastic. I didn't have to ask her what she meant—that was a pretty easy translation.

"We've got to save Alonzo!" I shouted trying to detach myself from the clingy bird and find the fallen maintenance man.

We are Flock!

"And he's my friend." I dropped the bird and found Alonzo's still form, then coughed at the acrid smoke and tried to drag the older man's body toward the door. The flamingo shifted tactics and got behind Alonzo, pushing him with her neck.

I lost my grip on him and fell backward, landing on the melted carpet, then struggling to stand. More images flashed in my mind, but these weren't from the bird, these were from the amount of smoke I'd breathed in. I saw what I could have sworn was a younger and decidedly more tattooed version of Alonzo looking down at me.

"Hey, we were trying to save you." I said before drifting off into a smoke-filled slumber.

13

BLACKOUT

I blinked my eyes.

I wasn't dead. Based on how my head felt this was a mild disappointment.

I coughed a few times, calling up what amounted to a considerable amount of soot, and spat it in the dirt.

The dirt? Where am I?

Wherever I was it was dark, very dark. I tried to take a deep breath, but again a bout of coughing sent my head spinning.

"Help."

My voice was rough, it had that sandpapery quality that I'd always imagined women found attractive.

If only Porter could hear me now.

I tried to wipe my eyes, but discovered my hands were bound.

This is all vaguely familiar.

The sharp metal of what felt like chains bit into the skin of my wrists.

I was more than a little surprised to find I had wrists again. I'd assumed them, along with just about every other part of my body had been lost in a collapsing house.

The house... Alonzo!

My eyes continued to adjust to the darkness, while slowly individual items began to appear in the gloom. I didn't know what any of them were, but they had a distinctly industrial appearance. Long chains dangled from the ceiling and gently held up all manner of oddly shaped lumps of steel and gaskets.

Engines?

While it took a bit of effort, the smell of oil and rubber slowly displaced the acrid aroma of burnt house still lingering in my nose.

Alonzo's words came back to me as I lay there in the oppressive dark.

'My brother works on small engines.'

I called out for my new boss, but my voice broke into coughing before I could finish the word.

Bright red and blue lights cut odd patterns across the room. They slipped in through distant cracks in the folded steel doors and cast their bright colors over me.

Police?

"Help! I'm in here!"

Try as I might, my lungs weren't ready for shouting yet. Nothing I said was going to make it beyond these stifling walls.

"That it?" a voice said from somewhere outside the machine shop. I twisted my head to try to pick up more of it.

"Yeah. That's it."

That was a different voice, surprisingly not unlike Alonzo's, but it wasn't him. This new speaker had a decidedly tougher edge to his tone.

"So you're telling me you came home and found your brother's neck cut and laying out in the front yard of your house?"

"Yeah." The tough voice didn't appear to be the talkative type.

"A house that was on fire and rapidly burning to the ground?"

"Yeah."

"You got a problem with your brother, Miguel?"

Miguel? Where had I heard that name? Alonzo's brother.

"No."

There was a crackle of static, someone's radio must have popped on. What I assumed was the police officer asking the questions paused to mumble something confusing to whoever had contacted him.

"What about my daughter?"

To hear Miguel say something more than a few syllables caught me off-guard.

"What about her?"

"You said you'd look for her."

There was a long pause, and while I couldn't see it, I imagined the officer was shaking his head. "We've already gone over this. I told dispatch. You got any pictures of her?"

"I did."

"Well, where are they?"

It appeared it was Miguel's turn to stay silent.

"They were in the house? Shit. Yeah, that's a problem. Listen, I'll tell the guys to keep a sharp look out for a hot chica roaming the street—that might be hard though, vice keeps pretty busy. Who knows, maybe you'll get lucky and they'll pick her up before some John does."

A snarl cut the tension beyond the steel walls of Miguel's small engine repair.

"Watch it, Miguel. You want me to call your probation officer?"

No response.

"Well, I think we've got what we need guys. Let's go."

"This is bullshit! You aren't going to do anything about Sofia." Even through the muffling metal the pain in Miguel's voice was evident.

"You're right. Dispatch?"

A radio crackled. "Dispatch, over."

"Cancel that 10-65."

Miguel must have exploded into movement because the bright red and blue light shifted and threw fresh shadows across the walls.

"I'll—"

"You'll what, convict? You know something, I've had it up to here with your shit."

Static from the radio broke up the conversation. "Roger. Confirm, cancel 10-65, missing person, over."

"She's my daughter! Have a shred of decency."

There was another pause before the officer answered his radio.

"Confirmed, dispatch."

What came next was impossible to follow. Someone was taking the brunt of more than a few blows. I winced at the sound of each impact.

It wasn't long after that the red and blue lights faded, leaving me in the oily dark of the engine shop, wondering what exactly was going to come next.

Thankfully, I didn't have to wait long.

Creak...

Somewhere in the distance what sounded like a door opened. I started to speak speak, then immediately clamped my mouth shut again. Alonzo's brother was missing his daughter, had just gotten beat up by the police, and had his house burned down. Would he be willing to listen to some guy he found on the floor?

Click.

I shut my eyes at the sudden flash of white light.

Scrape...

I opened them again to find a bruised and bloodied Miguel dragging what resembled a very large wrench across the table.

"Where is Sofia?" he said, his words direct and blunt.

"I don't know."

Clang!

He slammed the wrench against a long workbench, taking another step closer to me. "Lies. You're one of them. You're one of Deacon's boys. I told that girl to stay far away from him, but you wouldn't leave her alone."

"No, listen. That's not me. I work for Alonzo. My name's Eugene Law."

Miguel's bloodshot eyes didn't appear to give two shits about what I was saying. He hoisted the wrench to his shoulder and continued his advance, wiping the blood from his face and flicking it into the dirt.

"Nice try. You came into my house," he slapped the cast iron against his palm, "you took my daughter," he let the tool spin in his hand again before slapping down, "and now you want to lie to me."

My hands shook and had I had anything in my stomach it would have certainly been on the dirt by now. "No, I'm not lying. I swear. I live at The Oaks. I'm married. My wife's name is Porter. She works in the leasing office and Alonzo is the maintenance man. He offered to get you to look at my broken lawn mower. It's in the back of his trailer. I swear. I don't work for Deacon or have a job for that matter. We just moved here!"

Boom!

Miguel swung the wrench down against the workbench sending a cavalcade of loose bolts and screws into the air. "Ah ha! You do know Deacon."

"Wow, he has no idea you really are that boring, does he?" A burned and bloody Alonzo stepped out of the shadows. Its voice was close to the maintenance man I'd known, but off just enough for me to recognize the shape-taking thing for what it was.

You!

"What are you doing here?" I asked under my breath, trying

not to make direct eye-contact with the maintenance man doppleganger.

"I'm the one asking the questions," Miguel shouted, clanging his wrench again. "Where did you take her?"

Not-Alonzo shook his head and wandered into the space between Miguel and I. "Well, I'm trying to save your ass. It would appear you've got yourself in quite a bind here, Gene. Does this guy really think you know where his daughter is? That's really not your speed. I mean, I'm reasonably sure you could get another girl, but you've got this whole monogamy thing you're doing. I can't say I agree with it, but I'm progressive."

"I'm trying to tell you," I said, focusing all my attention on the angry younger brother. "I don't know what happened to Sofia."

"Let's start with what you do know." Miguel pressed the cold wrench against my cheek. "You saw Sofia, and I'm guessing Deacon too. Where did they go? You had to see something."

"Oh, my. He's really spun up, Gene." Fake Alonzo walked past his brother and ran a hand through the younger man's bloodied hair. "Yep. That's murderous intent. I'm thinking you've got about another thirty seconds or so. Unless we do something about that."

"I saw... A toaster."

Both brothers tilted their heads and focused their attention on me. "What?"

Nice one, Gene. Where exactly are you going to go from here?

14

OH, BROTHER

Sweat trickled down my neck, sliding between my tired shoulders and tickling at the boney edges of my spine—a spine I hoped very much would remain intact at the conclusion of this evening.

"A toaster?" Miguel said, his brain clearly struggling to wrap its head around my response.

The Alonzo looking thing didn't offer much in the way of assistance. "Don't look at me, Eugenio. You've dug your own hole here."

"Right, a toaster," I said, struggling against the chains. "But it wasn't just any toaster. That thing put out more heat than you could imagine."

"A toaster burned down my house and kidnapped my daughter?"

"Well, I suppose when you put it that way it does sound a bit crazy, but that's not all of it. It was Deacon's toaster."

Miguel placed the murderous wrench back on his shoulder. "So you are saying Deacon used Satan's toaster to set fire to my house and scooped up my daughter in the process?"

Not Alonzo chuckled and toyed with some small hand tools

on the workbench. "I've got to admit, Gene. That one's far-fetched even by your standards."

"I'm telling you, I don't know where she is, but what I do know is Deacon was there, and he had a toaster."

Miguel drew in a deep breath and let it out slowly, turning the wrench over in his fingers.

"Okay, so, Gene. This is what we call murderous rage." Not Alonzo stood behind his brother and held up a long screwdriver. "In about twenty-seconds or so tattoos here is going to get tired of asking you questions and will resort to bashing your head in with that wrench. Now, lucky for you, I happen to have lots of plans for that noodle of yours. So I'm prepared to make you a deal."

"Uh, you've got to believe me." My eyes darted back and forth between Miguel and his wrench. "That's what happened. I swear I didn't see anything else. That's all."

Miguel's facial expressions didn't change. His eyes remained focused, dead focused on mine. Alonzo's cherubic face appeared alongside his brother's. "Oh, snap. Yep, it's time Gene. Maybe a little earlier than I'd hoped, but 'tempus fugit,' right? Time to use that Magick and save your butt."

There was going to be no Magickal butt-saving today. My Magick hated me, and I knew it.

Alonzo placed a hand to his mouth. "What's that? You can't get it up right now, eh? It happens to a lot of Magicians. It's nothing to be proud of, mind you, but I can help you through it. You just need focus, a mission if you will. Here's what you do, you swear allegiance to me—whole heart and soul, no finagling out of it and all—and I'll get you right back in the Magickal game. Guys like 'Chuckles' here won't be a problem for the new Eugene Law. Not by a long shot."

The first hints of Magick tickled the air. This wasn't my Magick, and it certainly wasn't coming from Miguel. This was a strange and terrifying power I'd only felt once before, deep in the heart of the Gloom.

"I..."

The Alonzo shaped thing leaned forward as if he were coaxing a rabbit out of its hole. "There you go. Here, I'll help you. 'I submit to you...' I suppose you'll need to call me something. Hmm, what have they been using in this millennia?"

Miguel grabbed the chains that bound my hands and pulled me to my feet. "This is your last chance. Tell me where my daughter is!"

"Oh, why is it so hard to think of a suitable name? I've had so many over the years. We could go with—"

"That scar, the one on your left hand. You didn't get that working on a motorcycle." I shouted, hoping to hell my gamble would work.

"What?"

"You tell everyone it happened working on a motorcycle. It didn't."

"So?"

"So, when you were a kid, you took your brother's tools and ended up stabbing yourself in the hand. You didn't want him to get in trouble so you bandaged it yourself and it didn't heal right."

Miguel yanked on my chains, hoisting my hands above my head and hooking them to a conveniently hanging engine hook. "Nice try, but I've told a few guys that over the years."

"Gene," Alonzo's face reappeared next to mine. "Screw the name, we'll come up with something later. Just say, 'I submit to you,' and we'll be golden."

Miguel took a step back and with it a few practices swings of his wrench. "Last chance, kid. Tell me where Sofia and Deacon are and I'll leave you a decent face for an open casket."

"Get a load of this guy, eh Gene? He's no Magician. Once we're working together, he doesn't stand a chance. Should we crush his spine? Or would it be better to tear his heart out? I'm totally open to letting you choose."

I dug through my head trying to find something else, anything that might convince Alonzo's younger brother I wasn't who he thought I was. I played back that time on the roof from earlier today, when the boisterous maintenance man had been regaling me with stories of his youth.

"So, don't mention the scar on his hand, he's kind of sensitive about it," Alonzo had said, his face partially covered by a dusty bandana. "You know something, Eugenio, when Miguel got older he saved up his money and replaced the tools he ruined that day. After I'd opened the bag and thanked him, I found something hidden at the bottom."

"What was it?"

"A picture. A picture of him and I at the church carnival. It was one of his favorites. I still have it."

"Gene!" Fake Alonzo's shout jolted me to the present. "It's time buddy. Say the words and let's put this moron in the ground."

"You gave him a picture of you both at the carnival. It was your favorite picture and he knew it. Alonzo still has that photo today."

Thump!

The murderous wrench hit the ground. "I never told anyone that," Miguel said taking a step back.

"He cares about you—a lot. I swear I don't know where your daughter and Deacon went, but I have an idea."

The mechanic unhooked my arms from the chains and caught me before I landed somewhere near his wrench.

"Thanks," I said, my wrists really getting tired of being chained up.

Not-Alonzo was gone, but the faint hint of his Magick still lingered in the air.

"You know where she is?" Miguel asked as he undid the chains from my wrists.

"I have an idea, but there's no way we can get to them alone."

Trust me, there's a lot you don't know about Deacon and your daughter.

Miguel let the chains fall to the ground. "Shit."

"But, I might know someone who could help us. Just let me call my wife and tell her I'm still alive."

Miguel pushed twisted metal and wires out of the way and grabbed a cheap handset from the workbench. "Here. As soon as you're done we go."

"Go? Go where?"

Miguel pressed the corded receiver into my hand. "We go find Sofia."

Shit.

I tried to dial, but my fingers shook too much to press the numbers.

"What is it?" Miguel yanked the phone out of my hand.

I relayed our apartment phone number to him and hoped Porter would be home.

"It's ringing."

I pressed the receiver to my ear and yelped, startled at just how badly burned my skin was.

You were just rolling around in a burning house you idiot.

"Hello, you've reached Gene… and Porter," in spite of it all I smiled at the sound of my wife's recorded voice, "we can't come to the phone right now because we're all sexy newlyweds and stuff. So leave a message and we'll call you back!"

The beep came quick and caught me off guard. You don't typically call your own apartment. "Porter, it's Gene. I'm okay. There was a fire at Miguel's. Alonzo's in the hospital I think. Listen, honey. Miguel's daughter is missing, and I promised him I'd—"

The mechanic pulled the phone out of my hand and mashed the button down. "That's enough."

"Shit, man, she's going to wonder what's going on. You can't just leave her with incomplete information like that. She's going to lose it. We do *not* want Porter to lose it. That would be bad for everyone, but mostly me."

Miguel pulled a box off the shelf, he popped the plastic lid off to reveal a thick mass of rubber belts.

"What are you..."

The mechanic ignored me and instead dug through the box until he found what he was looking for—the largest handgun I'd ever seen in my life.

"Holy..."

Miguel checked the barrel then ejected the magazine. "Go get that box of air filters," he said, pointing to the far wall.

"Huh?"

"The one all the way on the furthest side. It's got a blue label and expired on April first."

"What do we need an air filter for?" I asked, willing my feet to move.

"We don't."

I pulled the box off the shelf but found it a lot heavier than I expected. It slipped out of my hand and tumbled open on the ground.

"Bullets?"

"Yeah, guns are kinda useless without em. You ready?"

I looked down at my torn and burn shirt and ash covered shorts. I was a soot-covered mess.

"Here," he said, grabbing a wadded up pair of coveralls off the workbench and tearing the 'Miguel's' patch off them in one fluid motion. "Put these on and let's go."

Two jobs in one day, lucky me.

I adjusted the ill-fitting coveralls. "This one is a little above my pay grade as weird goes. I need to bring in the cavalry."

Miguel advanced on me quickly, grabbing the edge of my loaner clothes and pulling me toward him in a rapidly violent movement. "No cops."

"No cops. Yes, sir. You got it. One hundred percent, but how do you feel about old people?"

15

PARTY CITY

*V*arious options for tomorrow's newspaper headlines played out in my head with each step up the apartment's stairs.

Ex-con shoots girly man and his geriatric friend over missing daughter.

Night ends in bloodshed when idiot lawn boy guides convicted killer to retiree's house.

Too much stupid and not enough ink.

I shook my overly anxious mind and tried to tamp down the cauldron of concern roiling in my gut.

Mr. Jenkins is a good guy. He'll help.

I wasn't quite sure where I'd come to the conclusion that Mr. Jenkins was a good guy, or even that he'd help. As it was, he had only been willing to throw out that half-hearted offer after I'd agreed to be his Magickal guinea pig.

I had a better chance of convincing Marco than the old man.

That's why you stopped at the grocery store.

I squeezed the bag of 'Mar-Vee-Poo' dog treats to my chest.

Please be the right ones.

"This is it." I stepped off the stairs onto Mr. Jenkins floor. It was after eight at this point and I had no idea if the old man would even be awake. "Let me do the talking."

Miguel grunted in assent. I wasn't exactly sure what he would do if my plan didn't work out. It had taken ten minutes in the car to convince him that I wasn't lying, and an additional five minutes to get him to go into the grocery store. Getting him to pay for the dog treats had been an even greater challenge entirely.

I set the bag down next to the door and took a deep breath. I wasn't sure exactly which fear was the one eating at my intestines—there were a lot to consider.

What would Mr. Jenkins do when we showed up at his place after dark?

I imagined him opening the door and unloading a shotgun into my midsection, then somewhere in that same delusion Miguel returned fire and the entryway to our Magickal savior's apartment became a bloodbath.

Before I could roll through the remaining panic-laden options Miguel leaned it to listen at the apartment door. "Sounds like a party."

"What?!"

"Listen."

The felonious muscle was right. I didn't know how I missed it before, but there it was, a driving beat coming from just beyond the door.

Thump! Thump! Thump!

Miguel gently pulled up the edge of his shirt to reveal the hidden handgun. "You better not be screwing with me, kid."

"No, sir, this is the—"

Before I could finish my statement Miguel pounded on the door with his fist.

"Mr. Jenkins," I said, leaning in to shout through the cheap metal. "It's me, Eugene Law. I... We've got a problem, and I think you could..."

The door swung in slowly and bathed the two of us in mist and laser light. Draping her body against the metal door was a half-naked woman that caught both Miguel and I completely off guard. "You guys here for the party?"

Her long hair had to be about five different colors, from brilliant yellow to a royal purple, with all the shades in between. Straight as a board it tumbled down a perfectly shaped set of bare shoulders and matching chest. Small sparkly stickers covered most of her nipples, but only just barely.

"Uh..."

Rainbow Bright smiled and grabbed Miguel's hand. The rough and tumble mechanic didn't object, and instead practically floated into the apartment.

"Miguel?"

The nubile woman spun around, the tiny pompoms on her bikini strings sparkling, and hesitated just long enough to wink at me before guiding my captor into the bright lights and writhing mass of flesh gyrating in the center of the room. Arms and legs moved in perfect rhythm to the pulsing beat, while somewhere more flashes of laser light cut across the smokey air.

"We'll take care of him, Magician. Viktor's on the porch. He says you should bring your supplication."

"Supplication?"

Miguel's shirt flew into the air like a cap at graduation. It caught on the ceiling fan before being cast off into some distant corner. One of the many dancers that bore an eerie resemblance to our hostess slipped the gun out of his bare waistband.

"Hey watch it with that!" Visions of stray bullets raced past in my mind.

Magick drifted through the room, catching the lights and settling on the warm bodies. The handgun passed from person to person until a voluptuous, pink-haired vixen handed the sweaty weapon to Rainbow.

"Here." She placed the gun in my hand. Her fingers were

practically electric, and the moment they touched my skin I'd have swore half the day's tiredness left my body.

"He's waiting."

"Who? Where's Mr. Jenkins?"

The rave shifted just enough for me to get a clear view of the porch. There was the old Magician, sitting in his plastic Adirondack chair, and still wearing the robe he'd been sporting this morning. He'd upgraded the rest of his ensemble to include what could have been Rainbow's most curvaceous sister in his lap, while at his feet Marco enjoyed being brushed by two equally beautiful dancers, their short hair laced with feathered braids.

Mr. Jenkins casually turned to face me and smiled, tilting his head gently while at the same time bright flashes of laser lights reflected off his glasses.

What the hell?

I'm somewhat ashamed to admit it took me a lot longer than it should have to cross the tiny apartment. Each caress, roaming hand, and finger through the hair was invigorating. I'd never felt anything like it before, but after the day I'd had, I wanted, no, I needed, every ounce of it.

"I see you're enjoying the party," Mr. Jenkins said as soon as I'd stepped onto the narrow balcony, dog treat bag in one hand, gun in the other.

"Uh... Yeah. I mean, yes, sir. I am. Wow."

"And I see you brought Marco treats?"

At the word treats, the large dog's massive tail smacked the ground in time with the music inside.

Whump. Whump. Whump.

"Why don't you ladies go back inside." Mr. Jenkins dismissed the alluring groomers, then scooted his voluptuous lap warmer back toward the party.

None of them looked pleased to leave, but the curvaceous beauty that had only moments ago been gracing the old man's lap took a second to run a hand down the nether-regions of my coveralls before stepping back inside and closing the sliding glass behind her. It wasn't until she was inside that my lungs figured out how to exhale again.

"What the—"

"Smart move, kid." Mr. Jenkins rubbed a hand on Marco's fur. "I told you he was a smart kid, Marco."

The mountain dog snorted.

"I did too. I said 'that kid's a smart kid, he'll go far in life.'"

Bark!

"Yes, that was after I called him a moron. Damn it, dog, it's not all cut and dry. This is a process. He's got 'performance issues,'" Mr. Jenkins put his fingers in the air like tiny quotes, "and its best not to talk about those. Gets in their heads…"

"Uh, what are they doing to him?" I asked, content to let the comments about my Magick issues to go by the wayside when I found Miguel disappearing beneath a mass of flesh.

"Who? The Kittens?" Mr. Jenkins propped himself up in his cheap plastic chair. "Oh, they're getting ready to consume him. It's nothing."

"What!"

Mr. Jenkins must have seen my face in the reflection of the glass. "Oh, come on, kid. You had to know something was going to happen when you brought your attacker here. I mean, I wasn't just going to let him saunter right out that door."

The party shifted. There really wasn't a better way to explain it. One minute the laser lights and pulsing beat felt invigorating, and in the next malevolent.

"Wait. You don't understand. That's Miguel, he's Alonzo's brother."

The old Magician tilted his head. "Who?"

The ladies parted, giving me a perfect view of Miguel on his knees, and while he still had a smile on his face, I didn't expect it would last long. The curvy women had him surrounded. They prowled like panthers in a tight circle, their bodies still dancing to the music, but in a much more muted fashion.

"The maintenance guy, you know? The one who keeps things working around here."

"His name's Alonzo?" Mr. Jenkins said, rubbing his stubbly chin.

Bark!

"Oh, like you remember everything? I seem to recall you can't remember a single trick I've taught you."

Marco snorted and rolled back over.

The dancer's circle tightened, their bodies continuing to sway in tune with the music, but their eyes never leaving Miguel. Laser light shot across the pack and for the briefest of seconds illuminated Rainbow's face.

Cat's eyes?!

The bright-haired girl's hourglass eyes winked at me, while her tongue gently licked at tiny razor sharp looking fangs. These weren't the same as the fangs I'd seen on Deacon or Sofia, these were positively feline.

Aw, hell.

16

FRISKIES

*M*r. Jenkins stared at what remained in the bottom of his cup. "His name's Alonzo, huh? Well, you learn something new every day I guess."

"And that's his brother in there." I pointed at the man in the center of what was beginning to resemble a bullseye. The circle tightened, and if I wasn't mistaken something about the young women's arms had changed. I hadn't noticed nails that long when we'd arrived.

I looked closer. Those weren't long fingernails, or at least they weren't anymore—they were claws. It took a flash of laser light to be sure, but there they were, protracted from somewhere inside the webbing of the ladies' hands.

Just like cats...

Mr. Jenkins twirled the ice in his largely empty cup. "What about that gun? Isn't that the same gun Mr. Friendly there was ready to use on you outside my door?"

"No! Well, yes." I threw my hands in the air. "It's complicated. You've got to stop them. His daughter's been kidnapped and I told him you'd help us find her."

The old Magician took what was most likely the last sip from his cup, the oversized ice cubes rattling against each other. "I told you this would happen, Marco. If you give the kid a hand, he's gonna want your arm too."

Mr. Jenkin's mountain dog snorted and turned to face the glass.

"Well, you insisted." Mr. Jenkins frowned at his canine.

Marco stretched and extended his body until his nose touched the bag of treats.

The old Magician shook his head. "Go ahead. He didn't buy them himself. He had this guy do it for him."

Marco snorted again and smacked the bag with an oversized paw.

The sliding door shook under my fingers, inside the music was reaching its crescendo. For the first time tonight I noticed tiny scratches on Miguel's face.

"Do something!" I shouted, yanking on the locked door handle.

"Listen, kid, I'd love to, but once the Kittens get their claws out they just have to use them on something and at this point I'd rather it not be us—or my furniture."

Rainbow caught my eyes again, her smile highlighting those fangs. Tiny and well-concealed, the wicked-sharp teeth sent my heart racing. In fact, the decidedly feline nature of her head was causing all manner of palpitations.

"I came to you because there was Magick!"

Mr. Jenkins looked at his empty glass, then inside past the circling cat-women to the liquor bottles on the far counter. "And? You think I'm some sort of Magick police?"

"They burned his house down—"

"That's really a shame, but he did threaten you with a gun and you don't need to be a master Magician like me to pickup on the fact he would have used it."

"—with a toaster."

Mr. Jenkin's hand froze mid-twirl of his melting cubes. "Wait. Roll that back. Did you say toaster?"

Fog drifted across the floor. I didn't know where it was coming from, but the mist had covered the cheap carpet, and with it, most of Miguel. Claws flashed in the laser light, and it certainly appeared they were reaching the end of the song, and with it what might be the finale for Alonzo's brother.

"Yes! Toaster!"

Mr. Jenkins closed the gap between us impossibly fast, dropping his cup on the hard concrete and using that hand to grab the seam of my loose-fitting coveralls. "Was it a toaster or a toaster oven?"

The music stopped.

Rainbow and the rest of her feline-like ladies dance came to an end. Their retractable claws slipped out as they advanced on a delirious Miguel.

"What? I don't know the differ—" I kept my head on a swivel between Miguel and the old Magician.

Mr. Jenkins pulled me back to face him. "Toaster's have slots. Toaster ovens have doors. Slot or door, kid? Which was it?"

Bright steel and black handles, a shiny face that shone like the sun, and two slots across the top.

"Slots!" I yelled, fighting the older man and reaching for the sliding door. "It had two slots. Mr. Monochrome, I mean Deacon, he undid the handle and carried it away like it was nothing, but I'm telling you, that toaster set the whole damn house on fire."

Mr. Jenkins let go and knocked me away from the sliding door handle in one motion. "And it would have burned more than that if he hadn't stopped it. The Five Star Toaster isn't something to be screwed with. If that damn thing is back in the hands of idiots we've got bigger problems."

"The Five Star Toaster?"

Mr. Jenkins' Magick snapped like the cracking of a whip. "Clauditis," he said, the sliding door flying open beneath his fingers. "Stop!"

The old Magician's voice was powerful, strong and commanding, and sure to have an effect on Rainbow and the rest of the ravenous women.

Nope.

What had been women certainly weren't now. With heads and faces like regal felines, their soft fur shifted in the misty air. The half-woman, half-cat that had met us at the door pounced on Miguel. She had him in her claws, with feral eyes that shined in the laser light. Blood dripped from tiny fangs, while all around her the others hissed.

Mr. Jenkins stepped into his tiny apartment with an air of authority. "I am the keeper of the Soul of Isis. You *will* listen to me."

Rainbow's claws hesitated, mere inches from Miguel's glazed-over pupils. "The Soul of Isis dances for your pleasure once every hundred years. Your dance is over old one, and we are hungry."

"Whatever you do," Mr. Jenkins' whispered to me, adjusting his robe. "Show no fear. They smell it, and it gets them all kinds of turned on. It's totally kinky, but don't do it. Just follow my lead and don't screw this up."

Before I could respond the old man sauntered across the room toward the tiny kitchenette, his arms suddenly jolly and carefree. "Are you sure? I don't think you're remembering right."

A chorus of hissing sent my short hairs on edge, but before I could start hyperventilating the old man shot me a withering look over his shoulder from behind those tinted glasses.

Right, no fear. No fear. Holy shit those claws look sharp—damn it, Gene.

"Are you not revitalized?" the rainbow-maned cat-woman

said, her claws leaving a bright red line along Miguel's throat. "Your loins are full now, are they not?"

Loins?

Mr. Jenkins gently unscrewed the cap on a bottle of what looked like tequila. "First, Bastet, my man parts are not up for discussion, but yes, now that you mention it, I am feeling rather virile."

It was my turn to shoot the old man a similar look.

"But that's not the point," he said. "The point is—"

"Are you trying to slip our covenant? A deal that has lasted this many years?" Bastet's claws left more narrow red lines in Miguel's skin.

Mr. Jenkins refilled his cup, then searched the countertop for something. "You got a copy of that deal, Bastie?"

If looks could kill, Mr. Jenkins and I would have fallen dead where we stood, Rainbow's withering gaze the chief murder weapon.

"You promised us, Bastet," the voluptuous cat-woman whined, the same one that had been sitting in the old Magician's lap when I got here. The claws in her fingers retracted and extended in rapid fire succession like a nervous tick. "I had to sit in his lap!"

"The old Magician cheats." Bastet pressed her claws against Miguel's neck. "We'll get what we were promised."

She's gonna kill him! Do something!

My eyes pleaded with Mr. Jenkins, but the old man ignored me and instead held up his glass of tequila. "Any of you ladies know where the limes are?"

What?

Miguel had seconds to live. All it would only take was a flick of the wrist for Rainbow or Bastet, or whatever the hell she was, to separate his throat from his body. I may not have liked the guy, but no one deserved to have DIY surgery on the cheap carpet of an old apartment.

"Wait!" I shouted, not exactly sure what I was going to do next.

All eyes turned to me, most of which were feline and blood-thirsty.

Mr. Jenkins white-knuckled his cup, the plastic popping beneath his fingers, but didn't say anything—he didn't have to, I could feel his anger from here.

A flick of the neck from Bastet and I was surrounded. The grooming twosome I'd met on the porch were on me in seconds, their claws out and pressed against my neck.

"This one smells sweet." The shorter of the two's green cat eyes narrowed.

Bastet took a series of feral breaths and sniffed the air. "You hid him from us. He's a succulent morsel."

Mr. Jenkins set down his glass and waved the young cat-woman off with his hand. "He's a day laborer—stringy and basically all tendons—you'd get him stuck in your teeth."

"No, old man. I can smell the Magick on him. He has a deep well of power, one that will be fun to roll in, along with his entrails."

My what?

"Ah ha, limes." The old man smiled at a small bowl of cut fruit next to the refrigerator. "Who prepared these?"

"I did." One of the taller cat-women waved, fighting to suppress a smile.

"Well, look at you, Sekmet. So proactive. This is some excep-tional work, sweetheart. You've got serious skill. I mean, these are just perfectly proportioned."

"Thank you, sir. I tried so very hard to please—"

Bastet cut off her fellow Kitten. "We didn't come here to cut limes. Stop changing the subject, old man."

Mr. Jenkins squeezed a slice over his tequila then swirled the glass a few times. "Right, right. You came here to give my loins a 'pick me up,' and in exchange you want dinner. Well, what are you waiting for?"

"What?" I blurted out, my gut bottoming out around my toes.

"Go ahead, you can have the Magician."

17

LET'S GET PHYSICAL

I may have been beat down, dragged out, and border line exhausted, but being offered up as dinner to a bunch of feral looking cat-women tended to wake you the hell up, and fast. "No!"

Yeah, you thought about adding 'bad kitty' to that? Maybe you have a feather you can dangle in front of their faces?

Bastet and the rest of her claw-flashing felines zeroed in on me.

"You don't want to eat me. I'm terrible, just like he said—all gristle and tendons!" I shouted, wondering just how many times I would get the chance to say something like that in my life and actually mean it.

A hiss from Bastet sent Marco's former groomers in motion, they had me pressed against the wall with enough strength to raise my feet off the ground. It was at this time it dawned me the dog was missing. Marco, the canine mountain, had chosen that exact moment to disappear—hard to do when you weigh in at over a hundred pounds of fat and fur—but somehow he'd managed it all the same. I honestly didn't have an opportunity to dwell on this discovery, because the grooming gals had extended their claws and they certainly didn't appear interested in fixing my hair.

"Help."

If the only other resident Magician had any interest in doing something about my predicament, he was doing his damndest not to show it. Mr. Jenkins continued to swirl his tequila and lick his lips in that smacking fashion all old men seem to have down to an art.

Bastet's fangs sparkled in a flash of laser light, and appeared poised to make short work of Miguel's face.

Think, Gene, think! If the old man isn't going to do anything, then it's up to you.

The thought of using Magick sent the cosmic power swirling around in my body into a tizzy. My Magick wanted out in the worst of ways, but thanks to what we were calling 'performance anxiety,' that power was more likely to add to our problems than resolve them.

Miguel's tattooed face lulled to one side—the poor guy didn't stand a chance.

Neither do I.

My Magick rumbled again, this time a good bit angrier than before. It didn't like being hemmed in and wanted out. I wasn't exactly sure how long I could keep it pinned down, but was terrified of what might happen if I didn't.

The music resumed, a strong and rolling beat that rattled my brain stem.

Bang! Bang!

There it was again, but wait, that wasn't the music, that was the front door. Everyone froze, the Kittens, Mr. Jenkins, and even Miguel in his torporific state.

The old man adjusted his robe and pressed his tinted glasses to his face. "Damn it, I told you ladies we had to keep it down. I had enough trouble with the downstairs neighbors after the last shindig."

I didn't know exactly how to respond to that admonishment. Miguel was only seconds away from having his face sliced up and passed around like a sushi roll, and I had two sets of claws pressed tight to my own body, and not in a way that was remotely pleasant, but heaven forbid we make too much noise.

I had half a mind to unleash my Magick right then, but there was something about the look on Jenkins' face, and the fact that my power was hellbent on escape that kept me quiet.

"Who is it?" the old man asked, holding his drink and leaning in to get a look out the peephole.

"It's Jeff, from downstairs."

Jenkins spun around and held his hands out to quiet the crowd. "Shit, it's Jeff. He's such a whiner. Okay, everybody stay still. I got this."

"You know I can hear you, right?"

The old Magician sighed and gently opened the door a crack. "Hey, Jeff. What's the problem?"

I couldn't see the man beyond the door, but just the tone of his voice was enough to tell me he was pissed. "Don't give me that, old man. Some of us have kids, you know? Some of us have actual work too."

"Yes, right. I'm very sorry. Listen, I'll be happy to make it up to you, I could—"

"You could start by shutting the damn music off, and maybe clean your place up. It reeks, you know that? You have a cat don't you?"

"I, uh, okay. I don't have a cat per se but—"

"Well then I don't know what the hell you are doing that makes the whole place smell like cat piss, but I don't like it, and my wife doesn't like it either. I swear if you don't get your shit in order I'm going to go down to the leasing office. I don't care how long you've been here."

At first I wasn't sure why a Magician with Mr. Jenkins' skill would put up with the likes of Jeff. Why not use a little of that cosmic power to send him off confused or assured that what-ever it was he'd wanted to accomplish had worked. It was some-thing Morgan excelled at, perhaps Mr. Jenkins did not.

It was right about this moment when I noticed the latent Magick slip out of the room like helium from yesterday's party balloon. I didn't know how he was doing it, but Jeff was like Magick kryptonite, and Mr. Jenkins was taking it full on. He gripped the door like it was the only thing keeping him upright, his shoulders stooping and the liver spots on his hands multi-plying like rabbits.

"You got it, music going down now."

"Off," the neighbor said, with a finality in his voice I found more than a little annoying.

"Yes, of course. Off it is. Thank you, Jeff, for letting me know I was causing you such distress. We'll get it figured out going forward, don't you worry."

Mr. Jenkins snapped his fingers behind his back, and one of the topless cat women turned off the stereo beneath the TV.

"You better." Jeff's voice didn't sound convinced, but he left just the same.

Mr. Jenkins held the door ajar for a few moments, waving politely to the neighbor and waiting for him to reach the stairs before closing it. "Fucking hell, damn physicist is going to be the death of me." The old man placed his back against the door and took a long drink from his tequila. "Where were we?"

No one moved.

"Oh, that's right. Marco, button!"

Magick flooded the room, and with it came the black fur and slobbery jaws of one boisterous mountain dog. All one hundred plus pounds of Marco appeared out of nowhere, crashing into Bastet and knocking her off Miguel. Together they tumbled into the television stand.

"Not the TV!" Mr. Jenkins shouted, but it was too late, the heavy set crashed into the floor sending glass and circuitry flying. "The button, damn it. Give her the button before you tear the apartment down."

Marco and Bastet tumbled end over end across the cheap carpet, while outside I could have sworn I heard the sound of pounding feet on the stairwell.

Jeff the Physicist.

The groomer girls turned their attention back to me, their claws raised and the fangs glistening in the flashing laser light.

"The button, damn it," Mr. Jenkins cried, downing the last of his drink while the rest of the Kittens cornered him in the narrow kitchenette.

Marco pinned Bastet beneath his paws before coughing something up on the floor beside her.

A button?

Sure enough, shining in a politely vile mound of semi-gelatinous dog vomit, was a white button not much bigger than a silver dollar.

"You couldn't get it in her hand, really? We go over this time and again, and you still couldn't manage to vomit it into her palm, some trained dog you are."

If it were possible, I could have sworn Marco was embarrassed, but, I didn't really have much time to dwell on that before the first set of claws raked my coveralls.

"Discordia!"

I couldn't help it—the Magick just came out. It had been hard enough to control myself up to this point, but now that self-preservation had kicked in there was no putting that genie back in the bottle.

Cosmic power streamed out of my hands and into the tiny apartment. It bounced off the walls and twisted in odd directions.

"Nice work, kid. I knew you could do—"

I would have liked to have heard the rest of what Mr. Jenkins had said, just like I would also have liked to have heard something other than the toe-curling wail of the broken television filling the tiny apartment with mesmerizing images, but I wasn't in any position to be making demands, let alone having them filled.

Somewhere hidden behind the hissing mass of advancing cat women, the old man groaned. "Whoa, kid, get that under control. Your Magick is going rogue."

Bang! Bang!

"What did I tell you about the noise!"

The physicist had returned.

18

WHAT'S ON?

*D*iscord.

Well, that's what I'd asked my Magick for, and it would appear I was getting exactly that—in spades.

The remaining Kittens had Mr. Jenkins cornered in the kitchen, their fangs out and claws extended, both of which detracted from their carnival-like pasties and jiggling breasts.

Not to be outdone, Bastet and Marco the mountain dog continued their tussle across the living room floor, while the vomit button lay in a gooey pile of dog puke not far from the television, but certainly not in the palm of anyone's hands as Mr. Jenkins had hoped.

Miguel lay nearby, his eyes closed but his face still stuck in a twisted smile.

Another set of staccato knocks against the apartment door told me Jeff the Physicist had reached his breaking point and was all but ready to smash the door and join the party, and if all that wasn't enough, there was the television.

Bright lights and flashing colors streamed from the broken tube. Buffeted on the winds of my off-kilter Magick, they took on a life of their own. Coalescing into vaguely human shapes, they crawled out of the TV and into the melee that was Mr. Jenkins' apartment.

All of this would have been more than enough to keep me occupied had I not had a couple sets of Kitten claws only moments away from helping me sing soprano.

"We're on the planet's surface," an oddly commanding static figure said, jarring me from my introspection, and getting the attention of the Kittens currently planning to detach rather important man-parts. "There appears to be some sort of mating ritual in process."

The figures no longer resembled late night TV static. A quartet shimmered into view, stepping out of the remains of the busted television tube. They wore long black slacks and tight-fitting shirts, each a monochrome color, and each one practically vacuum-sealed to their bodies.

"Captain, it would appear they are humanoid, and the air here is thick with a pheromone like substance." The blue shirt held up some sort of hand-held calculator.

Bang! Bang!

"Damn it, Jenkins, I told you to turn it off. I can hear the TV from here."

"Sir, one of them appears to be incapacitated." The same man turned his attention to Miguel. "Should I?"

"No. This might be part of the ritual. We do not want to interrupt the mating process."

I sensed my opening and went for it.

"Help!" I cried, pushing back on the two Kittens suddenly distracted by our new visitors.

A trio of color-shirts had something that resembled TV remotes out in seconds and aimed at my assailants. "Back away from him!"

Yes!

It was about damn time my Magick did something good, even if I didn't quite understand what it was. The cat women backed away from me, their clawed hands up, and their faces a mixture of confusion and frustration.

"Sir, we'll need to—"

Those were the last words the science fiction group said before exploding into a wash of static and bright light. Marco and Bastet had rolled across the remote and with it changed the channel on my Magick.

No!

A sullen faced young man appeared, stirring a spoon in what looked to be coffee. "Ross, you've got to tell Rachel how you feel about her."

"I know," said a second man, even more despondent than the first. He stepped out of the television and sat down on the beat-up recliner. "It's just, what if she doesn't feel the same way?"

The Kittens advancing on Mr. Jenkins stopped, and turned all their attention on the two young men conversing in the tiny room. I couldn't tell for sure, but they appeared mesmerized by the scene unfolding before them.

"Don't think you can just change the channel and I'll leave," our least favorite Physicist said from the other side of the door.

Jenkins waved his hands to get my attention from behind the counter. "Get the button and put it in her palm."

"Why?"

The old man slapped a hand against his face. "It's a Lost Button."

"Huh?"

"You don't know what a damn Lost Button is?"

"Not exactly."

"Fingers only." Mr. Jenkins pinched one of the liquor covered cubes in his drink. "Do not put it in your palm."

I found the white disc again laying on the cheap carpet, not far from the Magickal actor's feet. "I got it." I slipped between the pre-occupied Kittens and dropped to the floor, crawling past their tasseled bikinis and fuzzy boots.

"You really think she likes me?" the more whiny of the two men asked, his head in his hands.

A chorus of soft purrs from the Kittens told me any one of them would be willing to take the place of whoever my televised manifestation was moaning about.

"Hurry!" Mr. Jenkins hissed.

Marco and Bastet rumbled past me and I understood why Mr. Jenkins wanted me to wrap this up fast. Marco might have been a strong mountain dog, but Bastet was quicker, and her claws had already made short work for his soft underbelly. Judging by the tears in his thick skin Marco wasn't going to hold up much longer.

Shit!

In the commotion I found the button again, this time it lay just beyond a pair of shapely legs.

Just a little farther...

"Turn it down, damn it, or so help me I'm going to knock this door down."

My fingers brushed across the button, but I only succeeded in burying it further in the shag carpet. "Sonofa—" I yanked my hand back before the wrestling duo twisted sideways across the button and rolled over the television remote yet again.

Aw, hell.

The wimpy guys vanished in a burst of static, only to be replaced with a crashing wave—a brilliant blue crashing wave that included the bronzed bodies of a few bright red swimsuit wearing lifeguards.

You've got to be kidding me.

The Kittens swooned at sight of the wide chest of the leading lifeguard, and I had my opportunity. Legs cleared just enough for me to make another mad stab for the button.

"CJ." The Adonis-looking man directed a perky young woman who bounced her way through the broken television

screen toward Miguel. "He needs mouth-to-mouth resuscitation!"

All ninety-pounds of that blonde bombshell crash landed
onto Miguel and I swore his eyes fluttered open for a second.
"Dios mio…"

You don't know the half of it, buddy.

The button resurfaced behind CJ's voluptuous chest and I
knew this was my last, best option.

"You can't just keep changing the channels!"

Take a number, Jeff. It's a full apartment in here.

I dove for the button, launching my exhausted body through
the legs of an otherwise pre-occupied Kitten and scooping up
the plastic circle with my fingers.

"Don't get it in your palm, kid!" Mr. Jenkins shouted from
across the room.

"I know!" I fumbled with the slippery wet piece of plastic.
The Magick locked inside was stunning, just holding it in my
fingers was almost too much. The button's pull was like a
suction of an industrial vacuum cleaner. "What do I do now?"

"Don't get eaten by that shark!" The old man ducked behind
the kitchen counter.

"Shark, what are you talking—"

My words froze in my mouth as the coal-black eyes and
predatory body of a great white shark skimmed my head.

Oh, shit.

"That's it!" Jeff the Physicist yelled from outside the door.
"I'm coming in!"

Kittens screamed and leapt for cover, the massive predator
driving them into the corners of the tiny apartment.

Mr. Jenkins swung a half-empty bottle of tequila, then
ducked the shark's serrated jaws. "Get your Magick under
control, kid."

I tried to pull back, but the Magick wasn't having anything
to do with me. "I can't!"

Mr. Jenkins ducked the shark's second pass, the wide fins narrowly missing his head. "Put the damn button in her palm."

Bastet and Marco rolled past me, while somewhere nearby Miguel was getting the mouth-to-mouth resuscitation of a lifetime, and all I had was a lousy, albeit insanely, Magickal, button.

I can't make this stuff up.

The shark banked hard and turned its attention on me. More Kittens hit the deck as the great white zeroed in on my tasty mid-section.

Bastet raised her hand for what appeared to be the winnowing blow. Marco slowed, his blood matted fur and tired jaws not moving with the same speed they had earlier. The old mountain dog had fought well, but he wasn't a match for Bastet.

Button, button, who's got the button.

I launched myself over the remote and slammed the plastic button down in the palm of her outstretched claws.

Crash!

Magick exploded out of that white plastic disc in all directions, and at that same time the door burst open and sent my whole world to static.

IRON WILL

*T*he Kittens were gone, every last one of them, including Bastet and her ferocious claws. Where they'd split to I didn't know, but they'd left the button. I rubbed my head and rolled over, content to let the old man's apartment stop spinning before I even considered standing up.

"What the hell is going on in here?" The new voice was Jeff the Physicist—it turned out he was a good bit smaller than I expected. "Oh my God, your dog!"

I blinked my eyes a few more times before I zeroed in on Marco. Our resident scientist was right, but his expletives didn't do the situation justice. The mountain dog wheezed in a painful and bloody lump in front of me. His once happy tail now a matted mess.

Mr. Jenkins appeared behind the counter, also far worse for wear than before. Those liver spots were back, along with a set of terribly hunched shoulders. He tried to leave the kitchenette but his knees didn't appear up to the task. "Closet, kid... Soul of Isis... Cover..."

Jeff approached the dying animal. "Are you running some sort of dog fighting ring? I'm calling the police, but first I've got to get this dog to the vet. It's okay, boy. We'll get you patched up."

"No… vet," Mr. Jenkins muttered, his lips doing a lousy job of forming clean and complete syllables. "Closet, Gene."

Jeff ignored the aging Magician and slipped his hands under Marco, then hoisted him with a strength I wasn't expecting. "Screw you, old man. This is animal cruelty."

Mr. Jenkins white-knuckled the counter's edge and glared at me, then flicked his head at a closed door. "Move, now."

I stumbled past Jeff and grabbed the door's handle. If there was Magick inside it had vanished in the scientific aura of the apartment's physicist. "What about Marco?"

Mr. Jenkins slumped against overflowing counter. "Cover her eyes."

The door opened onto a dark storage closet. Piles of odds and ends stuck out in strange configurations. It was like someone had shaken out the contents of an old thrift store and poured them into the Magician's closet. "Uh?"

"Cat statue…"

Cat statue? Where the hell am I going to find a…

The slender bronze rendering of Bastet turned out to be pretty easy to find. It was right next to a large stack of old phone books, many of which were still wrapped in plastic. "Found it!"

"Cover…"

The nubile cat-woman's bronze eyes stared up at me, their chilling-gaze feral and hungry.

Magician…

"Shit." I grabbed one of the phone books and shucked its bag, then twisted the cheap plastic in my fingers and whipped up a modest blindfold. The cat woman's whispering voice disappeared beneath the crinkled wrapper.

"Hah, that worked."

"Marco…" Mr. Jenkins was fading fast.

"Get out of my way." Jeff clutched the dog to his chest and knocked the old man aside long enough to get the door open. "You guys are sick—"

Those were the last words to make it out of his mouth before a perfectly placed fist dropped the physicist and his cargo like a stone. Our favorite gun-toting mechanic had made it to semi-conscious and still functioned well enough to bring down Mr. Jenkins' neighbor.

"What the—" I scrambled out of the closet just in time to catch Miguel grin, give me a thumbs up, then crash land into the recliner sound asleep.

"Get... him... out of... my apartment..." Mr. Jenkins said, each word an agonizing drawl.

"But what about Marco, he's not—"

"Now!"

Jeff the Physicist had a compact frame, but he was still surprisingly hard to drag out of the room. I grabbed his wrists and flipped that downstairs neighbor on his back and did what I could to not injure the dog underneath further.

Marco's breathing was shallow. "He's not looking good."

Mr. Jenkins shook his head and clawed his way around the tiny counter, clutching it for dear life and trying not to fall. "He'll... be... fine."

I pursed my lips and dragged the unruly neighbor out the broken door, and into the hallway. I felt the pop as we crossed the threshold that signaled Mr. Jenkins' Magick was back.

"Idiot neighbor. Damn it, Bastet!"

"What do I do with him?" I shouted, still standing in the narrow hallway with an unconscious physicist at my feet.

"One damn thing at a time."

I propped Jeff up against the wall and hoped that would be enough, then scrambled back into the tiny apartment. Mr. Jenkins' Magick may have been restored, but he still wasn't back to his spry self just yet.

"The treats!" he said, pointing to the bag of dog treats I'd picked up earlier this evening.

"What about them?"

The old man ran a hand down his still wrinkly face. "Get the damn treats and bring them in here before we lose the only fucking thing that matters in my life."

My legs ached and my arms burned, but there was something about Mr. Jenkins' tone that turned on the jets. I yanked the sliding door open and grabbed the oversized bag and brought them inside.

The old magician directed me to place the bag at Marco's feet. Blood was everywhere, and the poor dog's breathing had been reduced to a barely audible wheeze. He extended a hand, and I helped him to his knees next to the broken mountain of fur and fat.

"You stupidly brilliant dog," he said, his wizened fingers running through the matted hair. "Who's a good dog? Marco's a good dog, yes he is."

The mountain dog's tail barely moved.

"What do we do?"

"*We* do nothing." Mr. Jenkins pushed his tinted glasses up on his face. "Your out-of-control Magick isn't getting near my dog, you hear me?"

"Yeah, but I just—"

Mr. Jenkins rolled up the sleeves of his robe. "You just need to shut up now, and go get me a steak knife."

"What?"

The old man snapped his hand out, grabbing my face fast enough to tell me that his power was coming back.

"Top drawer, second from the door, now!"

Mr. Jenkins let go and I found the drawer, as well as the worn out but impressive collection of serrated knives that lived inside. I grabbed one and returned to the old man and his rapidly fading canine. "What are you going to do?"

Mr. Jenkins yanked the knife out of my hand. "Magick, kid. Now shut the hell up and let me work."

"But he's dying…"

Mr. Jenkins pressed the knife's edge against his arm. "I know the rules. Hell, I invented them, but if you think that's going to stop me then you're dead wrong."

I raised my hands. "Whatever you have to do."

Mr. Jenkins pointed the knife at my face. "And don't get any ideas. The Viburna is dangerous. You hear me? If I catch you using it I promise you I will end you myself. Do you understand?"

I nodded, keeping a close eye on the blade's serrated edge.

"Good, now stand back. You're crowding me damn it."

I hadn't backed away more than a few inches before Mr. Jenkins sliced into his arm like I'd have cut into a steak. Blood trickled from the wound and the old man's Magick spun around it.

Mr. Jenkins' placed his bloodied arm on the dog's side, using his other hand to trace a pattern in the matted fur.

The sigil!

The old man's design was clearly better than the melted flesh version on William's chest, but the soul of it was the same. Broken and haggard lines swung like a mad EKG and cut through the fluff with crazed ferocity.

The old man's Magick continued to flood the room. It was a different sort of power, old and self-assured, but also oddly hungry. Something dark prowled at the edges of that Magick and waited to pounce like a jungle cat.

"Come on, Marco. It's not time to go yet."

The old dog's eyes fluttered, but his lungs remained still.

"Damn it, you stupid dog. We haven't stayed alive this long for you to die now, you hear me? You gonna let some cat send you to the great beyond? A cat, Marco? A fucking cat!"

The dog growled.

"There you go! That's the spirit." The old man placed both hands on the dog's side. "We're a team you and me. We made a pact remember. We go together, or not at all. Don't you forget that."

The Magick swelled, exotic and powerful. It rose like the tide, a great wave of power that threatened to drown us all. The old Magician's fingers clutched at Marco's fur even while all around him the cosmic energy surged. "Come, Marco."

Shadowy hands, strong yet supple, reached for Jenkins from inside the swelling wave of energy. With fingers like black iron, they grabbed at the old man's hands and pulled at his legs.

"Damn it, Marco. Come!" The old man shrugged off the strong hands, even as sweat beaded on his brow. "Come, now!"

Whump! Whump!

The dogs tail whacked the bloody carpet with a resounding thump, then, as quickly as it had come, the Magickal tide and hungry shadows left us, fading like the retreating sea.

"I don't know how many of these we've got left." The old Magician slapped a palm against his arm to stem the flow of blood. "You know how it works. Can't cheat fate too many times, she gets angry."

Marco growled.

"Yeah, I know, but rules are rules. Now, let's start a new rule. No more cats in the apartment, deal?"

Bark!

Mr. Jenkins scratched at the mountain dog's long ears. "Yeah, couldn't have said it better myself. Now, help yourself to some of Gene's treats."

The now healthy mountain dog pushed himself up and padded toward the open bag.

Mr. Jenkins collapsed against the tiny kitchenette's island, his tinted glasses slipping below his eyes. He stared at the self-inflicted wound on his arm. "That's the Viburna, kid. I'm the last one that knows it and that's for the best."

I wanted to say something, but I couldn't tear my eyes away from the two small fangs poking out of Mr. Jenkins' mouth.

"What are you looking—oh, shit," the old man said, feeling the diminutive canines.

"Vampire. You are a vampire?!"

The old Magician shook his head. "That's inane. There's no such thing as vampires."

I stood and backed toward the door. "I know a vampire when I see one, and you're like the fourth one I've seen in the last twenty-four hours. The other three had you beat though. They had unfolding faces."

"What?" The old man scrambled to his feet, the fangs in his mouth gone. "That's not possible. I'm the last Sanguist left."

"Try again," I said, pointing at Miguel. "His daughter's jaws unfolded like fleshy origami, and what sprung out of the inside had nightmare fuel written all over it."

The old man gripped the counter like he'd taken a gut punch. "What?"

HERO TALK

"Oh no, you don't get to jump over everything that just happened here," I said, keeping a healthy distance between me and the Magickal vampire. "Some cat-woman and her entourage almost eviscerates me and the mean mechanic, then you bring Marco back from the dead with a nasty-looking sigil and a trickle of old-man-negative. Oh, and let's not forget, the icing on the 'holy crap' cake—you have fangs. Fangs that look a lot like the ones in vampire movies."

Mr. Jenkins rubbed his temples. "There were others?"

"That's right, I said vampires. Or would you prefer Nosferatu, or Child of the Night, or—wait, what did you say?"

"You said I was the fourth you'd seen in twenty-four hours. There were more?"

"Yeah, I got the full treatment, unfolding faces and rib arms."

Mr. Jenkins shook his head slowly. "I have no idea what that is, but it's not the Viburna, kid. You've been watching too much TV."

"Oh, no. I know what I saw." I pointed at the old man's chin. "Go ahead, unzip that mess and show me."

Mr. Jenkins frowned. "I assure you, kid. My face does not *unzip.*"

I leaned in closer, extending a finger. "I don't know, that wrinkle there looks suspect..."

The old man slapped my hand away.

"Fine, what about your chest legs?"

"Chest legs?"

"Yeah." I pointed at Jenkins' shirt. "Show me yours. I'm sure you've got them too. Terrifying clawed appendages that spring out from the gaps between your ribs like really bad alaskan king crab."

The old man pushed me back. "What in the hell are you talking about?"

"Me?" I pointed at the dog resting next to Miguel. "I'm talking about the Viburna. I've seen it before, melted into one of your fellow vampire's saggy chests."

"Was this over top of the rib feelers or behind them?"

"Don't mock me, I know what I saw."

The old man grabbed a wet napkin out of the trash and slapped it on the counter. "Show me, then."

"Right now?"

Mr. Jenkins nodded, fishing a pen out of the kitchen drawer. "Show me *your* Viburna."

"Fine." I finagled the pen into action, spiraling it a few times before the ink got going. "It was like this..."

I closed my eyes and brought back the memories of a hungry William. Satisfied I had what I needed, I let the pen dance across the soggy paper. Jagged EKG lines, the confining circle, and more spilled forth from the felt-tip until I had the sigil I remembered. If Morgan had taught me anything, it was how to re-create complex sets of crazy squiggles.

"Yes, that's the Viburna, but..."

I spun the pen and added the arms—six radiating lines that hinged out like the legs of an insect.

"What is that?"

I scrunched up my face and held up the napkin. "Looks like a bug."

"Give me that." Mr. Jenkins snapped the design out of my hand and stared at it.

"Mosquito," I said, seeing the symbol from the backside. "Yeah, that's my final answer."

"What did you say?"

"Mosquito. You know, the things you didn't want to let in the apartment the other morning."

"Okay, hot shot." Mr. Jenkins folded the napkin over. "If this actually worked and put you in the firing line of a bunch of 'Mosquito People,' how did you escape? I mean, you aren't exactly rocking the Magick at present."

Shit.

The old man stuffed the design in his pocket and reached for the almost empty bottle of tequila. "You suddenly get over those performance issues?"

"Uh…"

"Yeah, I didn't think so. Listen, kid, I love a good story as much as the next guy, and I can certainly appreciate your memory having seen me do the Viburna once, but I think you need to hit the road."

"There was—"

"What? A werewolf? Did he offer to introduce you to the Queen of England?"

"No, I'm not making this up."

The old Magician smiled and pushed his glasses back on his face, then started herding me toward the door. "Sure, sure. I bet. These 'Mosquito People' sound terrifying. I'll order you some bug spray."

Mr. Jenkins opened the door and pointed me to the hallway.

Jeff's gone? Focus, Gene.

"It's been great meeting you, Eugene Law." He slid his glasses down his nose. "Really, great. Now, have a nice life. I'll take care of returning the couch crasher to Ybor in the morning."

"No, stop! I'm telling the truth."

"Oh yeah? Well then tell me, Mr. Magician. How did you escape multiple Magickal Mosquito people?"

"We are Flock."

The old Magician yanked his tinted glasses off. "What did you say?"

"There's this thing, I think it's called a—"

Mr. Jenkins yanked me back into the tiny apartment and slammed the door. "Duplickity. How did you join The Flock?"

"Uh, I wouldn't say it was a conscious decision. It was very heat of the moment. You know, on the one hand you have a fleshy face-pizza ready to suck up your abnormal plasma like a Slurpee"—I held up a palm—"and on the other, a beady-eyed, plastic flamingo offering free membership in the invisibility club."

"You didn't…"

"I did."

Mr. Jenkins spun around and grabbed the counter top. "Oh all the stupid—"

"Hey, listen. I'm alive thanks to that bird. She's saved me a few times so far and I've got to say I'm starting to appreciate this whole Flock business very much—although I could do without the extra plastic birds everywhere."

"She… did you say she?"

I nodded.

The old Magician took a deep breath. "Okay, so let me get this straight. You willingly joined the Flock, and in doing so, saddled yourself up to a nesting Duplickity."

"Nesting… that's funny, Deacon said the same thing."

"Is that one of the Mosquito People?"

"Yeah."

The old man ran a hand through his wispy hair and pulled a

clean glass off the shelf. "Here, you need this more than me." He pressed the highball glass into my hand and poured a few fingers of tequila into it.

"Thanks, but I'm not really a tequila sort of—"

"A nesting Duplickity... I'm going to assume based on your cavalier attitude you have no idea what that means."

"No..." The old Magician's tequila was starting to look tempting.

"Well, let's start with the simple stuff. Birds nest before they are going to have baby birds—not going too fast for you, right?"

"Right..."

Mr. Jenkins pointed to my glass. "Drink up."

Once I had a little tequila in me he continued. "So, Duplickities don't have baby birds."

"Oh... Do I *want* to know what they have?"

"You really don't have a choice—You are Flock, remember?"

I took the bottle from him and poured more into my glass. "What do they have?"

The old Magician sighed and wiped the sweat from his face. "Potential."

"Excuse me?"

"The Duplickity doesn't get pregnant often—in fact it's unbelievably rare—but when they do the result is possibilities, near limitless possibilities, and not always the good ones."

I set the glass down. "I don't understand."

"Imagine it this way, kid. Imagine if you could see everything that could happen, that has happened, and that might happen. Then, imagine you could change it all."

Shit.

The old Magician picked up my glass and powered it down what was left in it in a single toss. "A Duplickity's egg is pure potential. They have changed the course of history, and not always for the best."

I swallowed hard. "Oh."

"Still want to be in the Flock?"

I wanted to say no and find a way to unhook myself from that little bird, but something held me back, something kept me from closing that door. "Uh…"

"A Duplickity's pull is strong. I'm betting these 'Mosquito People,' should they exist, know what I know. That means they are going to come after your flamingo—hard."

Run.

The bare emotion hit me hard, like one of the little bird's images.

"I bet your first inclination is to run," the old Magician said, looking for the bottle. "That would be the Flock talking. The lure of invisibility is strong, trust me. I've been hiding for a long time, a very long time. I know what it's like to run, to hide, to slip in and out unseen. The Flock will mess with your head, kid."

"But she saved me."

"She owns you. It isn't a partnership. That creature owns you and she'll drive you mad in the process."

"What do I do?"

"Go home, get some rest. Tomorrow I'll help detach you from the Flock."

But do I want to?

"Isn't that what they want…"

Mr. Jenkins pointed me toward the door. "Trust me, don't be the hero, kid. Let them have their Duplickity and get your life back. That's what's important."

I stepped out into the warm night air with more questions than I had when I'd arrived, the old Magician certainly had that effect. "What about—"

"Your mechanic? Yeah, he'll be really disoriented by morning. Together we can drive him home."

"But his daughter—"

"Kid, don't be a hero, be a husband."

A warm breeze swept across the parking lot as I made my way back to the apartment.

He's right... You don't need this.

I didn't.

I needed to get my life back together, to find a decent job—a real one that paid the bills—and to put all of this behind me.

Be the husband she deserves.

Even though I didn't ask for it, Magick bubbled up gently in my chest with each step on the still hot pavement.

The Magick...

It had always been about the Magick. The power was intoxicating and all consuming. No matter how much I gave it, it still wanted more, and now it wasn't even listening to me. I kicked at a clump of cut palm fronds I'd missed this morning and scattered them across the blacktop.

Why won't you work?

A vision from the past rolled in my mind like it had so many times before. Morgan dangled on Ariadne's Thread, her soul in my hands.

I cut the Thread.

The words stung and forced me to think hard about my choice.

What right did I have?

Morgan had been a terrible person, cruel and destructive, but did she deserve that?

Does anyone?

Twinkling stars winked in the darkening blanket of night above me, while the wispy clouds that drifted by brought with them memories of the Gloom. I'd been the judge, jury, and on that night, executioner.

What happened to her?

Ed had assured me what I'd done was for the best and that it had been the only way.

But did I believe him?

I took a deep breath of the twilight air, half expecting it to be as cold as that night in the Gloom, but it wasn't, because the apartment was not that hellish nightmare place.

You told Ed Lovely you were out of the hero business. Having second thoughts?

I followed the sidewalk around the corner, my eyes no longer on the stars, but now tracing the rigid seams in the brushed concrete. Cracks spread through the ground beneath my feet like the twisted lines of complex sigils.

'Don't be a hero, be a husband.'

I didn't tell Mr. Jenkins, but I'd stopped being a hero a long time ago. I paused on the sidewalk remembering that fateful evening.

"Come on, Gene. I need your Magick. We can't let those frat guys summon a Gorgon. I know, if she turned them to stone they'd look cool on the quad, but that's not what we do," my old roommate had said, his fishing vest loaded to the gills with trinkets of various and terrifying artifacts.

"I'm out, Ed."

"Out of what? Beer? We can pick some up."

I shook my head. "I mean I'm out. You're on your own. This isn't my fight."

"What do you mean it's not your fight? All of these are your fight. You're the one with power. You're the one that the old dead Magicians lusted after like those rollerblading hotties we saw this afternoon." Ed pat me on the back. "Now, come on. You're my dump truck of awesome. Beep! Beep! Let's go run us down a snake-headed Demon bitch."

"No."

I still remember the look in my his eyes when he realized I wasn't kidding.

"You're quitting Magick?"

"Hardly," I'd said, like the cocky liar I was. "I'm just done with running around trying to save people from themselves. That's a bang-up way to get yourself killed, you know that, I know that. Let's not kid ourselves."

"But, you have an obligation—"

An obligation to kill? To murder? Is that what I am, a murderer?

"I have no such thing. My obligation is to myself and to Porter. I don't owe those idiots anything. If they want to turn themselves to stone, then so be it."

But that wasn't it. That wasn't why I stopped.

"You have a damn gift, Law! You think you get to just walk away from that?"

"Yes, that's exactly what I think. Now, good luck to you. I have no problems being your friend, and even inviting you to the wedding, but if you can't..."

That was the last time I'd spoken to Edwin Lovely. Without another word, he'd turned around and left me standing in the sidewalk. I'd checked the Alligator the next day and found no mention of new statues.

He must have handled it fine, just fine in fact, and the best part was he handled it without you.

I had a life to live and a beautiful woman to be there for. I didn't need the insanity of Edwin Lovely, Duplickities, or Mosquito People.

Movement in the bright apartment windows drew my attention—men and women, families, together having dinner and sharing their day.

How many people are missing because of Deacon?

"It's not my job," I said to myself.

Maybe it is? Maybe this is who you are.

A small kid popped up from one of the glowing windows and waved. I waved back.

Don't even think about it, Gene. You're not ready for that.

Would I ever be ready? Was this the sort of world I'd bring a child into, knowing all the dark and scary things just waiting to devour them?

The kid smiled and held up what looked like a plastic hook. I squinted my eyes.

Flamingo?!

The kid stepped away and let the plastic bird lean against the glass.

It's just another plastic bird.

I blinked and could have sworn the bird's head faced the other way moments before.

That was when I noticed them.

The kid's bird wasn't the only flamingo, there were more, lots more. I hadn't seen them before, but now that I was looking I found them all over the grounds of the complex. They were tucked into bushes and wedged against trees. I even found them stacked like firewood under the stairs of my building.

She's nesting...

The lights were off at my apartment, but they didn't stay off long. I hadn't made it across the parking lot before the bright yellow glow from our open blinds flooded the grass outside and gave me a fishbowl like view inside.

There was Porter.

The moment she stepped in front of the glass I remembered exactly why I made the decision to stay out of the way of every crazy thing that found itself in my headlamps —Porter.

She tossed her purse on the couch and grabbed the edge of the curtains.

Is she talking to someone?

Alyssa leaned against the door, saying something that solicited a laugh from my wife.

But which Alyssa was it?

Was that the Alyssa that couldn't be bothered to put on pajamas before noon? Or was it the Alyssa looking thing that haunted me in one of a dozen different skins?

What are they talking about?

Whatever it was, it didn't last long. Porter pulled the curtains shut and shortly thereafter the door opened.

"Thank you so much for calling me. I had a great time," Alyssa said.

My wife's response was tired but bubbly. "Oh, it was my pleasure. Sometimes I get so bored by myself. It was so much fun to go out just us girls."

"Definitely, another time?"

"You got it, sister," my wife called out before closing the apartment door.

I stepped quietly off the pavement and found Alyssa working the lock on her unit.

"Oh, hey, Gene!" she said, without a hint of that strange tone in her perky voice.

"You ladies have fun?" I asked, relieved to be talking to my neighbor.

"Would have been more fun if you guys came."

"That would have been bliss compared to where I've been." I pointed to the stained coveralls I was wearing. "I'd be more than happy to trade these in for a suit and tie."

Alyssa laughed again, and I chuckled at the absurdity of my comment before reaching for the apartment door.

"Work for me and you can wear whatever you want."

I froze solid, my stomach dropping at roughly the same moment my heart rate shot for the ceiling.

The thing wearing Alyssa like a sock puppet was back.

"I told you to leave me alone."

"And I told you that I won't be doing that." Alyssa's heel popped against the hard concrete. "You're precious to me, Eugene Law."

I reached for my Magick but found it fleeting, wherever it had gone, the cosmic powers I'd have loved to have at that moment were conveniently missing.

"Oh, performance issues again?" Alyssa said, practically on top of me, perfume mixing with the alcohol on her breath, both of which were muddling my senses.

"I said—"

"Gene?" My apartment door swung open and there was Porter, her hair down and her blouse partially untucked. "I just listened to the message. Are you okay? What happened to Alonzo?"

I turned back to Alyssa, but found the neighbor from hell had vanished.

My wife stuck her head out to inspect the empty hallway. "Who were you talking to?"

"Nobody."

22

TRUTH AND LIARS

*H*ot water beat down on my shoulders, digging into the creases of my skin and washing away a long day's worth of dirt and grit. The soaking spray was great for my body, but for all its power, the shower did nothing for my head.

"Okay, so you got to Miguel's house, then what happened?" Porter asked from just outside the shower—privacy wasn't something you had in the Law apartment.

"We parked the car."

"I figured as much," my wife said, clearly frustrated at the slow pace of my story. "*Then* what happened?"

How much do I tell her?

I'd already set a pretty terrible precedent as of late by not telling her about William, Deacon, or even the blood-drinking pink bird that appeared to be dropping duplicates of itself like candy throughout the complex. To make matters worse, I wasn't quite ready to cover the complex's resident Vampire, his half-naked cat-women, or the skin-walking thing that appeared to have a renewed interest in me.

So, you're going to tell her what exactly?

I popped open the bottle of shampoo. "We got out of the car."

"Argh."

I could almost see my wife wringing her hands on the other side of the shower curtain. "Next you're going to tell me you took one step, and then another. Would you like me to wait while you decide which foot it was you used first?"

"Now that you mention it..."

"Eugene Law, stop fooling around. Tell me what happened to Alonzo."

"What's to tell." I squirt shampoo into my hand. "Miguel's shotgun house was on fire. Alonzo ran in and I followed him."

And while I was inside I had a snap reunion with the king of the Mosquito People, and what appeared to be Miguel's daughter and her rib cage ticklers. I almost died no less than twice, and that was before I found Satan's Toaster.

"You ran into a burning house?"

I worked the shampoo into my hair. "Well, when you say it like that it makes me sound quite heroic."

It wasn't burning when you went in... Damn it, Gene. Keep the story straight.

"Or massively stupid."

"Yes, heroic, but it was Alonzo who went in first. I just figured it was part of the job."

"So you found Miguel inside?"

Now it's going to get tricky...

"Yes and no. As it would turn out he wasn't there, and neither was his daughter. We ran into an empty house for nothing."

"Gene!"

I rinsed the lather from my hair. "Yeah, I know, not one of my more brilliant moves, but what if they had been?"

I couldn't see more than the rough outline of her body, but I could tell my wife was pacing outside the curtain.

Ease up, Gene. You're starting to worry her.

"Is that when Alonzo passed out?"

My wife had a degree in journalism. I knew this because it hung on the wall in our bedroom. It also came with a near expert level ability to ask questions—tricky questions that were excellent at ferreting out lies.

"I think. It was all a blur, really. Nearest I could tell the smoke must have gotten to him. I found him on the floor and couldn't get him out. He's not a small guy."

"True."

It's working.

"Is that when Miguel arrived?"

I fished a dry bar of soap out of the tray. "Yeah, pretty much. He found me in the kitchen and together we dragged Alonzo outside."

"Wow," Porter said, her shadow dropping the lid on the toilet and taking a seat. "That's how it happened, huh?"

"Yep."

I had a nice rich lather going on my chest and was just about to wash it off when I noticed the shower curtain had been pulled back enough for my wife's head to poke around the corner. "That's just amazing."

"I know, right?"

Something's not right.

"Totally, except it's completely different from the one Miguel told to the police and reporters when he was on the evening news seven hours ago."

The soap slipped out of my hand and banged against the tub floor.

"Yeah." Porter shook her head. "You'd have thought he would have mentioned saving a stringy white guy in a maintenance man's work shirt?"

"Maybe it slipped his mind?"

I married Woodward and Porterstein.

"Possibly." My wife's voice slipped into that inquisitive tone she'd once used to get me to admit to eating the last powdered donut.

"Yeah, that's got to be it," I said, pushing my face under the water. I surfaced moments later to find her missing.

"Porter?"

"You know, there's something else that hasn't made any sense to me." My wife's shadowy outline rummaged through something on the floor beyond the curtain. "Maybe you can explain it."

"I'd be happy too."

"Well, when I last saw you today you were wearing a work shirt Alonzo had offered you."

Shit! This girl's a bloodhound.

"Right, I—"

"And now." Porter reappeared at the end of the shower with a set of coveralls in her hands, a set of oil-stained mechanics coveralls that didn't look anything like what I'd had on this morning. "I find these. So peculiar?"

"Well—"

Porter pressed a black stain against her nose and took a breath. "Yep, oil. So, how about we start from the top, Mr. Law? You tell me what really happened, and I'll sit here quietly and listen."

I turned off the water and accepted the towel from Porter 'the reporter' Law. "Okay, but you've got to promise not to worry. I've got it all under control."

My wife didn't say anything, she simply sat on that closed toilet with her arms and legs crossed waiting for me to sing like a canary.

Sigh.

"All right, here goes."

23

GUILTY PARTY

For the first time in forever Porter remained completely motionless. She didn't pace. She didn't ask questions. She simply sat there and listened.

I told her about the chains, the birds, William, Deacon, all of it. I even dipped into the past and told her about whatever it was that had visited me in the shape of Morgan and Alyssa.

She only broke her stoic facade once, and that was at the mention of my ex-girlfriend. Even now Morgan was a sore subject and one I glossed over quickly.

Since Porter didn't appear interested in moving, I got up and started pacing myself. I walked grooves in the newly cleaned carpet telling her about Bastet, Miguel, and the Lost Button.

It was cathartic in a way I hadn't been expecting. I'd been holding a lot of this in for far too long and taking a hand off the stopper meant unleashing the whole tale in one massive explosion of activity.

It was well after midnight by the time I finished—my voice raw and my nerves frayed.

"But none of this matters because I'm out. You are too important. I'm not risking what I have here."

Porter's eyes didn't waiver. "Is that it?"

"Yes."

"I see," my wife said, her voice perfectly monotone.

It was unexpected and downright terrifying.

"So, I think the best plan now that we know Deacon might come here is to move. You can get a new job. You're talented and I know you'll find something really fast. I'm betting if we sort of get off the grid for a bit they'll stop caring and then we'll be fine."

"And what happens to Sofia? What happens to Miguel? What about the rest of the people those things are kidnapping?"

"Now, we don't know for sure—"

My tranquil wife practically exploded out of the chair like a tripped landmine. "Like hell we don't. You think those trucks to Miami were loaded with good will and happiness pie?"

"No, but it's dangerous—"

"You're damn right it's dangerous. It would be suicide for someone like me, but you aren't me."

"What do you mean?"

Porter paced the room like a caged lion. "I try, I really do. I try to understand what you are. Some days I can. Some days I look in those eyes and I see the man I fell in love with. Other days... I see the man you've become."

"I'm trying to protect you."

"What's the point of protecting me if doing so means I lose you in the process?"

"I don't understand."

Porter walked into the tiny kitchen and started pulling open drawers, not finding what she was looking for she slammed them shut again.

I followed her. "I'm here for you. I made you that promise when we got married."

"But you aren't *you* anymore," Porter said, opening the

bottom drawer and pulling out a stack of photos. We couldn't keep pictures on display—we lived in the showroom model after all—so we kept them in a drawer. "What happened to this Gene?"

My wife slammed down a picture of Ed and me that she'd taken during one of our first 'quasi-missions.' Ed had a bead on a Poltergeist holed up in a farmhouse just outside of town. I'd almost lost a foot to his great uncle Bart's Ethereal Bear Trap, but my roommate's half-baked plan had worked—no small thanks to some fast thinking by yours truly. We had dissipated that Poltergeist and were rewarded with one hell of an apple pie for our efforts.

"You remember this?" she asked.

"Yes."

"No, Gene. Do you *really* remember it?"

"Yes." I brushed the photo aside. "Ed and I dissipated a Poltergeist outside of Alachua. So what?"

My wife shook her head. "Nope, still not remembering it. I'll try again." She fished out another picture and laid it on the table. This one was taken after a visit to the Ocala National Forest. Ed wasn't in this shot, it was just me. I had a big goofy grin on my face because I'd just successfully banished a New Dead. I didn't know it at the time, but they'd be a frequent pain in my butt in the years to follow.

"Ringing any bells?"

"Yes, I'd banished a—"

"Nope." Porter slammed her hand down on the counter. "You still aren't seeing it. Damn it, Gene. What do these pictures have in common?"

"Me?"

"Yes and…"

I shook my head. "Ed? I don't know."

Porter grabbed my hand. "Purpose, you big idiot," she said, her voice softening. "You had a purpose back then. A reason for getting up and facing the day. When you told Ed you were out you lost that purpose. You lost the fire."

"But I did it for you."

My wife shook her head and let go of my hand. "No, you didn't. You did it for her."

"For who?"

Tears welled up in my wife's eyes. "You did it for Morgan."

"No!"

"Yes, Gene. She's still here, isn't she?"

It was my turn to shake my head. "No. I told you she isn't. She's gone—lost to the library. No one comes back from that."

Porter frowned and placed a finger on my head, and then again on my heart. "She's here, and here. She got to you in a way I don't understand. You still carry that guilt with you. You walk around with it day after day and I can't get you to put it down."

"Maybe I don't want to."

There it was.

The words had come out of my mouth and I didn't know how to put them back. "I killed her, Porter. Me. Your husband is a murderer. Do you know what it's like to live with that?"

"No."

"Exactly, you don't. You don't know what it's like to wonder day after day if you made the right decision. Was there another way? Was there something else you could have done? It eats at you nonstop."

"You did the right thing."

"Ed said that too, but how do you know? How do either of you really know?"

My wife placed her hand against my face. It was warm and soft in a way I wasn't expecting. "I'm alive because of you. That's how I know. You saved my life, just like you've saved others."

"But—"

My wife kissed me, her lips salty with tears.

"That's the Eugene Law I want you to remember. The one

that does what's right. The one that trusts his gut. The idiot that runs in headfirst. The one I fell in love with."

"I…"

"Oh, just shut up and kiss me," Porter said, kissing me again.

"But what about the—"

"Vampires? Mosquito People? Screw em, they don't stand a chance."

"Very funny, but they're going to come here, and I don't know how to keep you safe. I've got to get you out of town."

My wife threw her arms around my neck. "Nice try, but I'm not going anywhere. I took a vow too, you know."

"Porter, this is some seriously twisted Magick. I don't think you realize what these guys are capable of."

"And I don't think they realize who they're up against. Promise me you'll get out of your own way and stop carrying her around in your head."

"I will."

"Promise me, Eugene Law."

"I promise."

"Good." My wife turned off the lights in the kitchen. "It's time for bed."

"Yes, ma'am."

THIN SHAFTS of moonlight snuck in between the blinds and cut a prison bar pattern across the sheets. Porter lay next to me, her body turned away and softly sleeping.

She doesn't understand.

The Viburna was way beyond my skill level, as was Deacon and the rest of the Mosquito People.

The clock ticked gently on the far wall.

Is she right? Am I wrong to carry Morgan's guilt?

I slipped out of the sheets and crept into the living room, then pushed the curtains aside and stared up at the stars.

Did I do the right thing?

I was tired of being manipulated, tired of feeling guilty, and tired of second guessing myself, but did I deserve to be?

You can do this forever.

I could. I could go right on beating myself up over decisions made long ago, but they wouldn't play out any differently.

I left the window and went back to that drawer of pictures, digging through it until I found what I was looking for. To anyone else it had been a mistake, an off-kilter photo of some wooden doors, but I knew differently.

This was where I took a life.

I held up the picture and stared at the mundane seams of heavy oak.

"It's over. I'm not letting you control my life anymore."

I tore the photo in two and threw it into the trash.

24

NESTED PROBLEMS

I drifted in and out of sleep much of the night. With the first light of dawn, my hand drifted over to my wife's side of the bed.

"Wow, that was a crazy night," I said, my fingers tracing the curve of her face—her cheekbones, her nose, and that lovely way her face unzipped like a gut fish.

What?!

I opened my eyes to find myself face to face with open folds of bloody jaws and a quivering stinger.

Hiss!

"He's awake," the Mosquito-thing said, a nose-ring shining above its parted lips.

"Excellent, is the sigil in place?"

The redhead Skeeter didn't break eye-contact with me, the open flaps of her jaws twitching gently inches from my nose. "Yes."

"Good morning, Mr. Law," a familiar voice said, pulling open the blinds to flood the room with light. "I'm guessing you remember me?"

Deacon!

The man-in-black wasn't alone. Miguel's daughter leaned against the wall next to him, her eyes unfocused.

"Sofia, help me!"

Deacon shook his head. "She doesn't hear you, Magician."

"How—"

"Don't bother reaching for your Magick, because the lovely Cynthia is making that impossible. Aren't you, sweetheart?"

"He's not doing anything." The Skeeter next to me tapped her fingers on my forehead. "Kilpsee's Burning Bind."

"Excellent. So, unless you want to boil your own blood, you'll do what I say, Gene."

I bat away the redhead's hand and pushed myself up. "Where's my wife?"

The monochromatic Deacon held my wallet in his hands. "She's with William."

No!

I tried to lunge for him, but Cynthia was faster, and had the advantage of those damn sharp chest legs. The insect-like arms sprung from the sides of her open tank-top and slammed me back against the headboard. Narrow lines of blood tickled down my skin and left red stains on the sheets.

"Eugene... Law?" Deacon held up my driver's license and let the rest of my wallet hit the floor. "We need to have a chat. You have something of ours and we would like it back."

"What are you talking about?"

Deacon sighed, and the redhead dug her spindly claws deeper.

"I'd really hoped it wouldn't have to come to this. I'm not an unreasonable man. I'm simply asking for the bird you took from us."

We are Flock.

"I didn't take any bird."

"Cynthia, if you would please. I don't believe Mr. Law is a fan of wearing pants when he sleeps."

The leather-clad Skeeter ripped off the thin sheets covering me, and yes, I was not much for wearing pants when I slept—something that if I survived this, I would be doing a lot more of.

My heart pounded the moment she pressed her claws against my thigh. "Do Skeeters know about shrinkage?"

"Gene, all she has to do is squeeze and she'll slice open your femoral artery. Do you know what happens then?"

"I win a prize?"

"Depends."

"What do you mean?"

Deacon tossed my license. "Depends on how many things you've pissed off that would like to take a crack at you the moment you die."

I should really keep a count.

Deacon fished a phone out of his pocket and flipped it open, setting it on my bare stomach. "Can you read that?"

"Motorola."

The lovely Cynthia squeezed my leg, her claws drawing tiny droplets of blood.

"That's cute. What time is it Gene?"

"Seven fifteen, time for you to get out of my apartment."

"I told William he could start enjoying your lovely wife's fingers if I didn't call him off by seven seventeen. He has such a hard time with numbers, hopefully he won't jump the gun."

"You're lying."

Deacon pressed the mute button on his phone and the tiny bedroom filled with the sound of William's whistling nose. "It smells so sweet. Will it be a tasty meat?"

"Porter!"

"Gene! Help, I'm scared—"

"Just breathe. I'm coming for you!"

William's whistling nose overpowered the tiny speaker. "Almost time, my tasty treat. Oh, which fingers shall William eat?"

The man-in-black scooped up his phone and turned off the speaker. "One minute, Gene."

"I don't have it."

"That's a shame, but I imagine your wife can survive without a few fingers while you figure out where it is."

I reached for my Magick. It rumbled in my chest, ready for a fight.

"I wouldn't do that, Mr. Law." A faint smile spread across the hairless man's face.

A searing pain hit me between the eyes. I'd accidentally burned my hand on a sparkler once as a kid, and this made that feel joyful in comparison.

"What did I tell you about Kilpsee's Burning Bind? Cynthia is good at that one."

The red-headed Skeeter brought her fangs just inches from my stinging face. "Let me take him, Deacon. We'll find the bird. He's simply too tempting."

Mr. Monochromatic stepped around the side of the bed and grabbed my leg, his thumb pressing against the puncture wound's barely visible scab. "No, he's bonded with it. The damnable bird will only answer to him. Besides, she's nesting. You saw all the simulacrums outside."

"How is that possible?" Cynthia asked, her jaws quivering.

"What can I say? Animals love me."

The Skeeter's claws dug into my leg harder.

Ugh! Come on, Sofia. Snap out of it!

"You have less than one minute, Eugene Law. Release the Duplickity to me now and I'll keep William from feasting on your wife."

"I'm telling you. I don't know where she is. I haven't seen her since Ybor."

Deacon slammed a hand on the nightstand. "There are copies throughout this damn complex. She's here, and she's nesting. The Duplickity has bonded to you and you're going to break that bond and hand her over to me now or William will tear your precious wife's fingers from her hand one by one."

Motion in the distance caught my eye, something big, hairy, and remarkably fast-moving given its body fat percentage was on a collision course with my bedroom window.

"Wait!" I shouted, trying to buy some time. "I'll bring the bird, but it takes time. Like you said, she's nesting and skittish."

Please work.

I had no idea if that was how Duplickities worked, but if the old Magician was to be believed, very few people had a clue what happened when they nested—I just needed a few more seconds.

"Do it." Deacon waved off the redhead, her pinning appendages releasing me from the headboard.

"Call off the finger eating Cat-In-The-Hat and I will."

He mashed the speaker button on his phone. "William, do not touch her."

A feral growl crackled from the tiny speaker.

"It is done." Deacon clicked off the tiny button. "Now, give me the Duplickity."

Damn it, Marco. A little faster please?

"It's easier if I have clothes on. The bird is a bit shy when it comes to man-parts and—"

Deacon's bone-white hand grabbed my neck, his fingers squeezing at my already sore throat. "Stop wasting time."

"I'm not." I pointed to the final bounding leap of Marco the mountain dog moments before he hit my bedroom window. "The dog's just slow."

"Huh—"

Boom!

Mr. Jenkins' pet hit my window like a wrecking ball. Over a hundred pounds of fur and fat shattered the glass, sending sharp fragments of the cheap window everywhere, then crashed into the unsuspecting Deacon. The resulting impact launched the man-in-black and I across the bed, taking out an equally surprised Cynthia in the process.

Not in the man-parts!

The four of us landed in a misshapen lump on the carpet. Cynthia took the worst of it, her head slamming into the wall with a sickening crack. I scrambled to my feet while Deacon tangled with the mountain dog.

And this is why I'm not a morning person.

I grabbed the hairless one's phone from the bed and mashed the speaker button. "Porter, do it! Just like I taught you."

"Gene!"

"Do it, now!"

An explosion of static crackled in the phone along with William's soul-chilling scream.

Deacon untangled himself from Marco and tossed the oversized dog against the far wall like he were taking out the trash, then turned his attention back to me. The sides of his jacket flared out, making way for six long and powerful arms.

Crap.

"Well I'll be. Will you look at that." A robe-wearing Mr. Jenkins waved from my broken bedroom window, then pointed at Cynthia. "Their faces *do* unzip."

I ripped the sheet off the bed and twisted into a wad. "A little help here."

"Holy crap!" The old Magician's reflection appeared in the unbelievably expensive floor mirror the apartment complex had insisted on. "Where the hell are your pants, kid?"

Deacon's crab-like claws slashed at my bare chest.

"Bigger problems." I caught the bulk of his claws in the sheet, but not before one of them cut a line down my sternum.

"Damn. Even rib arms," The old Magician said, hiking up his robe to climb over the jagged glass only to have it catch on a derelict shard. "You weren't pulling my leg."

Deacon's Magick ramped up and filled the room quicker

than I thought possible. "Illici—" The Skeeter's words broke up on his lips the moment my bedroom door opened and he took a formerly showroom quality frying pan to the face.

I didn't think I'd ever be that pleased to see those murderous, yet remarkably well-rested eyes again—boy, was I ever wrong.

Miguel!

25

DUPLICKITY

"Sofia!" My new favorite ex-con smashed Deacon's face with our unused kitchen tools on his way toward his fallen daughter. The one-color Skeeter's face crumpled in on itself, his cheek bones cracking beneath the crushing pan.

On the other side of the room Mr. Jenkins fought to undo his threadbare bathrobe from my broken window. "Stupid robe."

With Deacon clutching his face, Miguel's attention was on his daughter. "Sweetheart, what have they done to you?"

Sofia's vacant eyes held no love for her father.

"She's one of us," the nose-ringed Cynthia said, getting to her feet. "Take him. He's yours, Sofia."

"Daughter?"

The young woman's unfocused eyes narrowed, while the flesh of her jaws peeled itself apart.

"Holy—"

Miguel didn't stand a chance. Sofia's quivering jaws pierced his neck and sent a spray of blood across my formerly white sheets.

Rip.

His robe torn, Jenkins was in my apartment, but even he couldn't believe what he was seeing. "It's like fleshy origami…"

I turned my attention to the bind-wielding Cynthia. "Watch out for the chest arms."

As if on cue, the nose-ringed Skeeter's claws unfolded from the sides of her chest, while at the same time her Magick sizzled. Anger and frustration in equal abundance swelled within the pierced-woman's power.

"They've perverted the Viburna," a confused Jenkins said, placing a hand against his head. "How?"

"Think we could worry about that later?" I ducked a many-armed slash from Cynthia, tying it up in what remained of the shredded sheet.

"Look out," the old Magician cried.

Cynthia unleashed a whip crack of Magickal force against my chest and I hit the carpet with a resounding thump. The lovely Skeeter wasted no time closing the distance to dig her many arms into my flesh.

"Deacon wants you to turn over the bird. As far as I'm concerned you can keep it. I only want your blood—all of it." Cynthia's fleshy stinger glistened in the morning light.

Oh, shit.

"No." Jenkins wrapped a strong hand around her neck and pulled the pulsing jaws back. "This is not the Viburna. I will show you its true power."

Cynthia's insect arms ripped into the old man, but he ignored them. Magick swelled behind those tinted glasses, the same rising tide of power I'd felt before, except this time I was close enough to get the full effect of his crushing wave. The Skeeter's Magick paled in contrast and she knew it. Her jaws flapped recklessly in an attempt to reach the old man. Mr. Jenkins' fangs returned, this time bringing with them sharp and ancient claws. He tore through the leathers covering her chest and neck to reveal the melted outline of the twisted sigil.

"Nihil."

His Magick surged and Cynthia screamed. Her jaws and arms tried desperately to dislodge the old man.

An unmaking!

Mr. Jenkins' claw pressed against her scar, cutting and peeling at the distorted sigil, while around them his Magick pulled her apart. Arms broke and skin split, the many insect claws fell silent as what had been Cynthia collapsed in a bloody lump on my previously pristine carpet. The old Magician kicked her aside and turned his attention to the feeding Sofia.

"No, that's his daughter." I tried to get between Jenkins and the confused Skeeter.

The old man pushed past me, grabbing Sofia's neck and peeling her off like a hungry leech. "It has to end, Gene."

Blood and gore dripped from the Skeeter's quivering jaws with each hungry lunge of her stinger, while her insect arms exploded out of the sides of her tank top, keen to tear into Jenkins' flesh.

The old man and his Magick didn't care. "Nih—" Jenkins' words died on his bloody lips. The tip of a sharp blade appearing in his chest.

Deacon!

The man-in-black's long and powerful insect claws pulled Jenkins against the sharp edge and sent dark blood streaming down the old man's chest. The old Magician's Magick exploded in a burst of uncontrolled fury and knocked Sofia's head into my wall mirror.

Boom!

Jenkins and Miguel's daughter slumped to the ground.

Growl.

Marco had recovered and was on his feet, his deep-throated growl a small comfort. He put himself between me and the hairless Deacon.

I reached for my Magick and pushed past the burning pain between my eyes. "Ledo!"

A shock wave of force ripped across the room, but Deacon was faster, side-stepping the attack as his broken face continued to reassemble.

I had more in mind, but the Burning Seal lived up to its name. The twisted stamp's power cut through me like a buzz saw, piercing my body with the pain of a thousand tiny daggers. Digging and twisting beneath my flesh, they lit up every nerve, and set it screaming. I collapsed on the carpet in a twitching mass of muscle.

Marco pressed his nose against my side.

Deacon closed the gap between us, then stopped to direct his attention to Miguel's bloody remains. "Donom Viburna..." The man-in-black's insect arms carved the twisted mosquito-like Viburna into Miguel's chest.

No!

Satisfied with his work, Deacon called out for the bird. "He is in pain. Where are you, Duplickity? You are Flock."

Marco growled and pressed his body close to mine, but I was helpless, the pain had numbed my senses. Waves of heat rolled out from under the door seam behind me, burning my already overworked nerves. It was a supernatural heat that by now I knew all too well.

The Toaster.

The Burning Bind's Magick pulsed, pushing more pain into my already overloaded synapsis, and if that wasn't bad enough, flames appeared along the wall, racing up paint and licking at the ceiling.

"It's coming!"

Deacon was right, something was coming, but it wasn't the fire threatening to engulf the entire apartment building. This was something far more subtle. It moved beneath the darkness of my bed, bobbing along on narrow metal legs.

The bird... my Duplickity.

The tiny flamingo's coal-black eyes stared up at me from the shadows, her voice barely a whisper in my mind.

We are Flock.

I wanted to cry out. I wanted to call to that little bird and get whisked away on the unseen wings of invisibility, but my lips, along with the rest of my face refused to break free of The Burning Bind.

"I smell it," Deacon said, his head up and sniffing the air like an apex predator. "The Duplickity is here."

A fresh wave of pain sent me spinning, but the bird's gaze never wavered.

Flock?

No! He'll see you!

The tiny bird faded away before my eyes.

Deacon's insect-like claws spread wide, pouring more Magick into the room and pushing my already frayed nerves to their breaking point. "Come, little bird. Come out, come out, wherever you are!"

No. Stay hidden. Don't listen to him.

Like every other women in my life, the tiny bird ignored me. She exploded across the carpet like she'd been fired out of a cannon, and launched herself in the air. She twisted and turned those little metal legs to adjust her trajectory for my chest. I reached out with numb hands, grasping for my Duplickity.

Come on!

My fingers grazed her plastic feathers, but only just barely—Deacon was too fast. The Skeeter's spider-like arms stabbed the tiny bird out of the air, yanking her away from my clawing hands.

He pressed the Duplickity to his nose, taking a deep breath and reveling in his victory. "An egg is coming. Delia will be pleased."

Tips of flame slipped under the door, licking against my bare back and sending fresh flashes of torturous Magick across my body. I tried to grasp at the cosmic power but Kilpsee's Bind was too strong.

"I will come back for the toaster in a day or so. In the meantime, I will enjoy watching your life burn on the evening news," the monochromatic Deacon said, clutching the bird under his arm and stepping out my broken window.

Porter!

Flames roared and smoke raged across the ceiling. Ash and soot rained down on the mountain dog and I. Fire alarms kicked on in other units, their piercing wails making it impossible to think, while in the distance a siren rattled what remained of my broken window. I'd seen the Five Star Toaster in action before, and that had only been a taste, but all of that was background noise compared to the thought of my wife with William. If she'd done it right, the Magick I'd left her should have been enough. My mind played through a dozen scenarios where she hadn't been able to shatter the stone, but I couldn't dwell on those.

Miguel... Mr. Jenkins!

With Deacon's Magick gone, the pain began to subside, and I dragged my body toward the fallen mechanic. I ran an uncoordinated hand across his bloodied body.

There's no way he's alive.

It was faint, but it was there—Miguel the mechanic's heart still beat.

But for how long?

The whimpering of a crying dog broke above the wailing alarm and I scrambled to the old Magician.

"Jenkins?" I coughed into my arm at the rising smoke.

Dark and bloodied, the metal blade protruded from his chest as a painful reminder of Deacon's power.

Bark!

Marco pawed at the knife.

I pulled it out and tossed the wicked iron aside. "Mr. Jenkins, can you hear me?"

The old man didn't move.

Marco tugged on his robe.

"Get up!" I shouted, joining the mountain dog and yanking on the surprisingly cool threadbare fabric, but still he didn't budge.

The Toaster.

The Magick trapped in that infernal device wasn't going to stop. It would tear through my apartment, my friends, and everything that made its home in this building.

Your Magick is on lockdown.

I grabbed Marco's collar and pulled him back. "You've got to get out of here, boy. I'm going to stop the Toaster."

The mountain dog stared at me then tilted his head to one side.

"Don't give me that. I'll think of something." I grabbed the wadded up sheet to cover my bare body and trying to think of a way to do the unthinkable.

Marco snorted and bit down on the old Magician's robe, yanking it off his master's shoulders.

"We can't drag him out, there's not enough time!"

Bark!

I suddenly understood just how hard Timmy must have had it when everyone made him translate Lassie. "What?!"

Marco yanked the sleeve off Mr. Jenkins' shoulder and shoved it in my hand.

"You want me to wear the robe?"

Bark!

"Of course you do."

BLACKENED

I cinched the robe's worn belt around my waist. "Okay, better now?"

Bark!

"Right, I'm talking to a dog." I coughed through the dense smoke. Still, Marco did appear to have something going for him because the robe practically dripped with Magick. I tucked my hands into the sleeves and pressed my shoulder against the bedroom door. The smoldering wood felt oddly cool beneath my fingers. "Here goes nothing."

~

Now this is what Hell should look like.

The Five Star Toaster shined like a damned Christmas star on my kitchen counter. Its mirror-like finish provided a panoramic view of the burning carpet and ash-stained walls. Flames engulfed what had been a showroom-grade couch and reduced it to the devil's ashtray, while the nicest TV I'd never owned had long since cracked and spewed its electronic guts on the melted floor.

I shouldn't have been able to withstand the heat, but thanks to Mr. Jenkins' robe I felt fresh as a daisy.

"I've got just to get those handles up." I took a few steps around the tiny table we'd never used for dinner en route to the kitchen, but I didn't make it much more than a foot before the mountain dog yanked at the end of the robe and sent a wave of skin-searing heat up my nether regions. "What the—"

Marco pulled again and dragged me toward the underside of the table.

"I can do this," I said, yanking the robe back from the dog.

Crash!

Part of the ceiling gave way and shattered in front of me. It missed my head by mere inches and sent up a small could of choking ash and dust into the air in the process.

Perhaps he has a decent plan I haven't given adequate consideration...

Another large chunk of ceiling broke away and I scrambled under the table next to the dog. "Move over."

Snort.

Together we watched the world burn. The Toaster's fire melted my sink and curled the metal of an oven we'd never been allowed to use. Its flames spread further, licking at the hollow wood of the bedroom door.

They don't have much time.

A wave of heat across my chest caught me off guard. I glanced down to find stray threads curling in the Magickal fire.

I don't have much time.

It would appear even the robe's powers had its limits in the face of the Five Star Toaster.

Bark!

"I know." I pushed a scorched chair out of the way with my sleeve covered hands. "I've got to stop it."

Bark! Bark!

"Yes, that means now." I crawled out from under the table and picked my way through the bits of fallen ceiling.

The Toaster shined in the bright yellow and red fires of my collapsing apartment. I just had to reach it and pop those handles up, and the cosmic power creating the inferno would stop. Scorching hot tiles burned my feet, and even with the robe's Magick I had to dance from toe to toe to keep from losing skin. The devil's appliance was now only a few feet away, but its rolling heat rocked me back like a battering ram. It curled more loose threads and squeezed the air out of my chest. I coughed and pressed a sleeve to my mouth, then caught my reflection in the Toaster's mirror-like finish.

My eyes rimmed in ash and soot and the burning walls of our apartment sent me back to the Gloom. Mentally, I was there again, my hands clutching Ariadne's Thread.

"Don't let me go, Gene!" Morgan cried, tears streaming down her cheeks in that hellish place. "I always loved you!"

The blackened cord burned my fingers, while behind her all I could see were the massive doors of the library, flames licking at the seams and pulling the young Magician toward them.

The words I'd said then came back to my lips, the guilt lancing my heart all over again. "You don't know what love is."

Morgan's eyes caught mine, a haunting mixture of regret and fury. "Murderer!"

I snapped the Thread and sent her tumbling into the abyss.

What have I done?

Morgan screamed, her fingers on the edge of the door while what remained of her body burned away in the library's fire.

Crash!

I hit the tile hard, an oversized mountain dog knocking me from my memories. Marco licked my face, and I pushed him back. My lungs burned with the acrid smoke. I pulled on the robe's lapels, but yanked my fingers away the instant they touched the worn fabric.

The robe was burning.

Bark!

The Toaster loomed directly above us on what remained of the crumbling counter. Smoke billowed from its twin slots and filled my vision.

Bark!

Somewhere Marco barked, but I'd lost him in the soot and ash.

My reflection appeared again, the Toaster taunting me with it.

The handles...

Matte-black and almost lost in the smoke, the twin handles lay tantalizingly beyond my grasp.

Pull up the handles.

The edges of the robe's sleeves curled, no longer able to withstand the unholy fire, and forced me to pull my hands in as far as they could go.

You can't do it.

Five Star Toaster sucked the air out of the room and the wind from my sails. With my hands tucked deep in the sleeves I couldn't grab the handles. I couldn't stop it.

Bark!

There was only one choice.

Don't be a hero, kid. The Five Star Toaster won't stop until it's all ash.

How many people would have to die? How many would Magick take from me before I remembered who I was?

The evil appliance sucked the air out of the room, its Deep Magick throbbing.

I'm sorry, Ed. I made a terrible mistake.

I pushed my hands out of the protective sleeves. Fire raced out to consume my skin. Blisters formed then popped under the strain, but still I reached for the handles. A scream escaped my lips, but I didn't remember making it. It was only me and the infernal appliance. My reflection danced in the waves of heat.

Almost there...

Red and angry skin blackened, but still I reached for the Toaster. Porter's face appeared in the shimmering waves of reflection.

You can do it, Gene.

Flesh flaked away like spent ash, but I couldn't stop. My wife's face vanished, leaving me alone in front of the Toaster.

The blackened stubs of my fingers caught the handles.

Be the hero.

I pushed them up. The Magickal plastic slid along the grooves and clanged against the top of that malevolent appliance.

The heat vanished, but all around me the fire remained. The starter might be out, but it had done its job and the apartment blazed. I yanked at my melted fingers, but what flesh remained refused to release the malignant plastic.

Crack!

The cabinets above me gave way, tearing off the wall and crashing down like a comet. It was all too fast. I held the Toaster up in a futile attempt to block the coming destruction.

I'm sorry, Porter.

I closed my eyes and waited for death, but instead, a gut ramming of epic proportions sent me sprawling across the hot tiles and knocked the Toaster free. The mountain dog's warm fur pressed against my body, while his tongue licked at my forehead.

Marco, did we do it?

I strained to make out the shouts and sirens outside my window when the first drops of water stung my hands.

My hands...

Blackened and destroyed, those useless digits were the last thing I saw before my world faded to gray and ash.

NERVES DAMAGED

"Gene?"

A gentle hand traced my cheek.

"You okay, big guy?"

A soft beep pecked at the foggy edges of sleep.

"You had us scared." My wife's quiet voice echoed in the room's muffled silence.

"Porter?" I said, my throat raw. "Is that you?"

"Who else would it be, sweetheart?"

I opened my eyes, letting them gradually adjust to the harsh fluorescents. "Where?"

The hospital?

Surrounded by long curtains and tied up in plastic tubes sending God knows what into my veins, a hospital seemed like the safest bet. The sound of hard soles on a squeaky clean floor drew my attention.

"Mr. Law, is it?" A tall and lanky man said, his grey green scrubs covering a fit frame. "You are very lucky to be alive."

"I am?"

"Yes, your are. Your hands are going to be another story, but the fact your wife is visiting you in the hospital and not at the morgue is altogether miraculous."

"What happened?"

"I was hoping you'd be able to tell us that. The burns on your hands are extensive, if I didn't know better I would say you were exposed to nuclear fire, but you came in without a hint of radiation."

"Fire..."

My mind rolled backward and skipped like a bad record over gaps in my memory.

The doctor didn't bother to wait for me before continuing. "Yes, like I was saying, you've been exposed to considerable heat, enough that I'm contemplating bringing in a specialist. For now we've got your hands wrapped, but we really don't know the extent of the nerve damage."

I held up my mummified hands.

Nerve damage?

Flashes of memory popped in my mind like scenes from a movie I only vaguely remembered: a mountain of fur, tinted-glasses, and the unfolding face of a monster.

Deacon!

With that sudden thought out of the way, the first of many visuals pulled into the station. Deacon had taken my wife while the old Magician lay in a pool of his own blood along with Sofia, her face still red with the drying bits of her dying father.

"Jenkins, Miguel, Sofia? There was a dog, did the—"

My wife grabbed my shoulder. "Gene, it's okay. You're okay. I'm here. Don't panic. You're safe now. Take a deep breath."

I struggled against the frantic beating of my heart. "Did they get out okay? Did everyone get out okay?"

"Honey—"

"I'm sorry, Mr. Law," the doctor said in a perfectly perfunctory tone.

My stomach sunk into my toes. "Ugh."

"But, I have no idea. You're my patient. Do you have a dog?"

"No, but—"

"Good," he flipped a page on his clipboard. "I would hate to tell you that your hands may never work again *and* that you may have lost your dog."

"My hands…"

"Yes. We did all we could, but the damage was extensive. Now all we can do is wait and see."

"The robe!"

"What's that?"

"I was wearing a robe. It was a very important robe. Do you—"

"Your clothing had to be cut off, Mr. Law. I trust you will be able to find a new robe. Now, if you'll excuse me I've got more patients to attend to. Mrs. Law, I'd like you to wrap this up so your husband can sleep."

"From the fire?" I asked, my mouth tasting of cotton. "You have more patients from the fire?"

"Surprisingly, no. It could have been a lot worse than it was."

Porter thanked the doctor and guided him out the side of my curtained off room. They stopped to have a short conversation somewhere beyond the confines of my bed, their voices just low enough to make it impossible to hear them.

My hands…

Thick white gauze wrapped my fingers like macabre mittens.

Memories of reflected steel rolled through my mind in excruciating detail and painted a picture of hands blackened and flaking away like ash.

The Toaster!

The Five Star Toaster appeared in my head, its imaginary heat too great, but I couldn't look away.

"Stop!" I shouted, closing my eyes against the painful visions.

"Gene, are you okay?" My wife's lovely head peeked around the edge of the curtain.

"Porter?"

"I'm right here, honey," she said, letting the thin fabric swish behind her.

"I'm confused."

"I know—it's the painkillers. The doctor said you need rest."

I shook my head, each image coming back more painful than the one before it: a cellphone, Porter's voice, the noseless whistling of William.

Deacon's words rattled between my ears.

Tell me, or I'll let William consume your wife one finger at a time.

But she was here... How?

Porter, do it now!

The stone—it had to have worked—the human Phase Knot Magick I'd wrapped inside it must have worked. She'd had only one shot, pull the stone from its setting in her ring and smash it against the ground. Provided everything worked, she'd be safe in the Phase Knot—unable to leave—but safe. "Did the stone work? How did you get away from William?"

My wife tilted her head to one side then placed her hands on jean-covered hips. "Certainly, why wouldn't it have? You did an amazing thing today. You saved all those people. I couldn't be more proud of you."

I exhaled and let go of the worry that had wrapped itself like a snake around my heart. "I wasn't sure you'd be able to get the stone out of its setting, and then there was the Phase Knot itself. It'd been so long since I inscribed the stone, I wasn't certain it would work. Then, on top of all of that, I had no idea how you'd get out of the bind. How did you do that?"

Porter smiled and placed a warm hand on my cheek. "Ssh, you need to rest. It all worked exactly as you'd planned. You're a master Magician if ever there was one."

"But..."

"I'm here aren't I?"

You are.

I reached out with a gauze covered hand and took my wife's fingers into my own. "You are. We've got to find out what happened to Mr. Jenkins, Miguel, and his daughter Sofia. Oh, and the dog, what about the dog?"

"Dog?"

It was coming back to me now in great bursts of sound and fury.

"Marco. He's a mountain dog, Mr. Jenkins' mountain dog. You know, big, slobbery, brown and black."

My wife shook her head. "Honey, I don't know what you're talking about."

Porter words triggered more images: Miguel's wide eyes the moment before his daughter pounced, and blood running down Sofia's inhuman jaws.

"Miguel! Oh my God, Miguel. He had a pulse—I checked. I know he did, but there's no way he would have been able to walk out. She tore apart his neck, Porter."

"Who, Gene?"

"Sofia," I cried, each painful memory crashing into the next. "I couldn't stop him, and she couldn't stop herself. Mr. Jenkins, he tried to stop her... Porter, they were both unconscious in the bedroom."

"My bedroom? Gene, that room was barely big enough for two people, let alone more."

"I'm telling you, he was there. They were all there in the apartment after you were taken by Deacon. Where did they take you?"

Porter lay my hand back down on my chest and gently pressed me back against the pillows. "Sweetheart, you need to get some rest. The doctor said there was a chance you'd have a hard time putting together what happened. You inhaled a lot of smoke, and the nerve damage to your hands is unimaginable.

They've got you on some serious painkillers so I think it's best you stop fighting them and just get some sleep."

I am tired.

"Just tell me. Just tell me how you got away?"

"Honey, I will. I promise, but first you need to get some rest."

"Okay, you promise?"

"Of course."

I sighed and let my hands settle in my lap. "Could you at least check and see if any of them ended up here?"

"Any of who, honey?"

"Mr. Jenkins, Miguel, or Sofia," I said, my eyes drifting closed.

"Sure. I'd be happy to, but only if you promise to get some sleep. You've got a long road ahead of you, and I need you in one piece. I can't have my best man out there burning himself to a crisp."

"Thanks, honey." I nestled into the pillow and let my eyes close. "It's not a bad hospital."

"Rest, Gene."

"Right, right. I will." I let the stress fall away from my shoulders and stopped fighting the slow drip of the painkillers. "I wonder if this is the same place they brought Alonzo to?"

"Who's that, honey? Another one of your friends?"

WHEELING AND DEALING

My tired eyes shot open.

"Oh, damn." Porter took a step back and crossed her arms. "There are so many of you monkeys to keep straight. Honestly, it's like naming ants. There goes Hermonculus, and look, it's little Amberdesius. I'm thinking based on the way you are looking at me you've moved on from those names to something else? Genghis? Wilbur? Whatever, that's not important. What is important is that you survived—there are limits, Gene."

"Where is my wife?" I said, the painkillers overridden by my pounding heart.

The Not-Porter thing sighed. "Again, do I look like a monkey tracker? I don't know where your wife is. Well, technically, that's not true, but it doesn't matter."

I propped myself up in bed and swung my club-like hands at the plastic tubes in my arms. "Get me out of here. I've got to find her."

"Gene, she'll be dead before you get halfway to Miami."

"Miami?"

Not-Porter shook her head. "Ugh, there I go doing it again.

I've said too much already. Bloodsuckers being what they are, I expect she'll be consumed before dinner time. Your wife is a tasty treat, remember?"

"Shit. I've got to stop them."

"Oh yeah? How are you going to do anything with those hands?"

"What about my hands?"

Not-Porter gently pulled the edge of the curtain back to show me the rest of my tiny hospital room. "Go ahead, dip into that Magick of yours. Tell me, how's it working out for you?"

"It's fine." I reached for Magick, but found it gossamer and thin. It was like a spider's web stretched taut between the trees, and each time I tugged at it, the power vanished into the ether.

"Not quite doing what you want, eh?"

"Half a minute."

Not-Porter scooped up a wrinkled magazine from one of the chairs on the edge of the room and dropped herself into a smooth vinyl chair. "Take all the time you need. I'm going to learn about… 'The G-Spot and why you need it.' This is going to be enlightening."

I wrestled with my furtive Magick, but each tug at the pernicious energy only seemed to exacerbate the problem further.

Come on!

"Ah, so that's where it is." Not-Porter turned a page in the worn magazine. "So odd. It's like there are these little on and off buttons tucked away in the strangest of places. Speaking of 'off,' how's it going over there little camper? You got your Magick back yet?"

"I'm working on it," I said, suddenly discovering I'd been holding my breath.

"Great, you keep that up. There's a whole piece here on lipstick and push-up bras I'm going to dig into. Did you know they have wires? I've been doing this all wrong, Gene."

The tired muscles in my shoulders slumped, either my Magick wasn't there, or it wasn't listening, or both.

"Give up?"

"No," I said through clenched jaws.

"Spectacular! After I cover bras, I'm going into this section on 'players' and their 'games.' I'm expecting enlightenment, Gene. I've been among monkeys so long that I thought I knew everything, but according to this…"

"Magazine."

"Yes, this magazine, it would appear I was missing out on a considerable amount of critical information."

I let my breathing soften and concentrated on the Magick. It was still there, deep in my body, but it wasn't listening. It was like a whipped dog, hiding under the table, and unwilling to come out.

Come on. Porter needs you.

My Magick sniffed the air, then scurried back into the dark hole inside me.

"Damn it."

The thing laid the magazine flat on her crossed legs. "Now, are you ready to give up?"

"I… Yes," I said, my voice low and defeated.

"That's the ticket." Not-Porter folded up the magazine and tossed it in the chair. "Now, let's get you what you need to save that wife of yours."

"Great, get me out of here and give me back my Magick."

"Your Magick?" Not-Porter turned up her nose. "I don't need your Magick." She placed a warm hand on my face and the whip crack of cosmic power was electric. "I've got power to spare."

"Give it to me!"

"I could, but what's in it for me?"

I placed a mummified hand on hers. "What do you want?"

Not-Porter smiled and leaned over the railing, her hair brushing my arm. "Now you're finally speaking my language.

You monkeys might be on to something with this push-up bra thing." Not-Porter ran her fingers along the wraps of my hands. "Serve me."

"What?"

"How long do monkeys live again?"

"I don't understand."

Not-Porter stepped away from the bed. "Let's go with a hundred years. So, just to be on the safe side, I'm going to need you to serve me for ten of those lifetimes."

"A thousand years?"

The thing that looked like my wife smiled. "Look at you. I didn't even give you a banana."

"You want me to serve you for a thousand years?"

Not-Porter nodded. "Yes, we should get everything done by then. I never know exactly when its going to happen. Sort of the breaks of the game. Still, with you on the team we'll be in good shape for what's next. You've got a little something special, Eugene Law, and I like special."

"And if I agree?"

Not-Porter's eyes sparkled. "You would have power beyond your wildest dreams."

"I don't believe you."

"You want to feel infinity?" She slammed her palm against my forehead. "Take a deep breath."

Cosmic forces beyond all reasoning roared through my body. In my mind's eye, the infinite cosmos stretched out to eternity. Worlds turned within worlds. It was complexity rendered in exquisite detail. It was everything and nothing, and it was all of that at once.

"Whoops! I always forget just how much a human can take. Scorched poor Jerry's noodle in the sixties with that one—don't think those glasses will ever be the same again—but, everyone was on LSD then, anyway." She pulled her hand away, and yanked the bottom out of my scrambled head.

"I…"

Not-Porter slapped my face a few times. "Come on, snap out of it. That was just a taste, wait till you're dining at the big kid's table with me."

I fought to get air back in my lungs. "That's…"

"Yes, yes. It's amazing and awesome. True power of the universe. I get it. I'll wait a minute for your heart rate to slow down. Can't have it bursting out of your chest before I get your mark on the contract."

"Contract?"

Not-Porter brushed a loose hair out of her face and reached into the back pocket of those skin-tight jeans. "Yes, I used to just do these things in blood, but times change, and your people have become decidedly legal."

The thing unfolded a sheet of paper and placed it in my lap along with a cheap pen. "Now, don't worry about reading it all. I assure you it's very much above board."

I picked up the paper and squinted at the tiny writing.

"Or read it, whatever." Not-Porter pat me on the head then wandered back to her magazine. "I didn't read the section on selecting the right handbag based on my eyeliner, but don't take too long, Porter's life hangs in the balance."

I held up the paper waiting for my eyes to refocus, but didn't get much past the first words before the door to my tiny hospital room burst open. Mr. Jenkins and a somewhat crispy Marco rushed in and slammed the door behind them.

"Gene, you're alive!"

"Yeah, I—"

Growl…

Marco's tail went down and his teeth came out.

"Now, stop it, you silly dog. Gene's…" Mr. Jenkins words fell away the moment his eyes fell upon Not-Porter.

"Hello, Viktor," she said, folding the magazine in her lap. "It's been a long time."

RESET BUTTON

The color drained out of Mr. Jenkins already pale face.

"Viktor." Not-Porter tossed her magazine and practically sprung to her feet. "You've gotten old."

"That's what time does."

The thing that wasn't my wife shook her head and her hair twisted into dense curls. Her silky top and tight jeans vanished, and in their place was an elaborate gown. "Is this better?"

Whatever it was, it no longer resembled my wife. This new woman struck a chord with the old Magician. Mr. Jenkins looked like he'd taken a solid punch to the gut. He stopped to lean against the cold steel railing of my bed. "Beatrice…"

"You remembered! I wasn't sure you would. We had such fun you and I. You do remember fun, right, Viktor?" The buxom redhead batted her eyelashes like a mascara model.

"Gene, we need to get out of here, now."

Beatrice swept up her long dress and crossed the tiny hospital room in a flurry I didn't believe was possible. "Gene is not going anywhere until he gets what he needs to save his wife Portly."

"Porter."

"Right, what he said."

"You took his wife." Mr. Jenkins' knuckles turned white against the thin railing.

"I did no such thing. Those Skeeters did. Oddly like Leeches aren't they? And you do know how Leeches can be, don't you, Victor?"

"The kid already knows."

Beatrice removed a small fan from the folds of her dress, snapping it out with a flick of her wrist. "Does he? Does he know everything?"

"He knows enough."

"Oh." Beatrice leaned against the opposite railing and let her ample chest press against the lacy edges of that ornate dress. "You've told him everything have you? Does he know what you are? What you did?"

"I'm right here," I said, interrupting the two of them. "He told me about the Viburna."

"Kid, stop talking."

Beatrice smiled and fanned herself with the multicolored paper. "He left out a really important part."

The old Magician grabbed my arm and with it my attention. "Don't listen to it, kid. You can't listen to it. You can't reason with it, and whatever you do, you can't make deals with it."

"Now, Victor, just because you found a way out of our arrangement doesn't give you the right to interfere with my deal with Mr. Law."

A way out?

Marco leaned against the old man's leg, never once taking his eyes off the oddly dressed Beatrice.

"Oh, you poor dog. He's kept you around for too many years hasn't he? Viktor doesn't know when to stop, does he?"

The mountain dog held his ground, his sharp teeth shining in the harsh light.

"I know. You preferred someone else, didn't you?"

"Not her," the old Magician said in protest.

Beatrice twisted like taffy. Her skin darkened, and her nails turned pastel and sharp, while long and thick dark hair replaced those elaborate curls—gone was the gown, and in its place a sparkling black dress that left almost nothing to imagination.

"Delia..." The old man sighed.

The exotic goddess shook out her nubile shoulders. "It's really a pattern with both of you, isn't it? I wonder if that's part of the grand plan? Odd. You two and your femme fatales."

Marco's head tilted to one side, clearly confused by the changed appearance.

"There's a good boy. I know you liked this one, Delia kept you fat and happy didn't she?"

Mr. Jenkins took a few steps back, his mouth falling open like a cod fish.

"Those were the days, weren't they? We had so much fun, and through it all no one was supposed to know, were they? It was all a secret. You murdered all of them, but not Delia, never Delia."

"You... She didn't..."

The woman's stiletto heels snapped against the hard floor. "She didn't what? She didn't birth your children? No, she didn't, did she? You saw to that, didn't you?"

"No, it wasn't like that."

"It wasn't? Please, enlighten Eugene and I. Explain to us why you did it?"

The old Magician stumbled a few steps before grabbing on to the wall like a drunken sailor. "I don't owe you an explanation. You aren't Delia."

The young woman admired her nails. "Gene, don't end up like Viktor. Take the deal. It's a good one. You'll get your wife back, and together you and I will do amazing things."

"I..."

Delia smiled and gave me a wink. "Right, you need to review

the terms of our arrangement. Take your time." She spun on her heels, then adjusted her dress in the mirror.

Something glinted up at me from the edge of my bed. The same color as the beige sheets, it would have been easy to miss, if it hadn't been for the way it glittered in the fluorescent light.

A button.

Mr. Jenkins pushed himself up against the wall, continuing to play the stunned old man, but in the process he let his tinted glasses dip down just enough for me to see his eyes.

He winked.

A Lost Button!

I held up my wrapped hands.

But how do I put it in my palm?

The old man slapped a hand on his forehead in the universal motion for 'crap.'

Marco padded over to the side of my bed and placed his wide snout beneath the railing.

That's it.

I scooted the button under the sheet, then presented a hand for Marco.

"It's really a simple quid pro quo, Gene." Delia adjusted her dress in the mirror. "I will give you the power to get your wife back from those Skeeters and in exchange you will help me take care of something."

The large dog bit his teeth into the gauze and gave it a tug.

Rip.

I let Marco pull my burned hand below the edge of the bed while I bought him some time. "Right, I think I understand that, but what I want to know is exactly what sort of power we are talking about? I mean, are there limits?"

Mr. Jenkins poked his head up. "Don't do it, Gene. The power it gives is a curse."

Delia sighed and turned her attention to the old Magician. "The power is real and nigh limitless. There's no curse. What do you think I am, some sort of Demon? Really, Gene? A Demon?"

"Well, I don't—"

My hand stung, but Marco had gotten through the outer layer of gauze.

"Right, you don't know. Listen, I share too much with you too quickly and 'poof,' " Delia made a little exploding gesture with her fingers, "your brain is toast. You don't need that, *I* don't need that. None of us needs that."

"But if you were a Demon, then I'd need—"

"You need to get your head examined if you are thinking about signing a contract with that thing." Mr. Jenkins pushed himself away from the wall and took a few cautious steps across the tiny room.

"Gene. You know I'm not a Demon—brainless things."

Marco had the first layer of gauze off and pooling nicely on the far side of the bed.

"Right, okay, so not a Demon... most likely." I held the paper up to inspect it more closely.

"Most likely?" Delia cried, her voice rising a few octaves. "Do you smell sulfur on that contract?"

I brought the paper to my nose and used it to cover my face while I checked on Marco's progress. The mountain dog had most of the second layer of gauze off my hand, but the pain was ramping up with each tug—it was all I could do to not tear up.

"Well?" Delia asked.

"No, not particularly, but you have to remember I've been in a hospital for I don't know how long. My nose might not be working up to snuff. Mr. Jenkins, would you?" I held out the paper for the old Magician.

"Kid, I told you, you can't sign a deal with that thing," Mr. Jenkins said, closing the gap between us to stand next to his dog.

"Don't listen to him, Gene. He's trying to keep you from

saving your wife. What about Porter, Gene? What about the Skeeters? Would you trust a Leach to be honest with you?"

I leaned my head back and set the paper against my lap. "I need a pen."

"Gene, no." Mr. Jenkins grabbed my shoulder. "Don't do it."

Delia retrieved one from the clipboard at the foot of my bed. "Excellent choice, Gene. I get the sense that this is the start of a beautiful relationship."

Marco removed the last of my bandage and let the cool hospital air send a fresh wave of pain up what remained of nerves in my hand.

"Gene." A deflated Mr. Jenkins reached down to pet Marco. "You do what you have to do, just promise me one thing?"

I slid my hand along the bed sheet, each inch agonizing. "What's that?"

"Take a deep breath. The air's thin on the other side."

Delia's eyes flashed. She noticed my unwrapped hand, but the monster couldn't move fast enough. My palm pressed against the tiny button. Its Magick erupted like a shotgun blast and flooded the tiny room. I screamed, or at least it sounded like I did, it was hard to tell.

Porter!

The hospital melted away, along with my guests, and the rest of the world, until nothing remained but static and white.

30

GOD'S TEARS

A harsh wind blew across my face and sent the hospital gown whipping like a signal flag.

I opened my eyes to blue.

It wasn't the aquamarine of the ocean. It was a hazy indigo, the color of that pregnant pause before the sun rises on a new day. Soft sand crunched under my bare feet. I took a hesitant breath and was pleasantly surprised to find there was something to breathe, even if it did taste like salt.

Where am I?

The wind snaked across powdery dunes. The undulating mass of unbroken waves of sand seemed to stretch to the infinite in all directions. Thick clouds hung low in the sky. Dark and angry, they bunched at the edges of that lifeless ocean like a poorly draped bedsheet. Far beyond the desert, distant mountains offered the lone variation in that quietly shifting sea of blue.

"Hey, you made it." Mr. Jenkins waved from a nearby dune, his collar covering his mouth. "I was beginning to wonder if something had happened."

"Where are we?"

"God's Tears." The old man scooped up a handful of the sandy salt and let it go in the wind.

"Excuse me?"

"I know. It's a little melodramatic." He shrugged his shoulders. "A world so beautiful its creator wept at its destruction. The salt of those tears is all that remains of this forgotten place."

"I don't understand."

"The Lost Button, kid. This is where it took us."

"But where is this?"

Mr. Jenkins shook his head. "I don't think anyone really knows. Whoever wept for this world is long gone."

"We have to get out of here. The Skeeters took Porter. She's trapped in a Phase Knot, but I don't know how long it will hold. You've got to take me home." The wind stung my eyes with blast of rock salt.

"I can't do that."

"What do you mean you can't do that? That was your damn button. It was your idea to send us here in the first place, like hell you can't take us back."

Mr. Jenkins shook his head. "Can't use the button, kid. They're a one-way trip."

"What the hell kind of bullshit is that? Porter is in danger. Have you not been listening to what I'm saying?"

Mr. Jenkins whistled and a salt-crusted Marco jogged into view. "I know, Gene. I know *exactly* how much danger she's in, but it's not the Skeeters I worry about." The old man paused, then turned to the distant horizon. "It's you…"

I closed the gap between myself and the Magician in an instant, my bare feet leaving deep grooves in the thick salt. "What the hell is that supposed to mean?"

"You don't even know what that was back there, do you?"

"No, but I've got it under control. It comes and goes. I can handle it."

"It's stepping up the pressure, isn't it? The visits are more frequent, aren't they?"

"Whatever, I said I can handle it. It's Porter I'm worried about. My wife is in danger."

The old Magician turned his attention back to me. "I've been hiding from it for a long time—years… I walk into your hospital room, and boom, I'm right back on the menu."

I reached for my Magick, but the throbbing in my hands made it impossible. "Damn it!"

"The Five Star Toaster burns more than flesh, Gene." Mr. Jenkins reached for me but I pushed him away.

"I'll heal—I always do."

"Not this time."

The old man examined my melted fingers in the stinging salt, then let out a low whistle as he brought them up to his face. "Not good."

I pulled my hand back, grimacing at the sharp stab of pain. "Can you heal them?"

"Yes."

"Then do it." I held up my ruined fingers. "Do it so I can save my wife."

"You don't know what you are asking." Sadness ringed the edges of Mr. Jenkins tired eyes.

"I would become like you wouldn't I?"

"Eat my flesh and drink my blood and you shall have life within you. Yes, you would become like me."

It was like I'd taken yet another punch to the gut, but this time my hands dropped along with my heart. "I…"

"I'm not going to do that, kid."

I collapsed against the salt dune. My useless hand stinging in the salt spray, while the one that was still covered lay in my lap. "I have to take that thing's deal."

Mr. Jenkins dropped down beside me, stretching out his old

knees and letting his own shoulders droop. "You don't know what you're saying, kid."

"The Phase Knot isn't going to last forever. Deacon's too strong, and if it's not him, it'll be someone else. One of them will dismantle those protections and devour my wife."

The old man nodded. "Or they'll make her a feeder. She's strong enough to withstand the change."

My stomach churned. "A feeder?"

Mr. Jenkins shook his head. "Kid, you don't want to know."

"That's it." I tore at the wrap on my other hand, blinking back tears that came from more than the pain in my fingers. "I'm taking the deal."

"I can't let you do that." The old Magician's voice was firm but gentle. "I refuse to let our world end up like this one."

Wind swept the azure dunes of God's Tears.

"That thing back there did this?"

Mr. Jenkins nodded. "That's how the story goes, yes. You still don't know what it is, do you?"

"No."

Marco padded over to sit between us. "I don't even know its true name. I don't think anyone does, but I know what it is. I went toe-to-toe with it as a kid, and like you, got my ass handed to me."

"What is it?"

"I don't suppose you have any tequila?"

I frowned.

"I didn't think so." Mr. Jenkins ran a hand through the thick dog's fur. "You much for religion, Gene?"

"No."

"Me neither, but they get a few things right in those books. There are plenty of monsters out there and a lot more hells than they can cover in a library of religious texts."

"Is it the Devil?"

Mr. Jenkins shook his head. "Nah, nothing that pedestrian."

"Is it a Demon?"

The old Magician chuckled. "If it were, I wouldn't be hiding at the wrong end of a Lost Button."

"Just tell me what it is!"

Mr. Jenkins returned his attention to the horizon. "They all basically start the same way."

"What do?"

"The holy books: Bible, Koran, Torah. They all start with creation—the beginning of all things."

"And?"

Mr. Jenkins placed a hand on my shoulder. "In the beginning there was the formless void, the source of all chaos."

"Wait, are you telling me that is—"

"The Void, kid. It is the beginning of all things."

MAN'S BEST FRIEND

"What the hell does the Void want with me?"

"No idea." The old man pushed up from his seat and set off down the tall dune.

"Wait… What?"

"You heard me, I have no idea what the ultimate endgame is, but when an eternal force of chaotic Magick wants something from you, it's never good. Those are words to live by, Gene."

I scrambled to follow the wandering man, my hands throbbing in the salt spray. "Wait, you are running from something and you don't even know why?"

Mr. Jenkins squinted at the distant horizon. "I got a decent feeling it's something I don't want to be a part of, but no, I didn't stay around long enough for the grand reveal. I got out when the opportunity presented itself."

"Which was?"

"You don't want to know." The old man kicked at the salt.

"But—"

"Kid, Magick is all about sacrifices—haven't you figured that out yet?"

I stopped cold in the deep salt and sand. "No…"

Mr. Jenkins turned around and shielded his eyes from the stinging wind. "Well, it is. The whole stupid game is about sacrifice. It's about making you give up more and more of what makes you, you. It's a slippery slope of pain and regret."

"Magick's kept you alive though. The Viburna has—"

"Made damn sure I lost almost everyone I ever cared about."

"How do we stop the Void?"

"We don't." The old man dug his feet into the dune. "The best I could come up with was to trap it. Pin it down if you will."

"You can trap the eternal and formless void?"

"With the right piece of real estate, yeah."

"Wait," I said, scrambling to catch up with the older Magician. "Real estate? You mean like the house you showed me in your bathroom."

"Exactly, but we are here." Mr. Jenkins swung his hand wide at the stark majesty of God's Tears. "And not back there."

"But you could go back?"

"Yes, there's a way, but it's too dangerous."

"I don't get it, if it truly is the Void, an eternal force of the cosmos, doesn't that mean it's inevitable?"

"You feel that way about your wife too?"

The hairs on my arms stood at attention.

"I didn't think so. Just a few minutes ago you were willing to join team Sanguist if it meant saving your wife. So, where would that stop? What if to save the people you most cared about you had to be the lead off batter for the end times?"

"I wouldn't do it."

"Oh to be young. I hope you're right, kid, but for now we are safer here than back there. If that thing gets its hooks in you..." The old Magician shook his head.

"Stay here?"

"Not right here." The old man pointed to a distant, hazy gray blur. "There's a cave in those mountains, plenty of things you could call fish, and I can handle the blood cravings far better there. How do you think I survived so long?"

God's Tears stretched out in front of me like an endless sea of wind-swept blue. "You stayed here for years?"

"Oh, shit no, kid. This place doesn't run on the same clock we do. I'd say a month or so of roughing it in the old man cave and we can head home. By then the Void will have moved on to a new candidate."

I stopped, my feet refusing to take another step in the tinted salt. "My wife—"

"Will be dead by then." Mr. Jenkins paused his ascent up the dune. "But I cannot risk you making the wrong choice for the right reasons."

"I'm not leaving Porter to die at the hands of William," I said, my tone sharper than I expected it to be.

"And I'm afraid I can't let you leave. It's just too risky."

Marco padded up next to me, nuzzling his head against my hip.

"Not now." I ran the wrapped hand over Marco's fur before turning back to the old man. "This is bullshit. I'm not leaving her. I don't care if Hell itself is on the other side."

Marco coughed quietly, spitting something black and shiny on the salty earth.

A button?

Ahead of me the old Magician tilted his head at the sound. "Marco?"

The mountain dog didn't move.

"Marco, come, now!" Mr. Jenkins shouted, slapping a hand against his leg, but still the mountain dog remained steadfast beside me.

I scooped up the tiny black button in my gauze wrapped hand, its power immense even through the thick fabric. It was familiar, a power I'd felt before.

Was this somehow related to the button I'd given Bastet?

Mr. Jenkins turned around, the wind whipping at his pant legs like a clipper ship's sail. "Don't do it, Gene."

"Why not?"

"Bastet's going to be waiting for you on the other end of that button."

"What do you care? If she kills me that's one less person to take the deal with the Void."

Magick raced up the dune and dragged the salt around my ankles like the receding tide. Whatever it was Mr. Jenkins was preparing, he needed a lot of Magick to pull it off.

"I care about you, Gene. Don't make me do this."

Bark!

The old man pointed at his dog. "You're damn straight I care about staying alive too. We've been at this a long time, Marco. You think that happens by chance? Self-preservation has kept food on my plate and treats in your mouth. You weren't complaining when I brought you back from death's door at the hands of that cat, were you?"

The mountain dog growled and pressed his head tighter against my leg.

"I don't want to have to do this," Mr. Jenkins said, the power around him building to a fever pitch and pulling me like an undertow. "Drop the button."

I held my melted hand above the wrapped one, while all around me the sand and salt spun. "No."

The old Magician's power surged and sent the dune shifting under my feet. I lost my balance, tumbling into the sand, the button still caught in my gauze-covered mitt.

"Impetus Tempestatis!" the old man shouted, his words hard to make out in the swirling sand. Sharp gravel sliced at my skin and tore at my gown.

"Marco!" I swung my hands wildly, unable to see in the stifling spray.

The mountain dog rammed into my chest and knocked me

to the ground, then once again smothered me with this powerful body. That sandpaper tongue licked my face, and I knew what I had to do.

"You ready for this?" I said, pulling my shattered hands into my chest.

Bark!

"No, Gene!" the old Magician shouted, his words lost in the maelstrom.

I clasped my hands together and pressed the tiny plastic button into the melted palm.

The painful salt spray vanished, along with the rest of God's Tears, as once again my body tore itself apart atom by atom.

I'm coming, Porter!

3 2

TALL GRASS

"*H*ow am I supposed to know where we are?" I asked, pushing through a near infinite sea of waist height grass. "It was *your* button, remember?"

The mountain dog's head popped up from the yellow-green blades of grass ahead of me.

Snort.

"Oh, don't give me that. Yes, this place is better than God's Tears, but not much. This isn't home, and every second I waste in the middle of what looks like Kansas the worse off Porter has to be. She's bound up in a Phase Knot, but if Deacon has his way, I'm sure he'll figure out how to unravel it." I didn't like thinking about it, but the pain of my melted hands and the heat of a seemingly motionless sun were taking their toll on what little positive energy I had left.

Lost Buttons... nothing if not aptly named.

The Button had done its job. We were certainly lost, or at least I was. For his part, Marco appeared to be enjoying tracking something in the tall grass.

Bark!

"Yeah, yeah, I'm coming." I gently brushed aside the grass

that tickled at my man parts beneath a flimsy and now very dirty hospital gown.

Marco paused to sniff the air and then pushed off into the dense bush.

Grass... This world is in need of a decent mow.

I sighed and followed my four-legged navigator deeper into the sod sea.

We traveled for what felt like hours, the sun-bleached yellow and green stalks drifting back and forth around us in a never-ending breeze. Dark green clumps of trees huddled in the distance like small islands in the ocean of unceasing grain. Lazy iridescent bugs, like dragonflies with hooked tails skipped from blade to blade around us, their buzzing both annoying and better than the constant whistling breeze.

"Where are we going?" I asked for what had to be the fiftieth time, and once again the mountain dog simply snorted and continued to plow through the dense bush.

I did my best to ignore the throbbing pain in my hands, but the Five Star Toaster refused to be forgotten. I'd torn off the rest of the gauze a few miles back and now that I could see them both together clearly for the first time I was thinking that perhaps I was better off not knowing.

My hands were pink and blistered like melted crayons. The tender skin screamed out in pain with each caress from the soft breeze, and God forbid I let them touch the grass.

What am I going to do?

Every so many miles, I'd try again to reach my Magick, but every time I did I found it avoiding my grasp. The power was there, but like a scared animal it had burrowed deep in its hole and wasn't interested in being coaxed out.

Without your Magick how are you going to get out of here?

I'd asked myself that question often, and each time I did the panic set in just a little deeper.

It was so mired in one of these cycles of pain, worry, and

self-pity, that I practically rammed into the stopped dog's back-side. "Marco!"

The mountain dog panted softly, his nose pointing at something on the other side of some dark brown and black vegetation.

"What is it?" I leaned forward and used my elbows to push the tall blades aside. My own nose catching the faint scent of rot. "You find something?"

A Kitten!

My stomach churned, and I had to fight to keep whatever the hospital had given me from ending up on Marco. It wasn't a cat decaying in the tall grass in front of us, it was worse.

That's one of Bastet's girls.

The bloated and decomposing face took a few seconds to mentally reassemble, but when it did, I gasped.

Groomer...

When I'd arrived, they'd been brushing Marco's fur, but when commanded, they'd been more than happy to prep yours truly for an at-home testicle removal.

It was hard to tell exactly which of the groomers this was. The crooked dragonflies had long since begun to feast on what remained of her once smooth skin. Bright white bone and sharp canines reflected the hot sun, while cavernous sockets provided an unwanted view into the dark inside of a rotting skull.

"That's one of her girls," I said once I was sure I could speak without vomiting. "How?"

Marco padded up to the rotting corpse and sniffed at its distended gut.

I pulled up on my gown and pressed the thin fabric against my nose. "What is it?"

The mountain dog pawed at the gaping hole ripped out of the young cat woman's side.

"Did one of the other Kittens do that?" I asked, even though I knew the answer as soon as I'd said it. Bastet and her Kittens had dangerous claws and sharp canines, but that hole was too big, and far too vicious.

Something had taken a bite out of the cat woman.

The wind shifted and sent a fresh gust of decaying flesh over me. It was enough to force me to my knees. My stomach decided this was an opportune time to void its contents, but much to our mutual disappointment, there was nothing to vomit up. I ended up crouched in the grass fighting to get air back in my lungs for nothing. "We need to get out of here."

The mountain dog may have agreed with me, but his body language indicated there were bigger concerns. The shifting wind had brought with it a smell Marco didn't appear to approve of. He folded back his ears and bared his teeth, his thick legs pacing in front of me, and keeping that considerable bulk between me and whatever was coming.

Growl.

I reached again for my Magick. Mental fingers dug deep and demanded the cosmic power hiding in my body make its presence known—nothing happened.

Shit.

Marco scanned the dense grass, his eyes on alert and his fur at attention.

Snap! Snap! Snap!

The sound of breaking blades kicked my heart rate up a few notches and set my already frantic brain on fight-or-flight mode.

Where can I go?

I didn't have the dog's keen sense of smell, and my hands were all but useless. Would some future person find my decaying body in the tall grass, wearing nothing but the tattered remains of a dirty hospital gown?

Hiss.

Images flooded my mind, memories of snakes in the weeds from some of my earlier lawn mowing experiences. Most of the time they'd been harmless, but every so often they were worse: scaly, aggressive, and venomous.

Crack.

Marco's growl grew louder, as did the cracking and popping of crushed grass. Whatever was coming, it was big, and it didn't care how much noise it made.

"Come on," I said, tugging at the vigilant dog and directing him back the way we came, but Marco shook me off.

I turned back and discovered why, the sounds weren't just coming from in front of us—we were slowly being surrounded. Bright green and yellow scales like diamond-shaped manhole covers slid through the dense grass.

"We've got trouble."

Bark! Bark!

"Right, weapons..." I scanned the ground, but there was nothing. No sticks, and not even a rock to throw. Whatever those reptiles were, they might get scratched up by Marco, but they'd tear through me like the Kitten back there.

Think, Gene!

I dropped to my knees and yanked at a clump of grass at my feet. My hands throbbed and my fingers cried out, but still I pulled on the shallow roots.

Hiss.

More scales rolled past, this time closer than before. They were tightening the circle, and it didn't take much in the way of imagination to believe that once they were certain we couldn't escape, they'd strike.

My heart beat on overdrive as I tossed aside the clumps of vegetation to expose a rich and loamy ground beneath. I flattened out that jumbled earth with hands that screamed at me to stop.

Bark! Bark!

Marco's tail dropped down along with the rest of his

haunches. The mountain dog knew something was coming, and there was nothing he could do about it.

I dug my finger into the soft soil and traced a pattern I hadn't thought about in years—Eldero's Seventh Seal. I'd never been much more than pedestrian at the complex patterns of that Magician's designs, but the Seventh Seal should have been exactly what the situation called for, provided I could muster the Magick to power it.

Dirt parted beneath my melted fingers and sent waves of fresh pain up my hand and into my arms. The mountain dog growled and pressed his bulk against my exposed back.

Hiss.

The first set of viper-like golden eyes appeared in the dense grass and was quickly joined by another, and then another.

I didn't wait around for more.

I closed the seal and pounded both melted hands into the soft earth pleading with my Magick for our lives.

33

BALANCED SCALES

*M*agick danced just beyond the edges of my outstretched fingers. It was there, and then it wasn't. The sigil flickered like a broken bulb, Eldero's Seventh Seal dropping in and out like a cheap set of Christmas lights.

"Come on!" I squeezed my bleeding hands in the black dirt. Pain shook my fingers and wracked my arms, but still the Magick refused me. "Son of a bitch, do something,"

Growl.

Marco pressed against me, a comfort for sure, but he also kept placing his paws dangerously close to the sigil's lines.

"Hey, watch it!"

The mountain dog dug his claws into the dirt and broke three of my lines in the process.

"Crap!"

Eldero's Seventh Seal dropped, dead as the Kitten whose body slowly rotted in the tall grass behind us.

I pulled the growling canine toward me, then fixed the lines.

"Now don't break my—"

Hiss.

Thick blades cracked and splinted beneath the thick body of a monstrous serpent. Wide jaws opened to reveal an oddly alligator-like row of jagged teeth which sent what remained of my focus out the window.

Bark! Bark!

The mountain dog held position, his thick flank pressing against my side, and hopefully not breaking my all but useless sigil again. Marco wasn't going anywhere, and that would have been a comfort had I actually been able to erect some defensive Magick, but as it stood right now, it just meant we'd die together, our entrails left to rot in the unceasing sun.

My hands screamed at me, every cell in them crying out for mercy, but those jaws didn't care.

Do it for Porter.

The snake's head reared back and I closed my eyes. There was no running now, no escape. It was Magick or death, and I only had the strength for one. Visions of my wife came to me, her soft eyes and beautiful smile in the dark of our bedroom, but that image didn't last, as Porter was pulled away by William and his hungry jaws.

No!

The Magick drifted past my mental fingers and I clamped down on it like a vise, sending the power rocketing into the poorly inscribed sigil at my feet. "Argh!"

Boom!

The viper's jaws snapped out only to slam against an invisible dome. My Magick held, but the snake's head was like a solid punch to the gut.

Hold on, Gene. Just hold on.

More strikes hammered at my flickering dome. Eldero's Seventh Seal was strong, but only as much as the Magician wielding it, and my powers weren't what they used to be.

Bark! Bark!

Marco snarled and nipped but he knew enough to stay inside the makeshift Magick.

"Don't break the damn, sigil!"

My hands screamed and my arms shook with each blast against the wavering wall.

Don't let go.

Morgan's face appeared in my mind, her hair streaming out against the roaring fires of the library's doors. "Don't let me go, Gene!"

My hands no longer held the black earth, instead they held Morgan's Thread, its faint light pulsing against the darkness of the Gloom.

No!

I snapped that Thread between my hands, just like I'd done a hundred times before in every vision of that moment. The pulsing cord fell away and with it went my Magick.

"Shit," I cried, grabbing on to Marco's neck and diving into the dirt only to have the serpent's heavy body rake across my bare back.

The mountain dog and I scrambled to our feet while more oversized garden snakes closed in for the killing blow. I held on to the mountain dog's thick fur, my dirty hands red with blood. "I'm sorry, buddy."

Marco sniffed the air then licked at my knee.

"Thanks, at least that part of me will be clean while we rot in the sun."

The mountain dog sniffed the air again, and I'd swear he smiled before pawing at the ground.

"You do realize we're about to die a horrible death, right?"

Bark!

I squeezed his thick fur. "Whatever floats your boat, you crazy canine."

The snakes advanced, jaws open and golden eyes mesmerizing.

"If you've got any tricks up your puppy sleeves now would be the time to use them, got it?"

Bark!

"I thought so, well it was worth checking." I let go of the dog and held up my useless hands in a weak boxer's stance. "It's been nice knowing you, Marco."

Bark!

"Don't get sentimental on me."

"In the entirety of my existence, you are the single loudest Magician I have ever met," a woman's voice called out from beyond the mesmerizing serpents. "Kittens!"

Bastet and her pack of feral cat women tore through the tall grass like amazons. Claws slashed and fangs flashed as the feline woman and her soldiers engaged.

"Holy—"

"Save it, Magician," Bastet said, her claws tearing through scales.

The rest of the Kittens attacked like coordinated pack animals. They'd converge and score a few strikes, then vanish again in the dense vegetation.

Bark!

"Keep that dog safe." Bastet's claws hooked the jaws of a lunging viper before it could reach Marco. "He's our ticket out of here."

"What?"

Fangs flashed in Bastet's feline jaws. "You heard me."

I turned to the mountain dog. "Are you telling me you could have gotten us out of here at any time?"

The dog let his long tongue dangle in the air.

"Son of a b—" I didn't get to complete my sentence before a side swipe from one of the snakes sent me crashing into the tall grass.

Damn it.

I had barely made it to my knees before Marco knocked me back to the ground again. "I'm not talking to you right now."

Bark! Bark!

Red and green blood painted the grass in a splatter art pattern, while the sounds of slithering scales faded into the distance.

"Damn it, if there's a way we can get out of here then we need to do that now. That cat woman is going to cut my face off and eat it. Do I have to remind you of what she did to you?"

Marco licked my hand, sending a wave of pain rolling up my arm. "Argh! The hurts like hell."

Bark!

"I'm not Timmy and you aren't Lassie. I don't speak dog and you clearly don't understand what I'm saying." I tried to push the heavy mountain dog off me without using my hands. "Let's not get out of the frying pan by jumping into the fire. I happen to like my face and don't want it on the menu."

Snort!

"Not a fan of my face? Well, I don't like yours either. I promise you once we get home we can part ways and if we see each other again, it'll be too soon. Just get me home."

Marco's immense bulk pinned me against the bent grass.

"Off! Heel!"

The mountain dog placed his head on my chest.

"You're going to be the death of me."

"No, that would be me." Bastet crouched down next to my face, her feline whiskers streaked red, and her eyes shining in the bright sun.

"Bastet..."

The cat woman placed a finger on my lips. "I would choose your next words very carefully, little Magician." More feline heads appeared behind hers. What remained of the Kittens had us surrounded.

Stupid dog.

"So, how can I help you?" I asked, my words squeezed out beneath the monster dog laying on my chest.

"My Kittens are hungry."

"Food?"

"Blood."

Crap.

3 4

POKER FACE

*I*t took a bit of coaxing to convince Marco to climb off me, but the mountain dog eventually relented and found a soft spot in the otherwise dense grass to lie down in.

I tried to push myself up with my hands but the pain was too great. Blood and dirt rattled my nerves and set my hands shaking.

"You are injured," Bastet said, her tone flat and uncaring.

"I'm fine."

The cat woman found an open spot in the tall grass and sat next to me, while her Kittens kept a sharp eye on the drifting blades.

"It would serve you right for trapping us here," she said, licking at her blood-stained claws.

"That was totally the old man. I'm finding it's his thing, actually. He's got a soft spot for hiding people at the opposite end of Lost Buttons."

Bastet raised an eyebrow. "So, you are not here by choice? Odd that Viktor let you keep the Chinthe."

"Excuse me?"

Marco perked his head up.

"Chinthe. You do realize he's not just a dog, don't you?"

"Oh, that, well Mr. Jenkins didn't exactly approve of me taking Marco with me, but he was the one that put the Lost Button in my hand in the first place. It was his fault the three of us were on Salt World."

Bastet's face broke into a wide grin. "You took the old man's ticket home and left him stranded?"

"I did?"

Bastet nodded. "Oh, yes you did. The Chinthe is a compass."

Marco rolled over and scratched his back on the thick grass.

"A compass?"

"Dogs find their way home. It's one of their only endearing traits." The cat woman wrinkled her nose. "Chinthes are just that much better at it."

"Marco is my ticket h—"

Bastet's claws moved fast, too fast for me to see them coming, and certainly too fast to do anything about it. The cat woman had a razor sharp set of nails under my chin before I finished speaking.

"The Chinthe is *our* ticket home, Magician," Bastet said, her eyes inches from mine.

"Right. *Our.*"

"Good." She let go of my neck and patted me gently on the cheek. "Now, get the Magick started so we can go home."

The Magick... Shit.

I held up my dirty and blood-covered hands. Disfigured and angry skin peeked out beneath the sand and muck. My shoulders slumped and I let out a long sigh. "Yeah, about that..."

Bastet sniffed at my fingers and wrinkled her nose. "You've been burned by Deep Magick."

"Tell me something I don't know."

One of the Kittens had her claws out faster than I could react. A sharp look from Bastet was the only thing that stood between me and evisceration.

"There appear to be many things you don't know, Magician," the rainbow-haired leader of the Kittens said.

"It's Eugene Law."

"You Jean..." Bastet butchered my name like she was trying to wrap her mouth around a lake trout.

Or the jugular of a Magickless Magician.

"Just call me Gene. Everybody else does."

"He's no use to us. We should eat him," one of the Kittens said, her claws twitching in the dappled light.

"Is that true, Gene? Are you no use to us?"

"I'm the one with the Chinthe, aren't I? I'd say that makes me pretty damn valuable."

The suspect Kitten hissed and took a hesitant step toward me, while the rest of her pack mates watched Bastet intently.

"That is true, but without your Magick you aren't much of a Magician."

Bluff, Gene.

I wasn't much for poker. My lone win had come against a largely inebriated Ed Lovely over a Homecoming weekend, but scoring salted peanuts off my roommate was nothing compared to bluffing my way past Bastet and her Kittens.

"I have plenty of Magick." I let the power I couldn't touch swell in my chest.

Bastet's eyes glittered and the advancing Kitten stopped in her tracks. "I see that. Very nice, but can you not use the Chinthe to take us home?"

Here goes nothing.

"I could, but the end result might not be what you want. You see, without my hands to help me direct the Magick—something very important to all Magicians—bad things could happen."

Bastet raised an eyebrow. "Bad things?"

"Of course, have you been to God's Tears? Terrible place. What if my broken hands sent us there? Or an infinite number of alternate locations. Hell, what if my busted fingers send us to the Gloom?"

Bastet hissed.

"Yeah, it sucks—*a lot*. I've been there a few times and have no interest in going back anytime soon."

Bastet rose and paced the tiny clearing like the jungle cat she was. "You want me to heal your hands."

Can she do that?

"Yes and in exchange I will take you home."

The cat woman shook her head. "Home is not enough, You Jean Law. What you are asking comes at a high price."

Don't give up, Gene. It's a negotiation. Remember when you negotiated the fancy mower? Yeah, Porter worked that deal. Crap.

"Worth more than a trip home?" I said, trying to keep the concern out of my voice. "Best I can tell, you're stuck here. How many Kittens are you willing to lose? I've found one of them so far. I assume there are others."

The aggressive cat woman pushed past Bastet, launching herself at me with claws extended. Fangs flashed in her feline face and it was all I could do to hold my ground and hope for a miracle.

Shit!

My Magick snapped like the crack of a whip. Power I wasn't expecting and had little if any control of, split the cat woman's lip and sent her sprawling in the thick grass.

For a moment no one moved, clearly unsure of what would come next, but none more than me.

Now you decide to show up?

Bastet helped the fallen Kitten to her feet only to slap her across an already bloody lips. They exchanged words in a language I didn't understand, but the body motions were clear— someone had overstepped their position.

"Magician, I will allow that one transgression, but do not

mistake my generosity for weakness," Bastet said, standing in front of me and backed by her Kittens.

"Understood."

You've got this, Gene. You're doing it.

"Heal my hands." I held up broken and melted fingers. "And I will take you home."

"Not good enough. There is something else I must have. What you are asking for is Deep Magick."

"So?"

"What you are asking for is part of me. I do not give of myself lightly."

"What do you want?" I asked, my Magick already beginning to slip in and out of my grasp.

"The Soul of Isis has been blinded."

"The what?"

Bastet claws retracted. "The statue. He has covered its eyes and blinded me to my Magick, and for that he will pay dearly. Remove the bind and I will heal your hands."

Watch it, Gene.

"Do I have your word that no harm will come to me or my friends if I remove the blindfold?"

Bastet's eyes flashed, and the kittens hissed around her. "Are you negotiating with me?"

"It would appear I am. I'm your ticket out of here."

Bastet's claws reappeared. "We could end you here and now Magician."

I gestured a melted hand at the bloodied Kitten. "You could try. You don't know what I'm capable of."

The cat woman hesitated, confusion clear on her face. It was at that moment I decided to go for broke.

"I don't want to do it, but I will if you force my hand. Do not tempt me, Bastet. I survived God's Tears and walked the Gloom. I am the Breaker of the Thread, and a member of the Flock. I have held the Five Star Toaster and lived."

Bastet and her Kittens held their ground, but it was clear they didn't know what to make of me at this point.

Leave it all on the field.

I did my best to look physically imposing in a dirt smeared hospital gown that left little to the imagination.

"I hit like a dump truck and I don't think you carry insurance."

It was all a bluff, and not a very good one at that, as at the same time I was spewing crazy proclamations my Magick was trickling out like someone pulled the plug on a half-empty bath-tub. A real Magician would have been able to sense that and seen right through my posturing—I just hoped a Magickally blinded Bastet wasn't capable of that.

"I will heal your hands and let no harm come to you or your friends from my Kittens, however, you must unbind The Soul of Isis."

"Deal," I said, with as much bravado as I could muster.

"After this is finished, Magician, you will have made an enemy of me."

"Got it," I said, wondering what it meant to be Bastet's enemy. "I've got a list going. Now, fix my hands so we can go home."

35

PANTS AND PROBLEMS

"That hurt like hell." I examined my fingers. "Did you have to... lick them?"

Bastet shrugged. "They are healed, are they not?"

"Yeah, but that couldn't have been sanitary."

The cat woman hissed and bared her impressive fangs.

"Right, I'm sure they're fine. Look at that pink skin." I held up my restored digits and wiggled them. "Yep, happy little piggies."

"It's time, Magician." Bastet placed a paw-like hand on my shoulder. While it could have been considered a friendly gesture, I knew it was anything but.

"Yes, home," I said, trying to untangle myself from the woman's strong hand and having little in the way of success. "I just need to get to Marco so we can start the process."

"He will come to you. I am not letting go of your blood-rich body."

Well, that paints a terrifying visual.

"Sure thing. Marco, come!"

The mountain dog snorted and rolled over.

"Problem?" Bastet's claws dug gently into my shoulder.

"Nothing I can't handle. Come, Marco."

The mountain dog raised his head up enough to make eye contact and then slumped back into his grass bed again.

The cat woman squeezed the life out of my joint. "I am not amused, Magician."

"Dogs. Am I right? It's a process, just be patient," I said, then proceeded to call Marco no less than a dozen different ways. By the twelfth failed attempt a growing sense of unease was quite evident on the Kittens' feline faces.

"I say we eat him," one of them said, her fur a mixture of orange and black.

"I call the neck," another voice cried from further back in the pack.

The brindle cat rolled her eyes. "You always call the neck. For once could you try thinking of someone other than yourself?"

"But I like the neck."

"Marco, come on buddy," I whispered. "You've got to come over here before they start fighting over my intestines."

The mountain dog slowly pushed himself up, then shook out his mane. He started toward me, then stopped to stretch out his ample body like a hairy yoga instructor.

"Great! Now, come on over here."

Content with his stretch, Marco promptly flopped back on the ground.

"Oh, for the love of Ra." Bastet let go of my shoulder and stomped toward the truculent pup. "You will take us home."

No sooner had she let go then Marco jumped to attention, shooting past the cat woman with a top speed I didn't believe a dog of his girth was capable of.

"Stop them!" Bastet shouted, but it was too late. The mountain dog barreled into me faster than her Kittens could react.

Magick ripped through my body on impact. A strange and homesick power that tugged at my heart strings.

I want to go home.

Marco's thick fur and oversized snout were the last things I remembered seeing before my world went black and filled with Bastet's echoing words. "I will have blood!"

Bark!

I opened my eyes to find myself face to face with Marco the mountain dog.

Lick!

"Ugh," I said, pushing his head away and sitting up. "That's enough. You've become quite the pain in my ass."

Bark!

"Yes, I appreciate the trip home, but if you could have done that whenever, why not just do it? Why the side trip to see the crazy cat lady?"

The mountain dog nuzzled my newly restored hands.

"Was that your plan all along?"

Bark!

"You stupidly brilliant dog." I ran my normal and pain-free fingers through Marco's thick fur. "Now, where are we?"

Pushing the mountain dog's head out of my way I got my answer.

Jenkins' Apartment.

The tiny bachelor pad didn't look much different from the first time I'd visited, back then I'd just been looking to fix a toilet, little had I known I'd see more of this place than I ever wanted to. The blood stains and signs of a scuffle were gone, the old man must have taken the time to clean them up. A leather jacket on the couch give me the impression we weren't alone.

Did he find a way back?

I climbed to my feet and leaned against the couch to let my body adjust to what felt like a rapid change in cabin pressure. "Why didn't you tell me all this traveling was going to hurt?"

Sneeze!

The mountain dog ignored me and immediately turned his attention to the closed bedroom door, the hairs on his back at attention.

"What is it?"

Growl.

A smarter man would have reacted faster, but a smarter man also wouldn't have just spent the past hours at the far end of a few Lost Buttons either. Regardless of the cause, I wasn't prepared for what came next.

The bedroom door burst open and an almost feral looking Miguel tore into the room. Blood ran from the edges of his eyes like cheap mascara, while his jaws unfolded like a freshly gut fish.

"Whoa, Miguel," I said, stumbling backward on tired legs. "Chill man, it's me, Gene."

Miguel shoved the couch aside like it were made of foam board, his bleeding eyes trained on me.

"Marco!"

The mountain dog growled and pressed his flank against my leg.

I reached for my Magick, fighting against the exhaustion to try to find something, anything, to protect me from a terrifying Miguel.

"Led—"

I didn't get to finish the Magick before the surprisingly spry mechanic launched himself at us, his crooked fingers outstretched.

Bang!

Sofia hit him out of nowhere. The Skeeter dropped a bag of what looked like groceries at the door then slammed into her father and knocked the older man into the couch.

"What the hell?"

Bark!

Marco and I could only watch as the younger and more athletic Sofia struggled to restrain her hyper-motivated old man.

"Get back," she cried, her rib arms pinning Miguel and trying desperately to keep his claws from reaching me.

Not one to argue with a Skeeter, I scrambled out of the way, Marco staying between me and the insane mechanic. Sofia corralled her father. Her insect claws held him fast while her human arms tightened around his neck. It wasn't long before his ferocity tapered off and he lay unconscious on the couch.

"What are you doing here?" Sofia asked, releasing her father once she was convinced he wouldn't spring back up. "Is that a hospital gown?"

"Uh, yeah."

"Did you go mud wrestling in it?"

"Not on purpose."

Sofia sighed and turned her father over. She removed a small pack of tissues from her groceries and started dabbing at the blood around his eyes. "He's getting worse. Where's the old man?"

"God's Tears."

"Huh?" Sofia tossed the bloody tissue in a trashcan I hadn't noticed before. "Is that some sort of code word?"

"No, it's a... it's a shitty place I have no interest in going back to."

"Damn it." She pushed down on an overflowing trash can. "When is the old man getting back?"

"How long has he been gone?" I held my breath.

"Half a day."

Whew.

"I'd say he'll be back in just under a thousand years."

Sofia crumpled the pack of tissues in her hand. "No. He promised me he'd help keep my dad from becoming a feeder."

I thought back to the hospital. "Something came up,"

The Void.

"This is bullshit." The young woman's jaws unfolded, giving me a top off of fleshy nightmare fuel. "You're going to help me."

"Me?" I kept a healthy eye on her quivering fangs. "I'm wearing a hospital gown."

Sofia's insect arms dug into the front of that gown. "You're a Magician, and you appear to have adopted his Chinthe. You are going to help me unwind the Magick destroying my father."

"How does everyone else seem to know what his dog is but me?"

The mountain dog grinned.

"Seriously, I'd love to help you, I really would, but my wife's been taken by your blood brothers and I've got to get her back."

"Without pants?" Sofia asked, letting go of my gown and gesturing to the open air crotch.

"I'm working on that."

"Just not very hard?" The young woman let her insect arms retract into those hidden gaps between her ribs. "And you know where 'my blood brothers,' are?"

Damn it.

"I—"

Bang! Bang!

"Mr. Jenkins? This is officer Harold and your neighbor Jeff Plankens. We need to talk to you about your dog."

"And dog fighting ring. I'm on to you, Jenkins."

Jeff the Physicist, shit.

"Who is that?" Sofia asked, her jaws flared and quivering with hungry anticipation.

"Keep it under control, terror-lips. I've got this."

Sohia frowned. "Where's the dog?"

Bang!

Marco had vanished.

"Gah!"

36
STUNG

"Khakis?" I whispered, holding the edges of the old man's pleated pants, before taking a white shirt in the face.

"He's got some plaid ones in here too." Sofia waved a pair of gaudy orange and green trousers that appeared to have been cut from the same material they'd used to make the couch.

Bang!

"Stay in the bedroom with your dad. I *so* don't need him stealing anyone's nose the hard way."

Sofia nodded and pulled the door closed.

"Mr. Jenkins?" the officer asked from the other side of the door.

Here goes nothing...

"Coming."

～

HAT IN HAND, the officer stood in the old Magician's door frame, while next to him, Jeff the Physicist frowned. "Good afternoon, sir—"

"That's not him. That's one of his friends," Jeff said, clearly displeased that Mr. Jenkins hadn't been the one to open the door.

"Eugene Law." I extended a newly healed hand and hoped to hell the officer wasn't a fan of the squeeze grip handshake. "What can I do for you guys?"

"May we come in?"

I hesitated. This was Mr. Jenkins' threshold and his apartment. I didn't know what in the way of protections the old Magician had placed on it and couldn't begin to know how to undo it.

"It was right here." Jeff pushed his way past the officer. "There was blood everywhere. I swear right here in the living room."

Well, that works too.

I waved the officer in behind the brazen neighbor. "Come in."

"Thank you, sir."

Jeff swept the room like a bloodhound, overturning the rug and checking under the brand new television. "There's got to be something here. I know what I saw, and I saw a bloodied dog."

The officer scratched his head. "Mr. Law, how do you know the tenant?"

"I... I'm watching his apartment. You know, can't be too careful anymore, criminals everywhere."

"Uh huh and does he have a dog?"

"Never leaves his side."

Jeff tossed the rug aside and rifled through the kitchen cabinets. "There was booze everywhere, enough tequila for a frat party. I know it's here." He yanked open the fridge and found the shelves empty. "Argh!"

"When will Mr. Jenkins be back?"

"That's a great question. I'm thinking it might be a few years."

"Years?"

"At least. He took his dog, and they went to Europe. Sweden I think? Could have been Switzerland. I'm not sure."

Jeff was positively fuming by this point. He grabbed the closet door and swung it open. He knocked over boxes and bags in the process. "I know there's something here."

Bastet's statue rolled out behind him, the plastic wrap still clinging to her eyes.

Crap.

"Well. I'm not seeing anything. I'm sorry for troubling you, Mr. Law."

Jeff threw his hands in the air. "What do you mean you're not seeing anything? Where's the CSI treatment? Shouldn't we be running over this with a UV light? I bet this place looks like splatter art under the right light."

"It doesn't work that way." The officer placed his hat back on. "You need to spray it with a reactant first."

"Do you have reactant?"

"No."

"Gah!" Jeff threw his arms in the air again.

Act cool, Gene.

I took a seat on Jenkins' couch, gently fluffing the pillows like what I imagined someone watching an apartment for an out-of-town eccentric would do. "Well, guys. If there's nothing else I can do for you…"

"There!" Jeff shouted like he were preparing to pin the scarlet letter on my chest with a railroad tie. "Right there, on the back of that cushion, that's blood."

Miguel! Damn it.

That got the officer's attention. "Let me see that."

"It's nothing," I said, trying to wipe the damning substance off with my fingers and having no luck. "I think I got some pizza on there."

"That doesn't look like pizza sauce."

Jeff clapped his hands in triumph. "See, see! I told you. I bet there's more. In fact I bet the old man is hiding in the bedroom. I'm telling you. He's a sleaze-ball."

Thump.

"Ah ha." Jeff pointed to the bedroom door. "Did you hear that?"

The officer nodded. "Mr. Law, is there anyone else here?"

"Uh, well it's—"

Wham.

The bedroom door burst open, and a robe covered Sofia stepped out. She had a bloody tissue pressed up to her nose. "Hey, sorry about that honey. You know how I get those nose-bleeds. Oh, shit," she pulled the robe tight against her body, "why didn't you tell me there were people here?"

Jeff grabbed at his hair. "Who are you? Where is the old man?"

"This is my—"

"Honey, you can't lie to the police." Sofia stuck out a pale hand. "I'm his lover."

"Uh..." neither man knew exactly how to respond.

"My—"

Sofia tossed the waded up tissue in the trash, then slipped her arms around my waist. "Go with it," she whispered.

"My lover. Yep, we are big time on the loving. All the loving. We do that. The loving. All of it."

Sofia's hands squeezed my sides. "Take it down a notch, Fabio."

"Right, sorry," I whispered.

"Are you going to arrest us?" The Skeeter asked, her insect arms pressing against my back.

The officer removed his hat and ran a hand through his short hair. "Uh, no. I'm not going to arrest you."

Jeff stomped past him and into the bed room. "Ah hah! I told you. Come here, look at this. I found more blood on the bed."

"I'm sorry, honey," Sofia did her best to play the pity card, softening her eyes and wiping her nose. "I got some on the sheets."

The officer shook his head. "Oh, no. We are totally good. You two have a nice rest of the day. I'm sorry to have bothered you."

"That's it?" Jeff wedged himself in the bedroom doorway. "Where's the crime scene investigators? The forensics? I'm telling you. Those two are lying."

"We'll be out of your hair now."

"What?! You can't be serious? This is—" The rest of Jeff's words were lost in a bloody scream. Miguel was awake, and hungry.

Oh, shit.

The officer's gun appeared way faster than I expected.

"Sofia—"

"On it." The Skeeter dropped Mr. Jenkins robe, letting her insect arms unfold and snap the weapon out of his hand.

"Get your dad," I cried, diving for the officer. Jeff may be annoying, but he certainly didn't deserve to have his neck consumed by a hatchling Skeeter.

Sofia appeared to have it in hand, her claws making short work of detaching Miguel from the Physicist and pinning him against the wall. I, on the other hand, had my work cut out for me.

"Oof!" A knee to the gut sent the air out of my lungs. "Radio!" I shouted in a grunt of pain.

The Skeeter was in control. She sent two of her remaining insect arms into the officer's shoulder, cracking the radio and pinning his body to the wall.

"Don't kill me," Jeff cried, slumping against the door jamb.

"Sofia?"

The Skeeter's jaws split apart like the insides of a ripe melon. She grabbed the physicist by his shirt and pulled him to her horrific lips.

"Sofia!"

Jeff's eyes rolled back in his head the instant her stinger pierced his neck.

"What are you doing?! Stop!"

Sofia dropped the physicist and then turned her attention to the officer.

"Sofia, don't—"

Too late, she dropped the man-in-blue just as fast.

"What did you do?"

The Skeeter shoved her father back in the bedroom and slammed the door. "I solved our problem," she said, her jaws folding back into place. "You're welcome."

Gah!

TICKET PLEASE

"What do you mean they aren't dead?"

Sofia shook her head, her insect arms folding back beneath the edges of her tank-top. "Exactly that, they aren't dead."

"But I saw—"

"Gene, they aren't dead. Check their pulses." The Skeeter held a wrist up for me. Sure enough, she was right.

"Oh, this is just great. They're going to wake up and call in the calvary."

Sofia shook her head. "Nope."

"How do you—"

The Mosquito woman pointed to the door. "I'll explain it to you on the way."

"The way?"

"I'm going to get you to your wife, and afterwards, you're going to fix my old man."

The slight ripple in her jaws told me exactly what I could expect if I didn't fill in my end of the deal.

No pressure.

~

"I CAN'T BELIEVE you stopped for a Toaster," the young woman said, looking at her reflection in the shiny side of the Five Star Toaster.

"Damn it, woman." I took a hand off the wheel of Mr. Jenkins' Mazda to slap her fingers away from the handle. "Do *not* press down those handles."

"I know." Sofia pouted. "You've told me like twenty times already."

"And I'll tell you another twenty times if you keep testing me."

While it was nice of the Skeeter to hot-wire the old man's Mazda, I was decidedly uncomfortable with the bottom half of the dash rattling against my legs. I pushed that thought aside and took us onto the road.

Sofia set the Toaster on the floor between her feet, pressing her ankles against the shiny sides to keep it from moving. "So, how do you know the old man?"

"I fixed his toilet once."

"Interesting..."

"Not really," I said, slowing down for a stoplight. It was late afternoon and the sun was already low in the sky. "What came after I fixed his toilet—very interesting. The fixing part? Not so much. Now, what's going to happen to Jeff and that nice police officer back there?"

Sofia picked up the Bastet statue sitting in the cup holder. "They won't remember anything." She let her jaws ripple. "Think of it like chemical amnesia. They'll wake up thinking what I whispered into their ears."

"Which was?"

"They found the apartment empty, and could really go for burgers."

"Well, that's handy—in an entirely above board and not remotely terrifying way."

"Yeah." Sofia placed the statue back in the cup holder and adjusted it to face the windshield like a bobble-head doll.

"Cute." I pulled onto the highway. "Now, where is Deacon and the rest of the Swarm?"

"Miami."

My stomach dropped. "Damn it, that's over five hours away by car. There's no way the Phase Knot stays closed that long." I yanked the wheel hard toward the next exit, crossing multiple lanes of traffic in a panic.

"Wait." Sofia grabbed the wheel. "There's a Slip in Ybor."

"A Slip?" I asked, my eyes still zeroed in on the offramp.

"Yeah, a Slip. They're gaps in space time. It's how we get around the state. Sangre Reina has a few of them, no one really knows how many."

"My Spanish is rough—"

"The Blood Queen."

"Queen?"

Sofia nodded. "You think Deacon is the top dog?"

"Well..."

"Hardly," she said, running her fingers along the window seam. "He's up there for sure, but it isn't his show."

"It's..."

"Delia's. She runs the whole thing. Brings us food, takes care of the feeders, and keeps the family in line."

Delia...

"Is she the first?"

"Nearest I can tell, she's the top of the heap. Listen, Gene, you don't stand a chance against Delia, don't even try. Your best plan of action is to get in, find your wife, and get the hell out."

"What if she finds me?"

Sofia dragged her fingers across her neck. "If I were you I'd pray that doesn't happen."

I swallowed hard and pulled off the interstate. We were immediately greeted by a flock of chickens that skittered out of the street in front of us.

Welcome to Ybor City.

"How did you get tied up with her?"

Sofia sighed and folded her arms. "You've met my dad, right?"

"I have."

"Then you've got half your answer. Don't get me wrong, he's a great guy, but not much help when he was in prison."

"And you..."

Sofia jaws rippled briefly. "I did what I had to do. I was by myself. Maybe you had a great childhood, with family and friends, but I didn't. Deacon found me and gave me a purpose, and a family that would always be there for me—at least that's what I told myself—sometimes the lies come easier than the truth"

I took another turn and crossed on to Seventh Ave. "I'm sorry."

"Save it. I own my mistakes. I'm done with all of them. The old man promised he could get me out and I believe him."

I let the car roll to a stop at the light. The red bulb hue filling the cab with an angry glow. "Where am I going?"

Sofia pointed toward Eighth Ave. "The church."

"You're kidding."

"Nope."

"The Slip is in a church?"

Sofia smiled, the seam of her chin visible in the street lamp's glow. "He goes by the name Deacon doesn't he? Tell me you don't find this surprising."

I followed the Skeeter's directions, taking the turn on to Eighth, then pulling up alongside an ancient building. The church's dark bricks had held a thick layer of dust and dirt built up over an untold number of years. A narrow metal fence added to the general spookiness of the place and all but guaranteed they'd only be a hit at Halloween. All of that and a sign out front that indicated the city of Tampa had condemned the building was sure to keep the parishioners to a minimum.

"This is it?" I asked, slowing the car to pull alongside the darkened structure.

"You were expecting something else?"

"Oh no, this is plenty terrifying."

Sofia smiled—even her normal teeth looked decidedly feral. "I thought so too the first time they brought me here. Delia has better taste in decor. This is really Deacon's deal."

A light flashed within one of the bar-covered windows and Sofia rammed her foot on the accelerator. Jenkins' Mazda lurched past the building in a huff of exhaust.

"What the—"

"Deacon's men."

"Shit," I said, taking back control of the vehicle from the young Skeeter. "What do we do?"

Miguel's daughter pointed to a nearby alley. "Pull over there and turn the engine off."

"Why?" I did as she asked and parked the old man's car in the narrow alley.

Sofia's jaws fluttered and her eyes took on a predatory glare. "Because, I'm going to use you as our ticket inside."

38

COVER CHARGE

*M*agick swirled in my chest and I must have made my concern abundantly apparent because Sofia snapped her jaws shut. "Whoops, sorry, that happens. Here's the deal. We don't bring meals here often, but the special ones we are required to take to the Sangre Reina."

The young Skeeter hopped out of the car and dug through a trash bin not far away. She fished out a relatively empty trash bag and dumped its contents in the damp alley.

"What's that for?"

Miguel's daughter pointed to the devil's Toaster and the Bastet bobblehead. "They're not going to let you just walk those things through the front door."

"True."

Sofia tossed the toaster in the bag and my heart skipped a beat.

"What?"

"The handles!"

She rolled her eyes and looked in the bag. "No change. You know, I never knew my abuela, but I'm getting an appreciation of what having one might have been like."

"Easy!" I held my breath when the statue dropped into the bag.

The young woman smiled, twirling the top of the bag and giving me another heart attack when its contents clunked together. "Come on, Grandma. Let's get you to Miami."

~

I LEANED against the edge of the alley and kept a sharp eye on the dark church. Its brick walls did little to catch the light from the nearby street lamps. "What's the play?"

"First, you've got to look the part."

"Huh?" I said, turning around just in time to be on the receiving end of a fist to the face. "Son of a bitch!"

Sofia's jaws splayed open in the humid night air. "Would you prefer I use these?"

"No!"

The young woman's face resealed. "Didn't think so. Now, once that shiner gets going you'll be a more believable prisoner. How are you at shuffling steps?"

"Shuffling?"

"I like to get mine drunk before I..." Sofia's grin faded.

"Before you drain them?" I asked, rubbing my sore cheek.

The Skeeter grabbed my shirt and yanked me toward her. "Don't. Do not for one second pretend to tell me who I am or what I can and cannot do. I'm a survivor."

"I—"

Sofia's jaws quivered just inches from my face. "I'm not Deacon and I won't become him. Do you know how long I spend finding my..."

"Dinner?"

Sofia pushed me back against the alley wall. "The men I take are murders, rapists, molesters—the worst of the worst. I find them, I seduce them, and I bleed them dry. You think you know me, but you don't, so stop."

I had a lot of other things I could have said, like the fact her hair was thinning, or the fact she only went after 'bad people,' which left me wondering where her own father fell on that list.

"Okay."

You need her, Gene. Think of Porter.

I brushed the dirt from my borrowed khakis. "So, are we done?"

The Skeeter set the trash bag down and picked up what looked like an almost completely empty bottle of rum. A small amount of dark orange fluid swirled around in the bottom. She took a sniff of the contents and wrinkled her nose. "Now we are," Sofia said, splashing the liquid on what had been a decently white shirt.

"Was that necessary?"

The young woman tossed the bottle and turned my face with her hand. "Yes. That's a nice looking black eye. Now remember, no Magick, and don't make eye contact. Oh and try to shuffle like you drank the rest of Tampa's finest." She scooped up the trash bag and pushed me toward the church. "Do all that," she whispered, her hot breath on my neck. "And we just might survive."

I'm coming, Porter—I hope.

～

"REMEMBER." Sofia's hands dug into the soft skin of my neck. "Do not speak."

I let my head loll gently to show I was listening.

The Skeeter guided me up a narrow set of concrete steps that led to the church's arched entry. The doors were old, what lacquer they had was peeled in spots, leaving the wood beneath exposed to the elements. Black and mold eaten, they rattled beneath Sofia's fist.

"Let me in, bitches."

Ah, so she's just as charming with her fellow Mosquito People.

I played the part of the disheveled blood bag and let my hands drift and my legs sway. It wasn't hard—I couldn't remember the last time I ate something or slept without Magickally induced head trauma.

Someone moved behind the heavy door. "Been a while, Sof. What are you doing back here?"

"I need somewhere to eat in peace," my pretend captor said, banging me against the heavy door.

Was that necessary?

A loud clunk from the other side of the door told me it was.

Lots of diary material today.

I didn't get much time to contemplate this new nugget of wisdom before Sofia pushed me into the dimly lit narthex. The front of the old church still had plenty of reminders of its more pious days. A particularly bloody painting of the crucified Christ hung above multiple kneelers adorned with rows of votive candles.

Catholics.

"So, what have you brought me?" the door man asked.

"You? Since when do we share?"

The young man's jaws unfolded like a cobra's hood. Even with my eyes unfocused, he was clearly cast in the mold of what I would have considered one of Deacon's men—at a minimum they shopped at the same clothing store. This guy's all black ensemble may have lacked Deacon's sophistication, but it made up for that with spikes, lots and lots of spikes.

"Since Deacon's not here and I get to decide who comes in," Spike Lee said, letting his jaws ripple in the dim light.

"No fucking way."

The Skeeter ran a hand over his balding head. "Well, there

are always other options..." His grin told me those options would not be PG.

"Screw you, Cal." Sofia's jaws snapped open, and her grip on my shoulder tightened up.

"Exactly, now you've got it," Spike said, grabbing at the young woman's butt.

My captor didn't stand for those antics. She pushed me out of the way and slammed a knee into the skinny man's crotch. He crumpled like a folding chair, proud shoulders dipping forward, while his hands clutched at the air—at least they did until they landed on me.

The effect was instant and would not have been surprising had I not been so completely exhausted. He may have been in pain, but junior Mr. Monochromatic pushed all that aside the moment he discovered I was a Magician.

Shit.

"Bitch, you got a Magician!"

"Exactly, he's mine. Get the hell out of my way before I drain both of you tonight." Sofia pumped as much bravado into her voice as she could, but I was pretty sure I wasn't the only one picking up on her fear.

Cal regained his composure pretty quickly and as predicted ignored the young Skeeter's hollow threat. He yanked me out of her grasp and spun me around to face her. "This one's mine and if you don't leave now, you'll be next."

Sofia and I made eye contact. This wasn't what she was expecting and she clearly didn't know what to do about it.

Damn it, kid. First rule of plans. They never work.

Cal pulled my head back with his strong fingers exposing my neck, while at the same time giving me a beautiful view of the open trusses above. Alonzo and I had spent a few hours fixing some busted electrical lines during the day of mainte-nance hell, and in doing so, he'd provided more than a little sage guidance. "Old wires, see? Stripped, don't touch—would make for a very bad day."

I reached for my Magick, doing what I could to be as subtle about it as possible all while being inches away from having my throat ripped out. I could only hope that power would be willing to answer to take my call.

It's Eugene Law, do you accept the charges?

My Magick swirled.

Oh, come on. It wasn't that *bad.*

The cosmic power rolling in my chest didn't appear to agree with my assessment.

Crap.

39

JUICY

*C*al had my jugular in his sights and showed no interest in backing down. He pressed his nose against my unwashed neck. "So sweet..."

I didn't know if there were more Skeeters in the church, nor did I particularly care given the apparent high likelihood of my blood staining the narthex floor. Action was necessary, and fast. My Magick might not have been listening, but my elbow sure was.

Whump!

A sharp jab sent that joint directly into the skinny Skeeter's gut and folded him for the second time this evening—albeit not as impressively as Sofia had. Speaking of Miguel's daughter, the young woman didn't waste any time either. She launched herself at the two of us, her arms wide and on a collision course with the other Skeeter.

Together all three of us rammed into the far wall, sending a fine cloud of dust into the air. Cal hadn't completely released his grip on my neck, but Miguel's daughter had her rib arms unfurled and in his mouth keeping those fluttering jaws from making contact.

Insect arms and serrated stingers flailed, and while I hadn't been bitten yet, it appeared it was only a matter of time before I was. I reached for my Magick again, this time with a considerable amount of adrenaline to back me up.

"Veni," I cried, reaching a hand for the distant candles and pulling them toward me. My Magick got the hint, except it wasn't the candles that moved, it was the entire wrought-iron kneeler.

Screech!

The heavy metal etched nasty grooves in the old stone floor before going airborne and slamming into the Skeeters fighting for control of a delicious Gene Law snack.

Not exactly what I had planned, but it'll work.

The kneeler flopped down moments before impact. The wooden bottom blasted into Cal's head, while the rest of the iron candle stand spun and scraped Sofia off me like the peel on an overripe banana.

I scrambled to my feet to find Cal shaking off the kneeler, but Sofia had not been that lucky. My pretend captor was pinned like a mounted butterfly beneath a jagged iron that had once held candles.

Oh, shit.

Cal's jacket flared out to reveal long and hairy insect arms. The appearance of the young Sofia pinned to the wall and bleeding sent him into a tizzy. "Someone's eating good tonight."

He pulled apart his shirt to show off a heavily tattooed chest.

Is that another sigil?

"You think Deacon's the only one who knows Magick?"

Think, Gene! What is that?

The sigil's lines reminded me of something I'd seen before. Something I hadn't thought about in years, but the Magick that poured out of it make it difficult to think clearly.

Sofia growled and yanked at the pinning iron. "Don't let him get you. It's a confusion glyph…"

My world started to spin. I knew it was Magick, but I didn't understand exactly what. The lines and swirls criss-crossed, almost undulating along the Skeeter's pale skin. Sofia kept shouting something, but it wasn't making it past my fascination.

The lines and curves... I've seen you before.

Cal slowly closed the gap between us, his chest the only thing I could focus on. "That's it. You like it? I had it made special..."

My mind rolled back to a time I tried hard not to think about. Dark days from my past best left buried and forgotten, but the sigil's power dredged them up.

"Gene." Morgan's hair shone in the searing light of the library, and in her hands, Ten Spins' Infernal Constructs, the book I'd gone out of my way to forget. "This is it. Think of the power."

I didn't have to think of that power, because I was feeling it. Ten Spins' Magick was chaotic and uncontrollable, a darkness that resisted containment, and there it was drawn in ink on that pale man's chest.

"There you go," Cal said, mere feet away. "Now, tilt your head up nice and easy for Cal."

"Stop!" Sofia shouted, but it wasn't her voice I heard. It was Morgan's, and it wasn't the wires above me that I saw anymore, it was the fiery doors of the library and before them the drifting Thread of Ariadne. I reached out and felt the Magick. It was everywhere, swimming in me and through me. There was no fighting for it, there was no clawing for it. The Magick and I were one, and we knew what we had to do.

"Goodbye, Morgan." I snapped Ariadne's Thread in my hands.

"What the hell is he talking about?" Cal's voice and his hot breath shattered my vision.

This time I knew what I had to do, and thankfully, my

Magick did too. "Veni!" I shouted, my eyes on the ceiling, and no longer lost in Ten Spins' confusion. "Veni!"

Bare wires tore away from the exposed trusses like the cracking of a whip. Sparks spilled from the twisted copper as it coiled around my extended hand.

Cal's head shot forward, his jaws wide and hungry, but instead of taking a mouthful of Eugene Law, they got a fist full of live copper.

Electricity and Magick coursed through the line. The twin powers surged into that spiky Skeeter and snapped his jaws shut. Magickally enhanced ions closed all his synapses at once. Muscles contracted and his body shutdown. He fell backward toward the stone floor, but I didn't stop. I followed him down and let the anger I'd built up over all those months course through me. His face melted and his eyes popped. The whites bled down his cheeks like runny eggs, but still I pushed harder.

I let the Magick roar and reveled in the feeling. Months of frustration pinned the dead man to the ground like overcooked meat, but still I didn't stop, not when his face blackened to char, and not when Sofia screamed at me.

It wasn't some Skeeter's burnt face melted to the stone, it was Morgan's, and in that moment I caught myself reflected in the glistening remains of what had been Cal's flesh.

What have I done?

My Magick vanished. I crumpled, tired and broken, against the body of that blackened Skeeter.

"Holy shit," Sofia cried, still pulling on the pinning iron. "What the hell was that?"

"Magick." I dropped the charred copper wiring and pushed myself off Cal's remains.

"You... you melted him." The young woman's brain was clearly having a hard time reconciling what it had just witnessed.

I wrapped my hands around the bent iron and yanked it out of her.

Sofia grunted and clutched at her gut. Those little hands did little to stem the flow of blood pooling around her. "Shit! Shit!"

"Can't you heal or something?"

"That's iron," she spat, shifting away from the broken metal. "Iron. Fucking iron. There's nothing I can do."

"What do you mean?"

Sofia pushed herself against the stone wall. "I mean I could drink your blood, drain you dry, but it won't heal this. The iron is in my blood now. There's no coming back."

"But isn't blood full of iron?"

"Do I look like an expert? I don't understand it. I don't understand any of it." The young Skeeter's face was losing color fast. "You think I wanted this life?"

"No one does."

"What do you know? You just fried that asshole to bacon. If I had that kind of power I wouldn't have needed Deacon... I wouldn't have needed these." Sofia let her jaws reseal and those insect arms retract. "The Slip is in the third confessional. Go in and close the door, then flip the little red light switch three times. Try to keep the wires in the wall." She grimaced at her own joke.

"What about you?"

"I'm screwed."

No.

I retrieved a spiked lapel from Cal's jacket.

"What are you doing?"

I pressed the sharp spike against my finger and elicited a single drop of blood.

"I told you," Sofia said, her head down. "It's the iron, it won't work."

"Do you really want to tell the guy who just pumped a few

hundred megawatts into your colleague what will and will not work?"

Sofia's jaws quivered at the smell of my blood. "Whatever. Just try not to melt my eyeballs."

"I make no promises." I knelt next to the young Skeeter. "I've only seen this done once."

"What?"

I ignored Sofia, and instead, mixed my blood with hers, tracing the sigil I'd watched Jenkins do on his own dog only a few days earlier.

The Viburna...

I had no idea what exactly it did, or even whose design it was, but I'd promised Miguel, and I wasn't about to break that promise.

"This."

I closed the sigil and Sofia screamed.

40

WILD AND DEEP

*M*y heart pumped like a fireman's hose, each burst more painful than the last. The sigil complete, it acted like a magnifying glass, focusing what remained of my tired Magick into the Skeeter's broken body.

Sofia clutched at her side. Her dark blood mixed with mine in the Viburna's complex swirls and in that moment our hearts beat together. "What are you doing to me?" she cried, her eyes wide and jaws flapping wildly.

I wanted to tell her I didn't know, but the Magick demanded my concentration. The old man earned my respect as I collapsed against the bloody stone floor spent.

Sofia pulled her hands aside to reveal smooth and sealed skin. "What did you do?"

I rolled over and rubbed my eyes at the dull ache settling in nicely between them. "I'm not sure, but it appears to have worked."

The young Skeeter jumped to her feet. "Worked? This is amazing. There's an electricity in the air and I can feel it. It's like rumbling clouds before a storm—a pent-up anticipation ready to erupt—and I want it."

"Huh?"

Sofia pounced on me before I could recover, her strong and supple body pinning me to the blood-soaked floor. "I can feel it pouring out of you."

Magick.

Sofia's jaws splayed open, quivering erratically beneath her hungry eyes. "I have to have it. I can't help it." Her hand clamped down on my bare arm and the sudden jolt shocked us both. "What was that?" she asked, the crackle of power temporarily derailing her bloodthirsty intentions.

"Wild Magick," I said, too tired to fight back. "I don't know how, but welcome to my world."

Sofia's jaws sealed shut and she pulled back her hand, holding it up in the dim light. "Magick?"

"Wild Magick." I corrected her. "It's uncontrollable, danger-ous, and potentially deadly. It doesn't listen, it doesn't follow orders, and it's hell on the body."

"It feels amazing."

I sighed. "Yeah. That too."

"But how?"

"We'll have to ask Mr. Jenkins should we ever see him again. Give me a hand." Another jolt of Wild Magick greeted us as Sofia pulled me to my feet. "Now, let's get to the Slip." I took a second to lean against the wall and catch my breath.

"Sure, it's—" The sound of car doors closing outside cut Sofia off mid-sentence. She was at the door in an instant.

"What is it?"

"Deacon's men. Lots of them," the young Skeeter said, excite-ment in her voice.

"Crap. Let's not hang around."

Sofia didn't budge. "No."

Wild Magick rushed around her, unbridled and dangerous.

"Whoa, don't even think about it."

Sofia's jaws reopened and her insect arms unfurled. "You

don't know what they did to me. You don't know what it was like before I could stand up for myself."

The Wild Magick churned around the young Skeeter like the power chords of a rock concert.

"You can't control it," I said, pleading with the young woman. "You are just as likely to blow your own head off as theirs. This is Wild Magick. Don't you understand?"

Of course she doesn't. She's been a Magician for all of fifteen seconds.

"I'll be fine." Sofia pulled off her jacket and tossed it aside. "Take your bag and get to the Slip." She pointed to the trash bag I'd all but forgotten in the corner. The trash bag containing the Toaster and Bastet's Soul of Isis.

The Toaster.

"Sofia, is this building connected to anything?"

"Huh?"

"The church. Is it connected to any other buildings?"

"No."

"Standalone?"

"Yeah. Yeah. Yeah," she said, clearly anxious to unleash a power she had no way of understanding, let alone controlling. "Why?"

"Because." I pulled the infernal appliance out of the trash bag. "It's going down tonight."

THE TOASTER'S Deep Magick sucked the air out of the room, and even the newly minted junior Magician felt it. Her jaws rippled open in the reflection of its perfectly polished sides. "What is that?" she asked as if seeing the Five Star Toaster in a new light. "I can *feel* it."

"That's Deep Magick, kid." I handed her the trash bag. "It's Advanced Placement Magick. You're not quite ready for four-hundred level material yet. We need to get you past Gen Ed."

Sofia tilted her head. "Huh?"

A series of bangs against the wooden door kept me from brandishing a witty response.

"They're here." The Skeeter's insect arms exploded out of her sides, while Wild Magick thrummed around her.

"What are they doing?"

Sofia's jaws expanded to their full and horrifying length. "Secret knock."

"You're kidding."

The young woman's eyes told me she wasn't.

Boom!

"They're coming in," Sofia cried, tossing me back the trash bag and pulling Wild Magick like a mad fool.

"Let em." I tried not to drop Bastet or the Toaster. "They aren't going to want to stay, trust me."

"I can take them." The young woman's insect arms flexed in the gloom.

"I'm sure you can, but we've got to think of the big picture here. What about your dad?"

The Wild Magick flicked.

"What about him?"

Boom!

"Maybe we don't need Jenkins to fix him, maybe between the two of us we have what we need now, but we'll never know if you don't survive the night."

Sofia hesitated, the unbridled power slipping away from her neophyte hands.

"Come on." I shoved the Toaster into those insect arms. "I'll even let you pull the handles."

~

WE LEFT the narthex and raced into the main church. It shared the same dark, dingy, and ill-kept motif that the front entrance had so expertly presented. If there'd been an altar, it had long ago been removed, but the clergy chairs were still there, arranged in a regal setting. This was clearly where a man like Deacon held court.

Boom!

The door wasn't going to hold up much longer, and by the sounds of it more of Deacon's men had arrived. I'd faced one Cal tonight, I wasn't interested in facing another.

"So much power," Sofia said, her claws on the Toaster and her eyes lost in its shiny sides. "This is Deep Magick?"

"Yes and don't get too excited. It turned my hands to putty and reduced the apartment to ashes. The Five Star Toaster is Deep Magick not to be taken lightly."

Sofia looked at my hands. "They look fine to me?"

"Yeah, they're doing amazing things with cat woman saliva these days."

"Huh?"

Boom! Crack!

"I'll explain it later. We don't have much time." I pointed to the wooden confessionals that lined the side of the narrow church. "Which one is the Slip?"

Sofia nodded her head toward the last door. "That one."

"Good. Now, put down the Toaster and pull both handles all the way to the bottom."

Crack!

The door was coming apart, and the sound of very unhappy Skeeters on the other side told me we needed to pick up the pace.

"All the way down?" Sofia asked, her hands trembling at the Deep Magick wrapped up in the Toaster.

"You want to see this place again?"

"Hell no."

"All the way down it goes."

Crash!

An explosion of wood and splinters in the narthex indicated it was time to go. Skeeters spilled out into the main church like black ants. Their monochromatic attire a scathing reminder of just whose house this was.

"Do it!" I cried.

Sofia's jaws shuddered in a surge of Wild Magick.

What the hell is she doing?

Black clad Skeeters scrambled over the pews and down the aisles. We didn't have time to screw around.

"Damn it, Sofia. Pull the handles!"

Wild Magick exploded around the young Skeeter. It tore at the walls and shook the ancient building.

She's trapping them.

Pews ripped up from their moorings and slammed into the arched entrance. No one was leaving.

"Now!" I pulled open the confessional.

The young woman dropped the Toaster and slammed its handles to the bottom, filling the room with an unholy wave of heat.

"Argh!" She shook the pain out of her fingers. "Holy—"

"Less talking, more running!"

Sofia didn't have to be told again. She rammed into me and together we landed in a heap in the tiny confessional. It couldn't have been much larger than a broom closet, there was barely enough room for one, let alone both of us.

"The switch," she said, pushing off me and slamming the door before the first burning Skeeter could get through the narrow opening. "Three times!"

Heat poured through the heavy wood, while wisps of smoke and screams filled the air.

"One."

Claws shook the heavy oak in its frame.

"Two."

"Do it!" The door rattled against its moorings and sent a fresh wave of heat over our already sweat-soaked bodies.

"Three."

The tiny room flooded with Magick and in an instant my world went black.

PART III
DUPLICKITY

41

FAMILY

"**W**here are we?" I whispered, my eyes gradually adjusting to the warm dark. "Sofia?"

Soft blue and dappled light filtered in through distant windows. Large and imposing, their glass disappeared into the ceiling and afforded a view of the stars any astronomer would kill for. Below the eternal magnificence of that night sky, small white-caps rippled across an ocean close enough to touch.

Miami.

"Yeah," the young Skeeter grunted, her voice strained and tired. "I'm here. Welcome to Miami."

"Is that where we are?" I ran my hands along the smooth walls. We were in some sort of great room. Geometric shapes in the dim starlight spoke of furniture with a decidedly modern touch.

"I haven't taken this Slip before but most of them end some-where on her estate." Sofia struggled to her feet, the Wild Magick had clearly taken its toll.

Magick demands sacrifice.

"Estate?" I asked, slowly moving my way toward what I

assumed was a white wall. Large paintings jut out like black cutouts against the pale sea. In the darkness, it was impossible to make out what they were, but they dominated the room. Everything was ornate, grand, and imposing.

Sofia rubbed her neck. "Yeah, it's big. This is one of her main receiving rooms. Deacon brought me here once—I think."

"Great," I whispered, cringing at the sound of my borrowed loafers on the hard floor. "We just need to figure out where they would be keeping Porter."

"Your wife? If she's going to be feed, then she'll be in one of the guest houses."

"Guest houses?"

Sofia nodded, her fleshy jaws neatly collapsed and folded away. "Don't kid yourself. It's no vacation—chained up waiting to be fed to her children."

Porter!

The Phase Knot could hold a long time, but how long in the face of a Magician like Deacon? Or this Delia?

My chest tightened. The heat in the room was stifling.

"Why is it so hot in here?"

"You don't know much about us, do you?"

"No, and in all honesty, I don't want to. I want to get my wife and get out of here."

"What do you know about mosquitos?" Sofia asked, her voice oddly distant in the dim room.

"There's a spray for them. Listen, if it's all the same to you I'd like to focus on finding my wife and getting the hell out of here."

Sofia's hard heels clicked against the tile, while the outline of her body vanished against one of the large paintings. "You know it's the female mosquito that bites, right?"

"That's what they tell me."

The young woman's eyes were all but invisible against the dark swirls of paint. "They need heat to live, to breed, and to grow."

"This is really great. I appreciate the biology lesson on Florida's state bird, but I'd prefer you help me find my wife so we can get out of here, then go fix Miguel."

At the sound of her father's name, the young Skeeter paused. "You're a good person, Gene. I'm sorry."

The hairs on my arm stood at attention. Sofia might be new to the game, but if you get hit with as much power as I have, you know Magick like the sudden pressure drop before a storm. This wasn't Wild Magick, and it certainly wasn't some kid learning the ropes. This was old and exotic, almost tribal. Magick borne of ritual and sacrifice—so much sacrifice. The pain was palpable. The cries of countless lives screamed in the soundless dark of that power.

This wasn't Deacon. It wasn't anything I'd ever felt before.

What did you get yourself into?

Overhead canister lights kicked on and sent warm beams of golden-yellow hues across the room.

We weren't alone.

Her beauty pulled the breath from my lungs, while at the same time her Magick rooted me in my spot. Breathtaking, the newest addition to our receiving room showed off her warm smile. Olive skin and soft pink lips gave off an impression of vapidity, but her eyes said anything but. Those large warm ovals of deep brown held enough years and experiences to tighten a vise around my chest.

She ran painted nails down the edges of a short tan dress that left very little to the imagination. It cut in at all the right spots, providing tantalizing glimpses of the pleasures that lay beneath the strained fabric.

"You must be Eugene Law," she said, her voice pouring like warm liquor, softening the nerves while at the same time stirring up all manner of emotions.

"And you must be Delia?"

The beautiful woman smiled, her white teeth stunning

against those pastel lips. "I am." She took a seat on one of the boxy leather chairs. The top of her dress tugged just enough to hint at a potential wardrobe malfunction. "Please take a seat."

"This was all a setup, wasn't it? Sofia, you set me up."

"I had to." The young Skeeter's eyes welled up with bloody tears. "She promised to save my dad. Don't you understand? He's family. The only real family I've got."

Magick rumbled in my chest. Even in the presence of Delia's immense power I was hard pressed to keep my anger in check.

Think, Gene. You go off now it's over. Breathe. Porter is out there, you know she is, but you can't take them both on...

Delia dismissed me with a gentle wave of her hand. "Mr. Law, I assure you Sofia did what she had to do. She's my daughter, and I take care of my children, as they take care of me."

Sofia did her best to ignore me, but I could see the pain in her eyes. "He's bonded with the Duplickity. I saw the puncture wound on his leg."

How did she... the hospital gown. Shit!

Delia's smiled widened and she brushed a stray long brown hair out of her sculpted face. "So, Deacon was right. You are a peculiar one, Mr. Law. You managed to bond with the only pregnant Duplickity in a few hundred years, and you do it in one of my processing centers in the middle of the sticks. I'd say that was quite impressive if you knew what you were doing. Given Deacon and William's assessment, I get the impression you have been unfairly evaluated."

"Where's my wife?"

Delia gestured to the seat across from her. "Please, take a seat and I'd be happy to explain everything. She's perfectly safe, I assure you."

"You'll have to forgive me, but I don't trust bloodsuckers."

Delia's smile diminished just enough to set my already tender nerves on edge—Sofia's gasp didn't help either.

"Please, Mr. Law. May I call you Gene?"

"You can get me my wife." I dug into my Magick and let it swirl in my body. It was hesitant, like an unsure animal testing the air.

"Gene." Delia ignored my posturing and got up from her chair. Long hair tumbled down smooth and supple shoulders. "I can see why she cares for you. I think you may have been unfairly judged. That was your Phase Knot was it not?"

"Yes."

What is she getting at?

"Impressive." Delia's heels struck the floor and echoed off the high walls. "Not unbreakable mind you, but damn impressive. You have a tenacious power, Gene, one I wouldn't mind getting to know a lot better."

Did she break the knot?

"Sorry, I've only got room for one woman in my life."

Delia shook her slender shoulders and laughed, it was an exotic and intoxicating sound that wormed its way into my head and shook my resolve. "You've bonded with a pregnant Duplickity. Best I can tell you've got room for a few women in your life. What's one more?" Delia's eyes locked on me and I found it almost impossible to shake free. Like dark magnets they drew the fight from my muscles. "You truly are interesting, young Magician. You remind me of someone I knew a long time ago."

"What do you want?" I asked, my hands shaking as I tried to hold on to the Magick quietly slipping away.

"Want?" Delia said, now close enough to run a soft hand down my cheek. Her Magick was like the rolling tide. "I want you, Gene, but if I can't have that I'll settle for getting my Duplickity back."

"You have the bird." I tried to keep my voice from breaking at the beautiful woman's touch.

Delia's jaws peeled apart slowly, fanning out with an almost sensual glide. "I do have the bird, but she's yours now.

You are Flock, Mr. Law, and that means the egg will be yours as well."

"The egg?"

"Yes, Gene"—Delia's warm voice whispered in my ears —"and if you don't give it up, I will make your wife the newest member of my family."

42

WE ARE FLOCK

*M*agick surged in my chest, but Delia's soft and sultry voice pushed it down like the plunger I'd used on Jenkins' toilet. "You do love Porter? Don't you?"

The Sangre Reina lived up to her name, her power squeezing the air right out of my lungs. Short of the Void, I'd never felt anything like the Blood Queen.

"I do."

"Exactly." Delia's soft fingers slid down my arm. "Let's get your lovely bride shall we?" The Skeeter didn't wait for me to respond and gestured to a set of opening side doors.

Deacon and more of his men flooded in, their hairless faces and rippling jaws gleaming in the orange light. "Deacon, see that William brings out our guest."

The monochromatic man bowed gently, then motioned to one of his lieutenants.

Delia directed me toward the chairs. "Please let us sit and discuss this like reasonable people."

As much as I might have wanted to fight it, her silky voice and oppressive Magick made damn sure my butt was in a chair opposite hers.

"Excellent. It's very simple. In a few moments William will bring in your wife. That Phase Knot was impressive, like I mentioned before, but it is a *human* Phase Knot."

No, you didn't!

My heart pounded in my chest and I gripped the hard edges of the cushioned chair. "If you hurt—"

"Mr. Law, I recommend you don't make promises you cannot keep." Delia placed my wife's engagement ring on a small table that sat between us.

Lenar's Logic Loop shined in the room's orange glow. One of the stones was missing. Porter had done what I'd taught her. She'd ripped it off and shattered it against the ground. It was glass, but inside I'd left enough Magick and the sigils for a Human Phase Knot, a swirling Magickal prison that should have kept her safe, if completely immobile.

"Such a smart idea, brilliant really, and under other circumstances I'd be keen to see how far I could take that intellect of yours, and in doing so find out just how much power hides in that delectable body." Delia licked at her lips gently, letting her long tongue peel away at the edges of her unfolded jaws. "Please let me know if you change your mind."

"What have you done to her?" It took everything I had not to erupt in a wild rage, but we were in the viper's nest and even with my Magick I was no match for the dozens of Mosquito People hovering just beyond my reach. Add to that Deacon and Delia, and I was hopelessly outnumbered.

Breathe, Gene. You're no use to anyone dead...

Delia gestured to a set of double doors. "I haven't finished yet. You're going to decide how this ends."

William!

The sagging skin and flaccid jaws of the grotesque and twisted Skeeter entered the room. William dragged Porter still wrapped in the Phase Knot's energy. The Magick swirled around my wife and trapped her in a frozen cocoon of cosmic power. It wasn't good for her, or anyone, but she'd be okay if I got her out soon.

Porter!

William kicked the table out of the way, sending my wife's Logic Loop skittering across the hard floor, then tossed Porter at Delia's feet.

"Thank you, William," Delia said, her voice like steely velvet.

"Porter, can you hear me?" I jumped out of my chair and down to her level. It was my wife, and she still wore the thin nightgown she'd gone to bed in the other day, but her eyes— there was something wrong with her eyes. They weren't the sparkling gemstones I remembered. These eyes were dull and unfocused. "What have you done to her?"

"There's still time, but not much." The insect arms tucked against Delia's bare sides rippled. "Your wife is—"

"She's undergoing the change!" Sofia came off her perch against the wall, Bastet's tiny statue in her white-knuckled fingers.

"My daughter's right."

I slammed my hand down on the hard tile and let the Magick in my body erupt, dragging it up like a troller pulling from the deep. "Undo it, now!"

"You're in luck, Mr. Law. You didn't waste your time coming to see me. Had this gone another few hours there would be no way back. I like your wife, she's got a lot of 'spunk,' but I'm afraid the change would destroy that. She'd end up like William here, sweet as pie, but not someone you'd have a deep conversation with."

The broken man smiled, jagged teeth quivering in his loose jaws.

My stomach churned, bile building in the back of my throat at the sight of Porter's unfocused eyes and the thought of her ending up like William.

No!

"Now, Gene. Don't be so hasty. I can sense that lovely Magick of yours, but I promise you, you try anything now and your wife is as good as William's new playmate."

Oh, sweetheart.

My wife's dull eyes stared through me.

I clenched my fists and fought to contain the Magick inside of me.

"Excellent, now, let's see what we have here." The woman's insect arms erupted from her sides. She shoved them right through my Phase Knot as if it hadn't existed in the first place. Those claws probed my wife's soft skin like they were checking the ripeness of a piece of fruit. "Ah, yes, definitely cutting it close. Now would be the time to coax out that egg."

"Coax?"

Delia nodded, the Phase Knot's Magick wicking around her arm like tips of blue-green flame. "Deacon, bring his Duplickity."

The hairless one returned to the room with the tiny plastic flamingo by its neck. Scratched and broken, the bird did little to resemble my tiny savior on the sandy floor.

We are Flock.

Her oddly pitched voice echoed in my head and sent an already raging torrent of emotion into overdrive. Deacon dropped the plastic animal at my feet. Her scuffed and bent metal legs rattled against the hard tile.

"A pregnant Duplickity, and one of mine no less." Delia's eyes revealed a hint of the anger that raged under a mask of detached cool. "Do you know how rare that is? Of course you don't. I've waited too many years. You will give me her egg, and I will keep your wife from becoming William's."

The tiny plastic flamingo pushed herself up on wobbly legs and swayed gently in an effort to stay balanced. Clearly beaten, it took all the little bird had to lean against my knees.

We are Flock.

I placed a hand on her head.

I know, girl. I know. I need your help though. I need your egg.

Images flashed through my head, at first they were too fast to follow, but the tiny Duplickity's metal projector slowed down enough for me to catch up. A brilliant crystal and mirrored egg shined in my head, the multi-faceted work of art like something Fabergé would have cooked up in his wildest dreams.

Is that the egg?

The tiny bird's neck bobbed gently.

I have to give it to her or she'll destroy my wife.

The Duplickity snapped her head back to stare at me with coal-black eyes.

I have to...

The flamingo raised a metal leg and poked it into my thigh just enough to draw a hint of blood. Around me the salivating gasps of Deacon's men was more than a little disconcerting, but I didn't have time to focus on that when the Duplickity revved back up its mental projector.

Images of fire, pain, death, and destruction exploded in my head like some dystopian nightmare. It was as if hell itself had come to earth, or at least the version of hell I'd imagined.

Is that what would happen if I let her take the egg?

The Duplickity didn't really have a word for yes, but she did appear to have a feeling. She let that warm and friendly glow cover my body like a soft blanket.

I won't let that happen. We are Flock.

The bruised and broken bird crawled into my lap, resting her tired neck against my chest. Her Magick flickered like a candle in the wind.

Delia's eyes grew wide, and she leaned forward in her chair. "It's coming..."

The tiny flamingo's metal legs rusted away, their once strong steel crumbling to dust my lap. The Duplickity's plastic crumbled in my hands. Small pieces peeled apart like bits of ash in the darkness of the Gloom.

The black pupils of the Duplickity gently turned to gray as I sat powerless to stop it. Beyond them my own wife's dead eyes stared.

I'm sorry.

The flamingo pressed its sightless head into my chest one last time, its body spent in those final moments. There were no images, and no mental projector, just a few words in a voice so soft I would never forget it.

We were Flock...

The Duplickity was gone. Nothing remained of my little friend but broken pieces of plastic.

Goodbye, little one.

There, tucked among the shards where that strange little bird had been, was an egg. The most beautiful mirrored crystal I'd ever seen.

43

CATS AND DOGS

"The egg," Delia said, her voice breathless. "Give it to me."

I picked up the crystalline oval and cupped it in my hand. Not much larger than a golf ball, it was surprisingly heavy for its diminutive size. There was Magick tied up in that mirror and crystal, but it wasn't what I'd expected. Given the Duplickity's mental images, I imagined something terrible and deadly, but this was anything but.

The egg was potential, pent up, and waiting to be unleashed.

"Give me the egg, Gene, and I'll restore your wife." There was desperation in Delia's voice, and everyone could sense it. The oversized room felt much tighter than it had only moments ago.

"How do I know you will fix Porter?" I asked, pumping what bravado I could into my shaky voice.

"You don't have much time. Once it goes beyond twenty-four hours, there's nothing anyone can do. Give me the egg now before it's too late."

"Too late?" The crystal shined in my fingers.

The Skeeter's patience was wearing thin. "Another few hours

and she'll be too far gone. Once the change passes a certain point..." Delia shrugged her beautiful shoulders like a runway model.

"What?!" Sofia's voice rocked a mostly silent room. "You promised me you'd fix my father."

Delia waved her off. "Give me the egg, Gene. Give it to me now or your wife is as good as gone."

"No. She's lying, Gene." The newly minted Magician crossed her arms, and I felt the erratic tug of Wild Magick interwoven between the tapestry of power already present in the wide room.

The fiery tips of the Phase Knots seal licked at Delia's insect arms, but she held them firm against my fading wife. "Choose now! Your wife or the egg."

Wild Magick prickled my skin.

Don't do it, kid!

"She's lying to you, Gene. That's all she does. Everything about her is a lie." Sofia spat the words like she were clearing her throat. "Look!"

Wild Magick ripped through the room like the crack of a whip, shattering my vision of Delia. Hideous and blackened, the gnarled limbs and blood-red eyes of a grotesque thing that had been the Sangre Reina glared at me. Organs pressed against thin skin, revealing a heart that beat sickly black blood.

"That is who she is, a living lie. Behold the beautiful Sangre Reina," Sofia screamed, her voice broken with bloody tears.

The Skeeter's red eyes never wavered, her long and twisted claws squeezing my wife's body tighter. "My daughter is right, but is this what you want for your wife? Give me the egg."

My own Magick rumbled, unsure and confused. Porter's skin had begun to gray beneath the Phase Knot's shield. Was Delia telling the truth? Would she bring her back? Could she?"

The egg sparkled in my palm and pressed into it the weight

of unbridled potential. The tiny bird's sacrifice lay heavy in my hand.

Magick is sacrifice.

I held out the egg.

Please be right.

There was only one thing that mattered anymore. I could have run and hid like Jenkins, content to end up in some cave at the end of a Lost Button, but I hadn't. I'd decided to take the risk, to live a life, and to love. I could no longer see my wife's eyes beneath the swirling power of the Phase Knot, but I didn't have to. I had a picture of them tattooed on my heart.

Please be the right choice.

"Save her."

The Blood Queen snatched the egg out of my palm and yanked her claws out of the swirling Phase Knot. Porter's skin continued to sag like day old meat.

"You promised!"

Delia's long claws clutched the egg and pressed it to her own wilted flesh. "I lied."

I reached out with my Magick and dropped the Phase Knot, letting my wife's decaying body collapse against the floor. "Porter!"

Strong hands grabbed my arms and pulled me away from the woman I loved.

"She's yours, William," Delia said, her malevolent eyes lost in the sparkly Magick of the Duplicity's crystalline potential.

Giddiness spread across William's flailing cheeks, and his nose-hole whistled with delight. "William's..."

"No!" I reached for my Magick, but found Deacon's long claws against my throat, his own power stifling and oppressive.

"What do you want me to do with him?" The monochromatic Magician asked.

Delia waved him off with a single claw. "Consume him, or feed him to your men. I don't care. I have what I want."

"Porter, wake up! You've got to fight it," I cried, pushing back against the hairless Skeeter's claws. "Please fight it."

My wife's body shook softly beneath William's pawing hands.

"Fight it!"

"She can't hear you, Magician." Delia leaned back in her chair. "Your wife will not be coming back."

Coming back?

"Maybe she isn't, but if that's the case then none of us are. Sofia, take off the blind-fold."

Nothing happened.

Damn, cats.

"Does anyone know what he's talking about?" Delia asked.

A single feline voice shattered the silence in the room. "Yes. He just put you all on the menu."

Bastet!

The cat woman and her Kittens appeared at the edges of the room, naked from the waist up they resembled the regal felines of ancient Egypt, their fur-covered bodies strong and supple. Short, yet vicious claws shined in the bright orange glow, while impressive feline fangs rivaled the flailing jaws of Deacon's men. "This changes nothing between us, Magician."

"Best news I've gotten all week." I threw an elbow into the gut of a very confused Deacon. "Bastet, Kittens, it is my distinct pleasure to introduce you to the Mosquito People. Enjoy!"

The bloodlust of a long hunger glowed in those feline eyes.

Fangs flashed and claws glinted, death was coming and I was pretty sure not one of them was going to pay any attention to what they were tearing into.

Bark!

Marco the mountain dog crashed onto the tile floor, sliding past a confused William and ramming into the Sangre Reina.

"Chinthe!" Delia fell backward in her chair and lost her grip on the Duplickity's egg in the process. The sparkling crystal and mirrored oval banged against the hard floor and rolled toward some distant corner of the room.

"Fight it, Porter!" I scrambled across the floor toward my collapsed wife as the first sounds of tearing flesh broke the standoff behind me. I didn't have a hand on her for long before the boiling heat of that graying skin forced me to pull it back.

"She is William's now." The grotesque Skeeter's fetid breath rolled over its flayed jaws.

"Like hell she is." I reached for my Magick. "That's my wife you sack of bloated skin, and I'll be damned if she's going anywhere with you."

The cosmic power in my body roared, but for all his disheveled demeanor, William hadn't survived this long without guile and a decent helping of fast-twitch muscle.

"Le—" I didn't even get the word out before the twisted Skeeter launched himself at my chest. We hit the hard tile and slid, spinning on a surface already slick with blood. The first slash of his insect claws raked my chest and sent hot waves of pain across my tired body. I tried to brandish Magick again, but it slipped away, lost among the mental confusion, so I opted for the second best option and rammed my knee into what I remembered had made an impression on William the first time we'd tussled.

"Oof!" The bent-over Skeeter grunted and used a hand to clutch at his groin while the other slammed my head against the tile.

Bang!

A star-field of bright orange filled my vision, followed by the sharp crack of claws on bone. Sofia's claws shot past my budding concussion and caught William under the chin, pulling out the sides of wide jaws like stretched taffy.

"Get your wife," she cried, dragging the slobbering beast off me.

I didn't have time to respond. I scrambled to my knees on

the wet tile only to find myself face to face with what remained of my love.

Porter!

Dead eyes stared through me.

Great bags had formed under those sightless windows. They sagged like hot wax and had already grown large enough to carry loose change. Her lips opened slowly, peeling apart like an overripe banana, and showing me the budding tip of a serrated stinger. She reached for me, but not with caring hands. The spindly insect arms of a budding Skeeter tore through the sides of her nightgown.

What have I done?

44

TAPPED POTENTIAL

*L*ong insect arms reached for me, but somewhere they stopped being Porter's, in my mind's eye they became Morgan's hands. The feverish heat of her skin became the blinding fury of the library's doors. Dead eyes vanished, and in their place emerged the fear-filled eyes of my first mistake.

"Why? Why did you let me die?" Morgan asked, a lone tear glistening on her cheek.

"You did this to yourself." My hands shook.

"You could have stopped it, just like you could have saved your wife today, but you didn't? Why, Gene? Why do you choose to disappoint the ones you love, the ones who love you?"

Morgan's Thread drifted un-attached, floating free like a snapped line, and gently twisting in my imagination.

"I did all—"

The old flame's face twisted and was now an odd mixture of Morgan and Porter. The blended woman reached for me, her fiery hands and nascent claws grasping in the open air. "Nothing. You did nothing, just as you've always done. Your power is a waste, a great disappointment. You hide, Eugene Law. You hide in the darkness of your own fear and ignorance."

I pushed myself back and tried to stay out of the reach of Morgan-Porter's claws. "You had to be stopped."

"And then what happend?" Her face constantly shifted back and forth between my wife's and Morgan's. "You gave up, and with that, you gave up on your Magick. You became a broken and useless thing."

My back pressed against something—the wall? I'd gone as far as I could, and the thing that hunted me knew it. Hot hands clutched at my legs but try as I might I couldn't kick them away.

"Gene." It was Porter again, the Porter I met all those years ago, the Porter's whose cute smile and warm heart trapped me like the tightest of fishing nets. "Why did you let them do this to me?"

"I didn't." My words broke as I said them.

My wife's eyes grayed and her skin began to sag. "But you did, Gene. You did by doing nothing. You quit being you, and on that day the die was cast. You sealed me in this fate no different than when you snapped Morgan's Thread."

"No!"

"Yes." Her face was Morgan's again, and those fiery hands clawed their way up my battered body. "You failed because you are a failure, because you've always been a failure. You had a chance to be more than anyone, and you gave it up, just like you gave up on me."

"You would have done terrible things." Fire consumed the tips of Morgan's hair. "I did what I had to do!"

"Did you, Gene?" She was Porter again, on the day of our marriage, her long hair elegantly twisted and spun like brown gold above her head. "When we married you promised to give me all of you, did you keep your promise?"

"Porter, I..."

"Ssh, Gene," she said, her hair falling away and her eyes fading. "I'll take all of you now, and I'll enjoy it."

My wife's long nails dug into the flesh of my chest as her

jaws split apart, splayed wide like the wings of a predatory bird, a fleshy stinger surrounded by sharp and hungry teeth.

I'd failed, and I knew it. There was no bringing back my wife, and there was no winning. All around me the sounds of rending claws and tearing flesh reminded me of exactly what awaited me at the end.

It might as well be you. All I am is yours.

The thing that had been my wife, the love of my life, let the sides of her jaws press against my neck and in that moment I could feel the beating of our hearts.

Goodbye, Porter. I love you, and I always will.

My hand brushed across something, something I'd forgotten, but that hadn't quite yet forgotten me.

We were Flock...

The Duplickity's egg rested against my hand. Untapped potential swirled inside the facets of that silvery crystal and brimmed with possibilities. An infinity of options rolled over me. In the tiny bird's egg, I saw myself anew. I wasn't Eugene Law the broken Magician. I was something more.

Husband. Lover. Father?

The little flamingo's legacy showed me a world that needed me, a world where dark things thrived because I did nothing. A world where I had the power to make a difference.

But my Magick...

The egg filled me with hope. My Magick wasn't broken, any more than I was. The power I'd once considered separate was a part of me. I could no more deny it than I could deny myself.

We were Flock... You are Magician.

The little bird was right, and for the first time in my short life I realized it.

I squeezed the egg and let the sharp edges bite into the skin of my hand as the tips of my twisted wife's teeth pressed against my throat.

There were no words, no commands. If there was a formula

for what I wanted, I didn't know it. In another time I would have been afraid. I would have leaned on terrible people like Morgan or even Delia to teach me the patterns and confining rules, but now, with the Duplickity's hope I didn't have to.

I no longer worried about the power, about the choices I'd made, or even the choices I'd make in the days to come. There was a quiet contentment that settled over me, like a warm hand on a cold day. I knew me, and in that instant that was enough.

I was comfortable being Eugene Law for the first time in a very long time.

Morgan's voice echoed in my ear, her words trying to upset my fragile calm. "You let me die. You'll do it again, and the next time it will break you. There will be no coming back from that. You will fall again, Eugene Law, and no one will be there to pick you back up."

So be it—I'm done paying for my sins.

I released my Magick.

Like the running of the bulls, or the roaring of a jet's powerful engine, it swelled. My Magick hadn't felt like this since that day on the library's evil ground. Carefree and unbound, it caught up with the power of potential in the Duplickity's egg. Like fish chasing each other's tails, they swirled, each pass expanding and reaching beyond the limits of my understanding.

Somewhere in that Magick I found my wife's face. It wasn't the twisted and dead thing whose jaws were hungry for my flesh—it was the woman I loved, and always would.

I knew what I had to do. I may not have known the words, or the right sigil to focus my power, but in that moment I didn't have to. I wasn't Eugene Law anymore, he didn't exist.

I was Magick, and I was without bounds.

45

BAD LUCK

*M*agick demands sacrifice, and I finally understood why. Pain and desire, a willingness to give everything and expect nothing in return, all of this and more flooded my mind and threatened to drown my soul.

Porter's wide jaws peeled away in the outpouring of cosmic power, vanishing beneath newly soft and resealed lips. The long insect arms that only moments ago sought to tear flesh from bone retracted into the sides of her torn nightgown. Clawing hands returned to the gentle and loving fingers of the woman I'd fallen for all those years ago.

Unclouded eyes looked up at me, confused, but clear.

"Gene?"

"In the flesh." I brushed away a stray hair away from her face. "I told you I'd find you."

Porter pushed herself up, stretching like she'd just woken from a long sleep. "Took you long enough. What's that?"

The Duplickity's egg lay in my hand, its many facets catching the light.

"What would you say if I told you I was a father?"

My wife's eyes grew wide. "Wha…"

"Duck!" I pulled her against my chest an instant before William's six arms would have detached my wife's newly restored head from her body.

"She is William's!" the slobbering thing cried, frustration in its red and angry eyes.

"Run." I pushed my wife away and scrambled to my feet.

"It wasn't a dream..."

I put myself between Porter and the broken Skeeter. "No, it sure wasn't. I've got this. You need to get the hell out of here, now." I pointed to a distant sliding glass door, black as pitch and almost reflective. "There, get outside and as far away as you can. I'll find you, I promise."

"I'm not leaving—"

"Yes you are." I shook my head and kept one eye on the approaching William.

"But..."

Where is Sofia?

"Porter, I've got this." Magick crackled between my fingers, surprising both of us. "Go!"

"Damn you." Porter let go of my shoulder and made a break for the distant sliding glass door.

I watched as she ran, her tiny feet carrying her safely between the melee of fangs and claws, and I was still watching the moment she yanked the sliding door open and vanished into the darkness. Sadly, I should have been paying more attention to William in that moment and not my wife's butt.

"Led—"

For the second time tonight, I didn't finish the words before the twisted creature's fast-twitch fibers sent him tearing into me again, this time making contact with the egg hand and once again sending it spinning across the blood-covered floor.

Son of a bitch.

William's spindly insect arms ripped a fresh hole in my

borrowed shirt and in the process tore a deep gouge in my stomach.

"Argh." My Magick cracked back like a whip. "Ledo!"

The power slammed into William's face, splitting an already unfolded jaw, and casting out a few teeth in the process, but the twisted Skeeter didn't flinch, instead, he wiped his bloody lip and smiled. "It will be a tasty treat…"

I reached for my Magick and let it rumble through my body. "I'm not on the menu."

"Yes, I'm actually quite certain you are."

Deacon!

Black tendrils of sickly and corrupted power slammed me back against the wall. The hairless Skeeter had me pinned. Where the hell was Bastet?

"He's yours, William," Deacon said, before turning his attention back to Bastet and her Kittens.

"Like hell I am." I fought against the Skeeter's evil constraints, but my Magick hovered just outside my mental grasp.

Shit.

"It will be tasty…"

Shit, shit, shit!

A dull rumble rattled the distant windows. It wasn't the ocean waves, or thunder. It was something else, something oddly familiar.

William licked at his claws, his long and serrated stinger savoring my blood like a sommelier.

Come on!

I pulled at my hands, but the inky darkness held me fast. I was pinned to the wall like a mounted butterfly and directly in the path of that hungry beast.

"William will start with the tender bits…"

There it was again, the rumble. It was getting louder. It

wasn't rain, or the rush of wind. It had a distinct, almost mechanical sound.

The Skeeter's insect arms reached my bare chest. William traced those claws down the bloody gouge he'd made only moments ago, sending a fresh wave of pain through my body.

"Yes, the tender bits."

Gasoline?

The acrid smell of fuel mixed with the salt spray in the night air, and it was in that instant I knew what that rumbling was, I knew because that was the model we *couldn't* afford—high-end standing mowers are expensive.

Crash!

Like an avenging angel of motorized fury, my wife and the most powerful lawn mower I'd ever test-driven exploded through the open sliding glass door. Her grease-streaked nightgown flapping like the flag of a malevolent pirate commander, Captain Porter and the great clipper 'shreds-a-lot' tore its way into Delia's great room.

Hell yeah!

Furniture exploded in great bursts of splinters and fabric, while Kittens and Skeeters dove out of the way of Porter's killing machine. William turned around just in time to see the rending blades reduce him to a pulpy stain on the slick tile.

"Gene!" Porter shouted, yanking the handle and turning the mower before it could take my legs off. "Are you okay?"

Deacon's Magick dropped, and I hit the floor. "I am now. Where the—"

"You aren't the only one with a little Magick." My wife winked, then spun the destructive machine around and aimed it at Deacon.

Now, aren't you glad you let her take a test drive?

The one-color Magician's Magick surged.

"Jump!" I cried, but Porter was already way ahead of me. She threw the throttle forward and leapt off the seemingly possessed death machine.

Deacon might have been fast, but even he had to respect the 'shreds-a-lot,' and its thirty horses. The hairless Magician dove out of the way, vanishing in the pandemonium my wife had created.

"Gene," Porter cried, her nightgown stained with blood and black. "The egg!"

"What?"

She was right. The egg was moving, or rather something was moving it. I strained my eyes, fighting to see beyond the clash of fangs and fur.

There was only one thing that moved like that.

Duplickity?

A slender pink bird appeared, followed by Delia's long and luxurious fingers.

"Oh, hell no." I launched myself at the vanishing egg.

My fingers caught on the Duplickity's neck. Delia was there, her hands on mine, and fighting for the untapped potential of that shining egg. Her insect arms raked my sides. Razor-like claws worked hard to to dislodge me from the tiny bundle of potential, but a quick foot to her midsection kept me from loosing my grasp.

"It is mine, Magician!"

"Like hell it is," I said, twisting my body to try to stay one step ahead of the powerful woman's devilish claws. "She was my bird. *We* were Flock."

Delia's flamingo snapped at my face. Its pointy beak poked at my eyes and forced me to turn away, only to have the skin of my back shredded like confetti by her insect arms.

"You can't win," she cried, her breath hot against my neck. "I've survived countless years, and I'll survive countless more. You are nothing but an ink stain on the annals of history, Eugene Law."

I couldn't get the egg out of her hand, but I couldn't let her have it. The Duplickity had shown me Delia's untapped potential, and no world deserved that. Mental images of possibilities flooded my mind, visions not just of Delia but of me—dark images, scenes that filled my head with fear. There were too many potentials, too many options, and no clear path.

"Give it to me!" Delia cried, her claws again making contact with my tender skin.

Sometimes there is only one choice.

I cupped both hands against the egg, then using what strength remained, I slammed the beautiful crystal against the floor.

Boom!

Shards of glass and mirror sliced up my hands, while Delia's scream shook my soul. "No!"

46

MIRROR, MIRROR

*P*ossibilities, unconstrained by the bounds of the egg's fragile shell, raced like floodwaters over Delia and me. The stronger Skeeter pulled a piece of the spherical mirror from my hand, the last vestiges of the Duplickity's egg.

She held it to her face, staring deep into that reflection. "No, no, no. I've waited so long. I will not be denied."

Magick twisted and pulled in the confines of the room. Around us Kittens and Skeeters continued their dance of death, but Delia's eyes never wavered. She screamed at the mirror, her Magick boiling in rage. "I will have my prize."

The mirror's Magick flowed over the ancient woman, picking at the edges of her face and tugging at the curves of her once again beautiful body. Delia's smooth skin began to wrinkle, pruning in the strong light of the broken egg. "Give it to me!"

The mirror obliged.

Its power like a vacuum, it pulled at Delia's Magick, her vitality, and her soul. Once luxurious locks of hair tumbled to the floor like straw, while glowing skin reduced to a brown-spotted and splotchy mess.

Delia's broken and withered voice continued to shout into the mirror. "Give…"

Collapsing forward, her ancient and crooked hands limp, Delia dropped what remained of the Duplickity's egg. The evil mirror tumbled to the ground, rolling to a stop at my feet.

"Kid," said a voice I hadn't expected to hear again. "Do me a favor and *don't* look at that mirror."

"Jenkins!"

The old Magician appeared in the door frame, his signature tinted glasses pressed up to his face and a new threadbare robe flapping against his narrow legs. "In the flesh. You're a real pain in my ass, you know that?" Mr. Jenkins pulled down his glasses and stared, mouth agape, at the still rumbling shreds-a-lot. "Is that a lawn mower?"

"Yeah…"

The old Magician shook his head. "Points for creativity, but don't just stand there like a cod fish, get that Soul-Splitter." He pointed at the mirror. "Can't let her get her Magick back, now can we?"

"Huh?"

A cat-claw-shredded Skeeter collapsed at Mr. Jenkins' feet, its body not much more than a pulpy mess. "Oh my, you brought the Kittens back?"

"Well, I didn't have any other—"

Mr. Jenkins brushed me off. "Smart move, but be careful, that Bastet's a feisty one."

"Viktor!" The cat-woman's voice resounded from across the wide room.

"See." The old Magician winked. "Bastet, how are you? I see you've been able to feed your Kittens thanks to my protege. You're welcome."

My excitement at seeing Jenkins was short-lived—I'd forgotten about Deacon.

Black and twisted Magick erupted from the man-in-black, swirling like an inky whirlpool of corruption and pain.

The mirror!

Slimy tendrils shot out of Deacon's Magick, their sickly edges reaching for the mirror. I dove for the reflecting glass, but my finger came up just short. Deacon's claws had scooped up the capricious remains of the Duplickity's egg.

"That's a problem," the old Magician said, pushing his way into the room. "Gene, we need—"

Jenkins' words were lost in the roar of the 'shreds-a-lot.' Porter was back at the reins with Deacon in her sights. My wife threw the throttle forward and rammed the mower into the one-color Magician. His Magick snapped like the breaking of a twig and sent the mirror spinning in the open air.

Damn it!

I scrambled to my feet and made a play for the reflective glass. "Gotcha," I cried, but the instant my fingers closed around the mirror I regretted the decision. The Magick trapped in that shiny circle clawed at my mind and ripped into my sanity. "Jenkins!"

"Soul-Splitter, Gene. In the pocket, now."

"Ugh…" I blinked back against the pain and forced the tiny mirror into my pants while I surveyed the aftermath. Kittens and Skeeters lay dead in large numbers throughout the room, their bodies broken and bloodied. I turned my attention back to Delia, and found her barely breathing, an ancient and decrepit version of her once glorious self.

"Why did you do it, Delia?" Mr. Jenkins said, more to himself than to the fallen woman as he picked his way past the dead.

"You said you loved me," she croaked, her once melodious voice now a jagged and scratchy thing.

"I think I did, once." The old Magician crouched down next to her. "But, it wasn't real…"

"It was to me." Delia's cloudy eyes barely registered in overhead light.

"How? Why did you..."

Delia licked at her dry lips. "You hid the Viburna from me, while at the same time you shared it with your wife and family. Did I mean so little to you? Was I just your whore?"

Mr. Jenkins soft eyes turned dark in an instant. "Delia!"

"I made it my own..." the old woman said, struggling to push herself to a seated position. Her long dress now bunching in uncomfortable spots and making it hard for her to move. "It gave me power, Viktor—real power—it made me like you."

The old Magician's shoulders slumped. "It took away who you were. You were never this person."

"No, Viktor. You did that. You took away who I was."

"I'm sorry, Delia," the old Magician said, his subtle Magick rising like the surrounding tide. "I cannot allow..."

"You do what you think is best. You always have, and you always will, regardless of who you destroy in the process." Delia brushed straw-like hair away from her sunken eyes then held out her hands. "Do it."

Jenkins Magick swelled around them, but the old man hesitated, his hands shaking. "I..."

"Oh, Viktor. You always were too slow."

Click. Click. Click.

The sound of metal rod legs on the hard tile startled me, but not the Skeeter. With her hands open she clutched a suddenly visible Duplickity to her chest and vanished.

"Son of a—"

"Gene." Porter pulled me out of my confusion. "He's still alive."

She was right.

Deacon pushed away the broken metal of the shreds-a-lot, his body now a reminder of the power of commercial lawn equipment, and pulled himself to a standing position. "This isn't over," he said, his exposed bones already knitting back together. Dark and oily Magick shuddered in a tight knot around his mending body.

Clap. Clap. Clap.

A calmness settled over the room, like the final moments before a thunderstorm, or the quiet stillness the instant before a bomb explodes. Someone else was here, and that someone stood in the doorway clapping, it may have looked like Morgan, but the instant it spoke I knew it wasn't.

"Oh, Gene, Viktor. You guys are the best, really the best. First, you sneak off to who knows where, making me no end of pissed in the process, only to return and put on one hell of a show."

Bastet and her Kittens vanished.

"It smelled too much like cat in here for me, you?" the Void said, running its hands through Morgan's green hair.

"It's her!" Porter grabbed my arm. "It's Morgan. Gene, we've got to run!"

"Sweetheart, am I scaring you?" Morgan said, a twisted smile on her face. "I'm sorry, how about this?"

My ex-lover shifted, her body twisting like taffy until it resembled Ed Lovely. "You like this better?" He flashed his signature grin. "I know you used to like this—a lot." The Void pressed a hand to its face in a feigned expression of shock. "Whoops, you probably didn't tell Gene that."

My wife's hands shook and I could feel her heart beating in her chest. "Gene!"

"And, now, we need to deal with you." Ed turned his attention to Deacon.

The man-in-black pulled his Magick in like a spider folding its legs. "The Defiler sends his best."

"That worthless bastard can—" Ed started to say, but stopped when Deacon disappeared like a collapsing star in the infernal blackness that surrounded him. "Well, problem solved for now. Where were we?"

"Gene," Jenkins backed toward me and away from my old roommate. "Don't suppose you brought any buttons?"

"No."

"You two and your tricks," Ed stepped over the bloody body of a mutilated Skeeter. "It doesn't matter. I've got you both here now. You've used too many Lost Buttons. Can't you feel it? You've torn a lot of holes in this world, and in the process made it practically as threadbare as that robe of yours. Not that I mind, but still, I've got a big picture plan here and those damn buttons are a pain in my ass."

"Gene?" Viktor asked, his robe just within reach. "Did you happen to bring my dog?"

GOING HOME

"*S*ort of."

"Where is he?" Mr. Jenkins whispered, getting as close to me as he could.

"How should I know? He has this nasty habit—"

"Yeah, I know. The disappearing. I've been trying to break him of that for years. It was easier to house train him than get him to stop shifting."

"You two do know I can hear you, right?" Ed stepped over a body I hadn't noticed before. "I mean, I wasn't born yesterday."

Sofia!

The Skeeter waited until my old roommate passed to open her eyes and wink.

Do not move!

I tried to convey as much using only my eyebrows, but Sofia's scrunched up frown did little in the way of providing assurances my message had been received.

"Kid, how much Magick you got left?" Jenkins whispered.

Porter's hand clutched at mine. "Gene…"

"Enough." My heart pounded in my ears. "… I think."

"That's the spirit. Now, on the count of three. One... Two..."

"Three." Ed snapped his fingers like a stage Magician. "You guys really should think about who you're up against. I mean, come on you two. I *am* Magick. I am the shifting void, the unfathomable chaos, the beginning and the end. Need I go on?"

I wanted to respond, but I couldn't.

It's gone!

From the look on Jenkins' face he was feeling the same thing, in fact his was worse, like Delia before him, his body had decided to take the bullet train to Geezerville.

"Gene!" Porter tried to keep me from falling over. "What's happening?"

I reached for my Magick, but it was gone, and it wasn't just the Magick that was gone, it was the very act of reaching for it. There was simply nothing. I had a hole in my heart so large you could drive a semi through it. I dropped to my knees, my hands shaking, and my lungs gasping for air.

"I'll tell you what's happening, sweetheart." Ed flashed again what had been my roommate's signature smile. "Fish need water to breathe. It's just how they work. Your husband needs his Magick, or at least the ability to access it. I just cut them both off at the source."

Cut off...

I clawed at the yawning mental hole in my chest but found it wanting. The Void wasn't lying. I was normal, but worse—I couldn't even feel the Wild Magick of the world. My mind was like cauterized flesh.

"Let them go!" Porter clutched my arm.

My old roommate shook his head and dropped back into the same chair Delia had sat in not minutes earlier. "Nope, that's not going to happen until I get what I want."

"What do you want?" my wife shouted, tears glistening in her eyes. "Why are you doing this to us?"

"Us? You are a really sweet monkey, but in the grand

scheme of things you're just another banana-eater that will be here one day, and worm food the next. Don't kid yourself into thinking you are anything but expendable. Now, your husband on the other hand, and even 'Old Man and the Sea' over there, they're important—rare monkeys if you will."

As if on cue, Mr. Jenkins crumpled to the bloody ground, his words lost in the fading raspiness of his voice.

"Whoops, looks like we're going to lose one." Ed leaned forward in his chair and kicked at the fading Viktor. "But that's why I've got your husband. Think of me like the casino—I always win."

Sofia picked her head up and tilted it in my direction as if to say, "Now?"

No.

The young Skeeter rolled her eyes.

"So, Gene. Are you ready to get started?" Ed pushed himself out of the chair.

"I…"

"Listen. I'll make it easy on you." My roommate got up from his chair and shifted effortlessly back into Morgan. "I'll look how ever you'd like. Would this work for you?"

Porter pushed past me, going toe-to-toe with my old girlfriend's facsimile. "You want him? You have to go through me first."

"Porter…" I said, my own voice raspy and breaking much like Jenkins'. "Stand back."

"Better listen to him, monkey." Morgan's eyes sparkled with violent intentions.

"No."

Morgan's surprised voice dripped with venom. "What?"

Porter puffed up her chest and placed her hands on her hips. "You heard me. You need me to say it again, bitch?"

My Magick might be gone, but I didn't need it to know the

Void was getting angry, and was sure to be pulling in some serious Magick of its own.

"One less monkey in the world," Morgan said, her body shifting into a mirror image of Porter's. "But don't worry, sweetheart, your man will never know the difference."

"Now?" Sofia's eyes asked from just beyond the shifting woman.

Is there enough Wild Magick to do—to do what exactly?

"Now," I said with the faintest node of my head.

Here goes nothing...

I had to give the young woman credit—the girl knew how to make an entrance—even if she had no idea what I really wanted her to do. Sofia pushed herself up silently, like a jungle cat, then exploded into the shape-changing Not-Porter. It would have been an amazing tackle, had the Void not picked up on it at the last second and stepped to the side. Sofia crashed into my wife along with the rest of us.

"Enough games," Not-Porter extended her hand. "It's time, Gene. Come with me."

Mr. Jenkins voice, barely a whisper, echoed in my ear. "The house always wins. The house, Gene."

The house... 69 Mallory Lane.

I grabbed Sofia's arm. "Close your eyes and imagine a small, white house. Its yard is in disrepair, the paint is peeling and the doors are faded. Imagine it all, down to the last detail."

"Huh?"

"Just do it," I said, grabbing my wife's hand. "69 Mallory Lane. Do you understand me? 69 Mallory Lane. That's where we have to go."

"I don't think—" The confused Skeeter shook her head.

"Don't think, just do. Use that Wild Magick and get us to 69 Mallory Lane—all of us," I shouted, letting go of Sofia and spinning around to grab Not-Porter's extended hand.

"No!" the Void screamed, its body shifting back and forth between Morgan, Ed, and Porter.

Sofia closed her eyes and even cut off from my own Magick I could imagine the power surging through her. If I was right, she'd tap into everything the Void had brought with it—I just hoped it would be enough to trap the infinite.

48

69 MALLORY LANE

"Wake up, Gene," Mr. Jenkins said, his warm hand on my shoulder.

"Huh?"

"You did good, kid. Damn good." The old man's voice drawn and tired.

I opened my eyes to the peeling paint of a dilapidated porch. Yellowed newspapers slowly rotted in a loose pile near me, while the old Magician rocked gently in a faded chair, his dog at his side.

Bark!

"Marco thinks so too…"

"Where are we?" I asked, propping myself up.

"69 Mallory Lane, kid. You did it."

A dark malevolence bore down on me like the evil-eye from the tiny bungalow's front door. The window shades drawn, the house lay quiet like a hungry predator waiting for the right moment to strike.

"Where's—"

"Your wife and that young Magician are safe. I sent them home, it was the least I could do before the end."

"End?"

Mr. Jenkins sighed and removed his tinted glasses, rubbing gently at the bridge of his nose. "Kid, someone has to make the sacrifice. I've been around long enough to know as much."

"I don't get it."

"Magick demands sacrifice, Gene. That's how it's always been, and that's how it'll always be."

"Did it work?" I stretched out my hands and my Magick, recoiling at the force of Jenkins' power and the Void trashing beneath the floorboards.

"For now," the old man reached down and scratched behind his dog's ears, his hands old and spotted, "but nothing lasts forever I'm afraid. Once you step off this porch, it's up to you."

I brushed the dirt from my borrowed pants. "Me? But I..."

The old man smiled. "Khakis? You look good in those. Are they mine?"

"Yeah, I borrowed them, along with your car."

"Nice. Keep em, I don't need them where I'm going." Viktor fished something out of his pocket and tossed it to me.

"Keys?"

"Three to be exact."

"What are they—"

The old man leaned back in his rocking chair, his body tired and his eyes drifting. "First, you can have the car. It's a great Mazda, treat it well, okay?"

"I didn't mean to hot-wire it. In fact, it was Sofia's—"

"Kid," the old man coughed, "shut up for once and just listen."

"Okay."

"The second key is to the apartment. It's yours. Might be good to have a place to stay. I have a hunch you're going to need more space soon though. Do me a favor and keep a close eye on the storage closet. Oh and don't lose The Soul of Isis. Bastet's a pain in the ass, but when it comes to avenging angels, well, you could do a lot worse. You follow?"

I nodded, the keys cold in my fingers.

Jenkins opened an eye. "Kid, I'm practically blind at this point, you think you could humor me with a 'yes' or 'okay?' "

"Sorry. Yes, I'll do it."

"Great." Mr. Jenkins closed his eyes again and settled into the chair. "The last key is the most important."

I held up the simple cut steel key. "What is it?"

"It's the key to 69 Mallory Lane, kid. It's yours now."

"Why not just—"

"Destroy it? Couldn't even if you wanted to. Trust me, I've tried." Mr. Jenkins broke into a fit of coughing, so much so that Marco sat up and pressed his oversized head into the old Magician's lap. "Good boy, is it time to go?"

Whimper...

"Yeah, dying sucks, but listen to us, Marco. We've seen the world and more, we've done things no mortal and his Chinthe should have been able to do."

Bark.

"Fine, you could have done all those things without me," Mr. Jenkins said, trying to raise his hand enough to place it on the dog's head. Marco didn't wait for him and instead pushed his snout under the man's frail fingers.

Whimper.

"I'll miss you too, old man. I'll miss you too."

"What do I do with the key?" I asked, afraid to interrupt this moment.

"Kid, I don't have all the answers. I just know you can't open this door, and you can't come back. The House will see you, it'll know you, and then it will find you. It's up to you now, Eugene Law."

"I don't know if I can."

"Of course you don't. I wouldn't have left the key with you if you did. You're a complicated person and life likes complicated people."

"What happens next?"

"You leave." Mr. Jenkins' rocking slowed, his legs no longer pushing the old chair. "You go and live your life. You love your wife, and check in on that young Magician from time to time. Go be the hero, Eugene Law. It suits you, far better than it ever did me."

"But, what about you?"

"Turn around, Gene."

My heart caught in my throat. "But—"

"Don't make me get out of this chair and smack you."

"I won't forget you."

"Thanks, kid, and for what it's worth, I believe in you—I have no idea why—but I do." Mr. Jenkins' hand drifted off Marco's head. "Now, get off my damn porch before I kick you off."

I turned my back to the old Magician, his power fading with the coming dawn. "Goodbye, Viktor." I stepped off the porch and down the narrow steps. Tall grass swayed gently in the faint morning breeze. It rubbed at my legs and brought with it memories of Bastet and her Kittens.

The Soul of Isis...

I waited until I reached the sidewalk to turn around and take in the bungalow. It was small, even by old house standards. Bleached white in the Florida sun, it lay nestled in the long blades of dense weeds. Birds and squirrels did what they could to avoid the wires and tree branches that dared cross over that ill-fated house. The rocking chair was empty, Mr. Jenkins and his majestic mountain dog were gone.

Goodbye, old man.

69 Mallory Lane seethed.

Drawn windows, like angry eyes, stared out at me, and at a

world they wanted badly to reach, but thanks to the old Magician, could not.

The House always wins.

I stepped off the sidewalk and found the Mazda waiting patiently on the curb. The seats smelled of Old Spice and tequila, a heady combination I wasn't sure would ever completely go away. I placed the key in the ignition and turned over the engine. The old wagon rumbled to life, and something bounced in the back seat. I adjusted the mirror to find a small pink yard flamingo sitting on the cushion, its coal-black eyes staring up at me.

"Well, look at you..."

The tiny bird wasn't my Duplickity, but she bore an uncanny resemblance to the little friend that had saved my butt more than once.

"You ready to see what this thing can do?"

The tiny flamingo bobbed its head.

"That's the spirit."

I punched the gas and together we left 69 Mallory Lane choking on our dust.

49

TIDINGS OF GREAT JOY

"She's moving out?" Porter asked, putting away enough groceries for a small army. "It would have been great to know that before I bought all this."

I nodded, keeping one eye on the monster receipt on the counter. "I know, but Sofia's got a bead on a new Flock of Duplickities. She's hoping to find an egg for her father, and in the meantime she'll be living with some swamp rats outside of Jacksonville."

"Gene!"

"What?" I took out an oversized box of mac-and-cheese and put it on the high shelf. "That's what they call themselves. I'm not being derogatory."

"It's one thing if they call themselves that, it's another entirely if you do it."

"So many rules..."

Porter's engagement ring shined on her finger. "Damn straight. Besides, she was nice enough to scoop this up before we left that hell-hole."

Lenar's Logic Loop sparkled in the morning light, a reminder of the darkness that existed beyond these apartment walls. I let my mental fingers dance through the Magick in my body. There was work to do to improve that charm, but it was work I was ready and excited for. I scooped my wife up in my arms and kissed her, surprising both of us in the process.

"Gene!" she said, doing nothing to stop me.

"What? I'm excited to get the place to ourselves. It's been hard to—you know—with Sofia coming and going."

My wife pressed her hands against my chest, those soft fingers warming my heart. "It hasn't been as hard as you think." She pushed me back and opened one of the drawers in what had been Jenkins' kitchen, then removed a narrow plastic stick.

"Is that—"

My wife held the plastic to her chest and smiled from ear to ear. Porter's face lit up with an exuberance I sorely missed. "It is! You're going to be a father, Eugene Law," she cried, shoving the pregnancy test into my hands.

"I..."

Porter hesitated and the excitement in her eyes diminished. "What? Talk to me."

A thousand possibilities rolled through my mind. Would my child be a Magician? What about the House, Deacon, Delia, and even Morgan? Was she still out there? Could I do this?

"Gene..." My wife's eyes swelled with tears. "If—"

But I wasn't alone, and I wasn't going to be alone anymore.

We were a team, and one hell of a force for the rest of the world to reckon with. Porter had proven that in spades.

I placed a finger on her lips. "I love you, and cannot wait to be a dad."

"Oh, Gene," Porter cried and threw her arms around me. "We're going to have a baby."

Oh, boy.

MARTIN SHANNON'S WEIRD FLORIDA

Short Stories

0 - Danderous Delivery (Newsletter Subscribers Only)

1 - Hook, Line, and Slinker

2 - Ballroom and Chain

3 - Bahama Blues

4 - Plasma Pistols

5 - Lights Out

6 - Mourning Paper

7 - Ignorance and Unleaded

8 - Black Valentine

9 - Soulless

10 - Ten Turns (Coming Soon)

Novels

1 - Dead Set

2 - Gathering Gloom

3 - Beaten Path

4 -Bloody Deed

5 - No Fury (Coming Soon)

NO FURY

TALES OF WEIRD FLORIDA

Evil is marshaling forces for an end Eugene Law never saw coming, and it isn't long before he finds himself in the Dad Wagon's driver seat for a reset of cosmic proportions.

The Calamity's cleansing fire sweeps across the hot sands of Hell. Atop the Demon Steed Obelleron, a dark angel of wrath and vengeance brings with her a promise of hope to a world without. Yet in the tarry-eyed aftermath of that destruction will all her vows ring hollow? The Defiler, New Dead, and just about every mistake a broken father has ever made, come back to haunt him in this stunning conclusion to a story that began at the clipped end of Ariadne's Thread.

In the tarnished edge of the silver saber, our hero will learn that Hell hath no fury like a daughter forgotten.

AFTERWORD

Bloody Deed was made possible by my years of lawn mainte-nance beneath the unforgiving Florida sun. Just like Gene, I never had the bucks for the standing models, but I kept our 'sir shreds-a-lot' long past his expiration.

God's Tears and the Ocean of Grass were just a few of the many crazy worlds I imagined at the end of Lost Buttons. The same little plastic circles are frequent visitors in my dryer lint.

Lastly, it was cathartic to finally put the 'House' in its place, but as you know, things rarely stay where you put them.

Martin
Under the Cypress
May 2020

ACKNOWLEDGMENTS

This book and all of its Magick could not have happened without the help of the following people:

Fay Lane, my cover artist and personal confidant—thank you for your vision, your art, and your unceasing support.

Amber Townsend, Keeper of the Mythos—thank you for always being there, when I'm excited about the story, or lost in the forking possibilities of a Duplickity's black eyes.

The Flock—thank all of you for keeping me sane, and believing in the story.

Last but not least, thank you, dear reader. To know you've made it this far warms my heart more than you can imagine.

ABOUT THE AUTHOR

Martin Shannon's been using his imagination to avoid weeding since he was in short pants. His first series, *Tales of Weird Florida*, is an homage to the Sunshine State he knows and loves, and spent countless hours riding his bike through as a kid. It's got mystery, mayhem, and more than a little Magick. He hopes you enjoy the supernatural side of the upside down state, but if not, he's got a banjo, and he knows how to use it. You can find out more at www.martin-shannon.com.

ON NEWSLETTERS, WRITING, AND REVIEWS

Thank you for making it this far. It is my sincere hope you enjoyed the story, and the opportunity to slip into the sometimes too tight shoes of Eugene Law and company. If you did, please take a few seconds to help me spread the word, and in exchange I promise to send out free short stories as well as keep you up to date with each new novel in the Tales of Weird Florida world.

Writers live on reviews, newsletter sign-ups, and tiny scraps of praise. The writing life can get rather lonely, as evidenced by my social-media presence. So, drop by, say hello, sign up for the newsletter, and if you feel strongly enough, write a review or tell your friends. Remember, every time you write a review, an angel gets its wings.